LOST

Kc Poe

Order this book online at www.trafford.com
or email orders@trafford.com

Most Trafford titles are also available at major online book retailers.

Printed in the United States of America.

ISBN: 978-1-4269-6810-5 (sc)
ISBN: 978-1-4269-6811-2 (e)

Trafford rev. 07/12/2011

 www.trafford.com

North America & international
toll-free: 1 888 232 4444 (USA & Canada)
phone: 250 383 6864 ♦ fax: 812 355 4082

Chapter 1

It all started one bright Thursday morning in early April. It was one of those days that seems to lead to nothing. Just a normal day. But this Thursday was different, because this Thursday Nichol Deanne Varson would meet someone who would change her life forever. (For the good or the bad, you ask? Well, that you will have to decide for yourself.)

Nicky was deep in history, studying for the test she had to take after lunch, when the speaker clicked on...

"Nichol Varson, please report to the office. Nichol Varson to the office."

Tina looked at Nicky, "What did you do?" she whispered.

Nicky shrugged as she slowly stood. Her heart flip-flopped as she walked to the office. Her mind raced, why was she being called to the office. *I hope daddy doesn't find out,* she thought. *What if he does? What did I do? It doesn't matter what I did or if I did anything, if daddy finds out I've been called to the office I will be in big trouble.*

She stopped outside the door and glanced in the mirror, making sure her hair fell over her neck covering the scares her father had given her the night before. She sighed, her long blond hair fell in place, but dark blue eyes looked scared. Though she wasn't quiet seventeen she was in the senior class. She had few close friends and her father made sure it stayed that way.

To look at her no one would have ever guessed the pain in her life, and she wasn't aloud to talk with anyone or be friends with anyone, because her father feared she would tell.

Slowly she opened the door. Miss Clam, who was sitting at her desk, looked up and smiled. "Come in, Nichol. This won't take but a minute. Mrs. Sharp just wanted me to check with you to be sure you knew that the school senior picnic was tomorrow. She was wondering where all the things were that you were suppose to get."

Nicky went pale. "It's tomorrow! I thought they were going to move it because of the rain. She told me last week not to get the stuff, because they weren't sure when they were going to have it and she would let me know when."

"Oh, we decided it would be in the gym. If it is raining. It isn't suppose to tomorrow. I know that is no guaranty but we decided to go ahead and have it. After all the rest of the month could be more of the same." Miss Clam smiled. "Now, don't worry about it. She said you all discussed it in class, as far as what all you had to get, being the class treasurer, and she said just bring the stuff tomorrow and put it in the band room. The boys will see that it gets to the picnic. However, if you already have it just put it in there today and she will see that everything is taken care of."

Nicky smiled weakly. "Yes, Miss Clam, I'll take care of it. Thank you for letting me know."

Miss Clam smiled again. "Now, you better hurry on so you aren't late for lunch."

Nicky stood. "Yes, ma'am." As she hurried back to study hall she sighed. "Well, this is just great. Now, what am I suppose to do?"

As the bell rang dismissing the students to lunch Nicky hurried out the door. *If I run all the way and hurry while I'm at the store I just might make it back without getting into trouble.* She hurried off down the street. If she had to get all the supplies for the picnic tomorrow she had to do it now. There was no way she could do it after school. "Just another thing to go wrong today." Nicky muttered.

Even though she ran every step of the way, Nicky was soaked by the time she stopped at the door to the market to catch her breath before going in. A bell tingled as the door opened. The smell of fresh bread and raw meat met her and for a moment she felt sick, though she wasn't sure if it was the smell or the anxiety she was feeling.

Grabbing the things she needed she hurried through the store and dumped everything on the counter. She kept her head down hopping Mr. Bates wouldn't recognize her. What if he told her father!

"Good afternoon."

The cheerful voice startled her and she looked up amazed to see a young boy, not much older than she. His brown hair was neatly combed and his deep brown eyes sparkled. "I wouldn't have guessed you to be old enough to be out of school yet. You wouldn't be skipping now, would you?"

Nicky flushed and for one moment she thought of lying and saying she was out of school, but she knew that would never work. "No. I just had to get some things for the class picnic tomorrow."

His brown eyes seemed to laugh as he looked into her deep blue eyes. "Nice weather for a picnic."

"It's not suppose to rain tomorrow." she snapped. Then bit her lip. If Mr. Bates caught her talking like that he would probably tell her father how disrespectful she was. "I'm sorry." she said softly. "I'm just in a hurry. I'm going to be late back to class if I don't."

The boy smiled and nodded as he started to ring up the stuff. "Name's Dustin." He said looking up at her again.

Nicky flushed. "Nichol." she said shortly. She didn't want to get into any kind of a conversation. She knew her father would never allow her to talk with a boy, even in polite conversation. Her stomach knotted painfully, thinking of what he would do to her if he knew anything about her day.

"Ten dollars and fifty-two cents please."

Nicky handed him a twenty just as Mr. Bates came out of the back. "Well, hello, Nichol. Is school out early today?"

Nicky jumped and turned pale. "No, I - I ah - I just had to get a few things." She turned quickly away.

Mr. Bates smiled. "Say hi to your parents for me."

Nicky smiled slightly as she reached for her stuff. "Yes sir. I'm sorry, but I have to go or I'll be late getting back to class."

"Nichol, wait!" Mr. Bates called after her. "Dustin is on his way home for lunch right now and passes right by the high school." he turned to Dustin and smiled. "Why don't you give her a ride?"

Nicky bit her lip. "No, thank you. I'll walk." she took a step back.

Mr. Bates smiled at her. "Now, you don't need to worry about this boy. You'll be all right. Might get sick walking all that way in the rain. Go on and let the boy help. You'll be fine. "

Nicky trembled as she looked from Mr. Bates to Dustin. She flushed as Dustin smiled at her.

"I would love to help." His smile was warm and friendly and made Nicky feel safe though she didn't know why.

"Okay." she finally consented.

"Great." Dustin smiled as he reached out and took the bags from her. Then going out into the rain he led her to his car.

"I hope Mr. Bates didn't make you to uncomfortable offering for me to give you a ride. I guess since he knows you and he knows me he figured it would be okay. I hope you aren't to late getting back."

Nicky trembled as she tried to smile, yet the thought of what would happen if her father knew any of what was happening was making her feel sick. "I guess I didn't sound to grateful did I?" her voice shook and she looked quickly away. She hadn't wanted to agree, but she was afraid Mr. Bates would say something if she didn't and she didn't want her father to know she was not in school.

"That's all right." he chuckled. "I understand." He looked over at her and grinned. "I guess I should properly introduce myself. I'm Dustin Davis."

Nicky smiled. "Nichol Varson. My friends call me Nicky."

Dustin stopped at the school. "Do you need help with this stuff?"

Nicky glanced at the clock. "No thank you. I'll just take it. I don't have much time before the bell." she started to get out but turned back. "Thank you for the ride."

He nodded. "You are welcome. Nicky," he paused, "This will probably sound a little odd - I mean I know we just met and all, but can I see you again? I don't want to make you uncomfortable, but I would like to get to know you. I mean if that is okay with you."

Nicky stepped back quickly, trembling as she thought of the consequences. "No I don't think that would work. I'm sorry. Maybe sometime, but -" she turned quickly. "I have to go."

Dustin was stunned by how gray she turned. "Nicky, are you all right. I didn't mean to up set you I just -" .

"I'm sorry." Nicky interrupted as she shut the door. She turned and fled to the school so he couldn't see the tears in her eyes. *Why did it hurt to tell him no?* she wondered. *I've turned down guys before.* She couldn't explain why it hurt, but it did. *Well, there is nothing I can do about it now. He's gone and I will probably never see him again.* Quickly dropping off the things in the band room she went on to her next class.

Tina nudged her as she sat down. "Are you coming to the party tomorrow? Andy was really hopping you would."

Nicky jumped as she looked at her friend. "I really doubt it, I'll have to ask."

Tina sighed. "Nicky, please try this time. You haven't made it to any parties this year. It's just going to be pizza and a movie and it's at Ben's so nothing should be a problem."

Nicky turned away. "I'll have to see, Tina. You know my dad doesn't want me to get mixed up in parties."

Tina sighed. "Well, please ask."

Nicky sighed then nodded. "I'll try." she whispered.

As the bell rang after the last class Nicky hurried to the door. Suddenly the speaker came on.

"All seniors to the gym for a meeting. All seniors meet in the gym for a class meeting."

Nicky groaned. "Oh, no. Not today." She turned to the gym, but her heart sank. "Daddy's going to kill me for being late." she bit her lip and looked around to make sure no one had heard. No one had and she breathed a little easier.

As soon as the meeting was over Nicky ran toward home even though she knew she was late and would be in serious trouble. The rain had slowed, but was still a miserable drizzle. Tina had offered her a ride home, but since she was already late she decided to enjoy her freedom for the few moments that she had.

Tears stung her eyes. Why did things have to be like this? Why couldn't things be like they were at Tina's? Her family at least got along, and her parents never even hollered at her. "I hate it." she muttered to herself. "Someday I will go away. I don't know where I'll go, but some day I will get away from my family. I'll leave and never come back." She bit her lip as she fought back tears. "I guess I probably won't -"

She stopped mid thought as a car pulled up behind her. She turned quickly, then relaxed a little when she saw that it was Dustin. She smiled as he stopped.

"Can I give you a lift home?" he asked.

Nicky hesitated. *Would it be alright?* she wondered. Then slowly shook her head. "Thank you for the offer, but no."

Dustin smiled as he sensed her hesitation. "I realize I don't have an excuse this time, but I would really love to give you a ride."

She glanced around quickly. "Okay," she whispered. "if you really don't mind."

He smiled. "I wouldn't have asked if I didn't want to."

She smiled and climbed in. "It was nice of you to stop. You didn't need to. I was almost home."

He grinned. "No problem." he pulled his seatbelt back on and put the car in gear. "Which way?" he asked kindly.

"Straight. For about three more blocks. You can let me off there."

"Then I'm sorry I didn't get to you sooner." He smiled at her.

She flushed and her heart skipped a beat. "Thank you for the ride, but you really didn't need to stop."

"No problem, wish it could have been longer. This the place?" He slowed the car.

"I can walk from here." she said briskly reaching to open the door. She had fully intended to say yes, but suddenly she couldn't bring herself to lie.

"I'd like to drive you home. I don't like it that you should have to walk home in the rain." he said softly. Then with a teasing smile added "I wouldn't want you to melt."

Nicky smiled. "Thanks, but I - I'll just walk from here."

She jumped out of the car before he had time to say anything else and ran down the street.

He watched her for a few minutes then sighed. *Why has this girl made me feel this way,* he wondered. Soon his jumbled thoughts became a prayer. "God, I thought you wanted me to go to collage. I thought you wanted me to go into the ministry and be established before I got serious about someone. Did I misunderstand? If I did, God, that is fine. Please show me what to do." He smiled as he looked down the street, then drove on. "I really want to get to know her."

Slowing as she reached the house Nicky tried to calm her heart. She saw her fathers car parked in the drive and she trembled. *May as well face it now. The longer I take getting to the house the worse it will be.* She felt sick as she walked up to the door. Slowly she stepped inside.

"You are late!"

Nicky jumped as she turned to face her father. "I - the rain slowed me." She tried to stop trembling, but couldn't.

Her father walked over to her and slugged her jaw. "Don't you lie to me, girl. You are forty-five minutes late. Do you really expect me to believe it was the rain that slowed you?" He looked at her hard. Hate radiated out of his eyes.

Nicky bit her lip. "We had a class meeting, to get things ready for graduation." Her voice trembled slightly she could tell her father was drunk again, even though he hadn't been off work for long. "I'm sorry I was late, but I couldn't help it."

Her father grabbed her arm as he slapped her across the face. "Don't you dare lie to me. You were out trying to make eyes at the boys again weren't you?" He slapped her again, "Answer me!"

Nicky trembled as she looked at him. "No, Sir. I'm telling the truth."

He pushed her to the floor and kicked her. "You better be." he snapped. "Go get dinner ready, your mother won't be home for a few more hours. Don't wait till it is cold to tell me. And bring me a drink first."

Nicky trembled as she stood.

"Now!" he screamed as he pushed her into the kitchen knocking her to the floor again. "You lazy brat."

Chapter 2

The next morning she washed in the bathroom trying to get all the blood off her face and back. The bruises were there no matter what she did but she would just have to make the most of it. "Why do you have to do this to me, daddy? If you don't want anyone to know, why do you do it?"

Looking in the mirror again she shrugged, "I guess that will have to do. I don't think it will get any better. I just have to come up with some excuse to not go with Tina tonight. I don't want to go anyway." She glanced in the mirror again. "Maybe no one will notice. If they don't look close, it looks almost normal. I'll just have to stay away from Tina." Trembling she picked up her school bag. She dreaded facing the day, yet staying home seemed a whole lot worse.

As she walked into the living room Her father looked up seaming to study her. "Well, I suppose you'll have to do." he grunted. "Don't be late today. Your mother will worry about you. I expect a good report when I get home."

"You'll get one." she said calmly.

As she turned to flee out the door her father stopped her, "And Nichol, remember what I said last night."

"Yes, sir. I'll be home on time." she said softly. "And I will be good. No looking or thinking about boys." she trembled slightly. "Promise." Quickly she crossed her heart.

"Good." he answered. Then he stood and gripped her arm tightly. Nicky bit her lip to keep back the cry of pain, her father's grip could brake a bone if he was angry or drunk enough. He lifted his belt and struck her seven or eight times. Then he turned her to face him. "That is to help you remember. Now, get out." Angrily he pushed her towards the door. "And don't get into any trouble. If you do I will find out, and you'll get what you deserve."

Slipping out the door she almost ran to the sidewalk. *All I have to do is get through today. Hopefully Tina won't see the bruises during gym, she's the only one that would ask.* Suddenly she remembered the picnic. "Oh, yea. I forgot about that." she smiled so relieved that she spoke out loud. "Sweet, we don't have classes or gym today. That will help." Completely absorbed in her thoughts she didn't hear a car pull up behind her.

"Hi, Nicky." came a friendly voice.

She turned her head, then flushed, it was Dustin. *Was he waiting for me?* she wondered. Then quickly pushed the thought away, *No, probably he just happen to be on his way to work at the same time?* She smiled and waved as he pulled up beside her and stopped.

"Can I give you a lift?" he asked gently.

Nicky thought for a few minuets. What could it hurt? She glanced quickly around to be sure no one saw her then smiled. "I guess so, that is, if you want to."

He reached over and opened the door for her, "I wouldn't of stopped if I didn't want to. Climb in."

She slid in to the seat and shut the door. "Thank you." she whispered feeling bashful, yet on alert for any sign of danger. She may not be able to control her father, but if someone else tried to hit her she would just walk away. Thinking that made her feel a little safer. She had control over what happened to her, and no boy was going to hit her. She would leave and never talk to him again if he did. Suddenly she forced her mind back to Dustin and what he was saying.

"No problem." he smiled at her. "All ready for the picnic today?"

"I suppose. My responsibilities are done anyway. All I had to do was get the supplies the boys are suppose to see that they get there. I'm just glad school is almost over."

"I guess you were right about the weather, for now any way." he looked at her and grinned. His eyes twinkled with laughter.

"Ah, thanks for the confidence." she said teasingly. "We are having the picnic in the gym any way. I guess they didn't want to worry about the weather."

He smiled at her. Then looked a little closer. *Is that a bruise on the side of her face!* he wondered. *I'm sure it wasn't there yesterday.* A concerned look came into his eyes. "Nicky?" he said softly yet his voice held all the question she needed.

She flushed knowing he saw marks from her father, "I uh, I just-I fell." she stammered turning to look out the window.

"Uh-huh." he said softly.

Something in his voice told Nicky he didn't believe her. She squirmed uneasily, feeling her pulse beginning to race. *What if he finds out? He'll never want to talk to me again.* She knew she didn't want that to happen, but why? She had only met him yesterday. She suddenly felt panicked. What if he found out and told someone else? What if he turned her father in? She bit her lip. *Please don't ask any more questions.* she thought. Nicky sighed with relief to see that they were at the high school. "Thanks for ride." she said as she quickly opened up the door and got out before he could say anymore.

"Can I give you a ride home? I get off about the same time school gets out and I'm going your way." he looked at her pleadingly.

She smiled. Something in his eyes said he wanted to say more, a whole lot more. For now she was just thankful he didn't. "We'll just have to see." she said weakly. She smiled as she shut the door and turned to run to the high school. Turning she waved then hurried inside.

Dustin watched her and sighed. What secret was she trying to keep? Was she in an abusive relationship with someone? He shook his head as he shifted in to drive. If she was dating someone she surely wouldn't be accepting rides from him, after all he had sensed her hesitation yesterday as though she wanted to say yes, but was nervous. Maybe sometime he could find out. It would just have to take time. "After all," he told himself, "she is basically a stranger to me. She probably wouldn't want to tell someone she hardly even knew her family is hurting her." Dustin felt his pulse race. "Should I try to find out, God, or should I just let it lay for a while? Please tell me what to do. I prayed last night that you would show me if you want me to pursue a relationship with her and I am still waiting, God. Please tell me what to do." He smiled as he looked back at the school then drove on.

His mind raced. Was he wanting to get to know her or did he feel a need to find out what was happening to her, because he had seen so many kids in abusive homes, thanks to his mom and dad doing faster care for so many years? *Do I want to get to know her and possibly have more, or is it just that - I don't know, should I tell mom and dad my concerns or just leave it alone?*

Chapter 3

Most of the time the seniors tried to act grown up, today it just didn't seem right to be that way. They played games that most of them hadn't played since grade school, They had a good time just being together as a class and though it wasn't graduation yet it seemed to many of them that they were saying goodbye.

"That was the best day I've had in a long time." Nicky commented to Tina. "I can't believe the time passed so fast. Most school days feel like they are never going to end."

"I know. I was dreading today, but I really enjoyed myself. I'm going to miss our class. Most of us won't be together in collage next year. It's kind of sad. Though we have a few new students, most of us have been together since kindergarten. I think I'm going to miss a lot of things about our school."

"I know. Me too. I can tell you one thing I'm not going to miss and that is homework. I am so sick of righting turn papers." Nicky smiled. "I'll just be glad it's over and we don't have to worry about making good grades anymore."

Tina grinned. "I didn't know you really worried about that, Nicky. I thought you were just naturally a good student."

Nicky laughed. "I wish. Then I wouldn't have to study."

Tina looked up at Nicky. "Are you coming to night or not? Andy was watching your every move today. This could be your big chance." Tina nudged Nicky as she teased. "What do you think?"

Nicky sighed. "I just don't know yet. I haven't had a chance to ask."

"Nicky, please. I really want you to come. One party surely wouldn't upset them would it?" Tina pleaded.

"I'll try." Nicky promised. "But that is all I can do. If you don't hear from me just assume I couldn't come. Fair?"

Tina sighed. "I guess it will have to be. As long as you try."

Nicky laughed. "I will tell you right now, Tina, if I go it has nothing to do with him, it will be for you. And if I go I don't want you to ask me to any more this year please." Just then Nicky stopped laughing and looked down at her watch. "Oh no, I've got to run. My mom wanted me home on time today."

"Okay. See you tonight hopefully." Tina called as she headed for her car.

"See ya." Nicky called as ran toward the street.

Slowing her step slightly Nicky sighed. "I don't know that I want to go to your party Tina." Nicky muttered as she walk on. "I like Andy just not in that way. Besides I'm not aloud to date. And even if I were I don't think I would date Andy." She trembled as she remembered her fathers threats from the night before. *Especially after last night.* she thought to herself.

What if Daddy would have seen me getting in and out of a strange boys car? What if he suspected something? Would he really do what he had threatened, she wondered to afraid to even say the thought out loud to herself. She shivered again.

Yes, he would. She knew he would. She bit her lip. What if he had followed her to school this morning? What if he had seen her with Dustin? She groaned as she slowed her step even more. "The last thing I want to do is go home." she groaned. "I'm tired of living like this. I'm not ready for what is coming."

All her life she had tried to obey. She wanted her mom and dad to like her maybe even love her. "What does it feel like to be loved?" she wondered. "Is it feeling safe the way I do when I'm around Dustin? Or is it something else? Do I like him?" she flushed. Would she ever know, would she ever have the chance to find out? Or would she go through life never knowing love or comfort. Never having someone to hold her or protect her?

At that moment a car pulled up beside her and stopped, the driver rolled down the window. "I thought you said I could give you a ride." Dustin called.

Lost in thought Nicky jumped, then felt her pulse race when she saw who it was. *Why is he doing this?* she thought. *Does he like me, or is he trying to do something to me, or maybe he is just trying to be nice? He hasn't tried to do any thing to me, and I don't feel afraid of him.* Nicky struggled with her thoughts. *He has been a perfect gentleman with me. Maybe it will be okay as long as my parents don't find out. There is no telling what they would do if they ever found out I was accepting rides from a stranger, especially a boy.*

But Mr. Bates had started it, maybe it was okay. She struggled with what to say knowing it wouldn't matter if it was started by Mr. Bates or not if her father saw her. Finally she answered, "I had to get home. I'm sorry. Maybe another time."

"Can I give you a ride the rest of the way?" he asked kindly.

Nicky trembled. His eyes looked so pleading she almost gave in, then remembering the way her father had threatened her, she hardened. "Not today, thanks. I am almost there anyway. I'll just walk today." she smiled slightly hoping she didn't sound to cold. "It was nice of you to stop, thanks."

"Are you sure I can't give you a ride the rest of the way?"

"Another time." she said softly not meeting his gaze. "I'll let you give me a ride another time."

"I'll hold you to that." he said with a teasing smile.

She smiled looking up at him. He sat back in his seat and waved. "I'll be seeing you soon." he said as he drove off.

Biting her lip she continued on her way home. "I hope so, Dustin." she whispered. "I hope so." Quickly she wiped away her tears.

Trudging up the drive she slowed even more. Dreading going in the house she paused, her hand on the door as her parents voices floated out to her.

"I told you I don't want to be left at home with her. She is the most disobedient child I have ever seen." Her mother hollered. "I have business to take care of also. If you are gone on a business trip then I am that is one thing, but we can't both be gone at the same time. I told you last week I needed to go to New York next Monday, and that I would be gone about a week."

Her father grunted and mumbled something Nicky couldn't hear. She leaned closer to the door trying to hear. "I don't have to leave till Thursday. I won't be gone more than over the weekend. Can't you try to make it home in time to be with her Thursday after school."

Her mother sighed. "What are we going to do when she graduates? I am not staying home just to make sure she behaves."

Nicky heard her father snort. "She will learn to behave with out us here. Don't worry she'll be to busy through the summer to get into any trouble. I know she is getting older but as long as I can help it she will keep herself clean."

Nicky trembled. *What does he mean by that?* she wondered. Then she heard her father again and leaned closer to the door to listen.

"Where is she anyway? Late again, I suppose." he growled. "If she don't learn to listen to me-"

Her mother sighed. "Yes, I suppose she is late. Isn't she always?"

Her father grunted. "You planning on staying here tonight with her? I'm sorry but I have to go to work."

"I suppose I have to don't I." her mother snapped. "Just don't count on me being in a good mood when you get home. And if I can't be back in time next weekend it might be a good time to see how good she will be during the summer.""

Nicky took a deep breath. "If I let them go on I'll be in even bigger trouble." she muttered. Slowly she pushed open the door.

Both parents turned to look at her. Nicky trembled as she stepped in. "Sorry I'm late." she said quietly. "I guess I just walked a little slow today."

As her father walked towards her Nicky closed the door and stepped back against it, trembling in fear.

Angrily he reached out and grabbed her arm. "Get to your room this minute. I'll deal with you later." He pushed her towards her bedroom.

Nicky fled to her room. As she pushed the door shut she sighed. "That went better than I expected." she thought. She relaxed a little when she heard her parents arguing again. "At least he won't come in here for a while." she said to herself as she pulled out her books. "Might as well get some homework done while I can. I know I won't be able to later."

After about an hour her father knocked at her door. "Nichol, I'm leaving for work. I don't have time to deal with you now so be prepared for later. And don't bother your mother tonight."

"Yes sir." Nicky called.

Soon she heard her father leave. Slowly she relaxed. After a while she opened her door. Her mother was sitting in the living room watching TV. She turned to look at Nicky.

"Get out of the house, Nichol. I don't want to have to deal with you tonight."

Nicky stared at her mother in shock. "Yes, mama." she said softly, stepping back into her room to change. "Guess I'm going to your party after all, Tina." she mumbled.

When Nicky got to Tina's she was just getting ready to leave. "You made it!" she cried. "I hope it will be worth it." her eyes twinkled with teasing.

I hope so too. Nicky thought. Out loud she said, "I'm sure you'll make it that way."

Tina grinned and they climbed into her car. Soon they arrived at Ben's. He and Andy were waiting for them.

"Glad you finally showed up." Ben called as he stepped up to the car. "We were about to start the movie without you."

Tina laughed. "I was waiting to see if Nicky would show."

Ben smiled at her. "Glad you did, Nicky. Otherwise Andy here would have been left out."

Nicky flushed.

They all went to the basement to watch a movie. After it was over Ben and Tina went upstairs to get some more popcorn, leaving Nicky and Andy in the basement alone.

Andy looked at her and smiled. "Glad you could come." he said softly as he put his hand on her leg.

Nicky felt her pulse begin to race, but not in the same way it did when she saw Dustin, instead it was more of a tremble. Quickly she pulled her leg away. "I am to. I had a good time."

Andy slid closer to her. "Want me to show you how it can be an even better time?"

Nicky backed away. "Cut it out, Andy." she tried to push him away but he backed up with her.

As though he hadn't heard her he slid his arms around her and leaned closer. "You don't mean that do you?" he whispered softly.

Nicky trembled. *What can I do?* she wondered. "Yes I do mean it! Please don't, Andy."

Without giving her time to think Andy pushed her to the floor and laid on top of her. He slowly began to rub his hands over her body.

Nicky tried to push him away but he was to strong for her. "Andy, please don't I don't want things to be like this."

He laughed dryly. "Don't worry if it's your first time. I'll go easy." he leaned down closer to her.

Without thinking Nicky screamed.

Andy slapped her. "What are you doing? You want everyone back down here?"

Nicky trembled again, but before she could say anything she heard footsteps on the stairs. Then Ben and Tina ran into the room.

Andy quickly rolled of Nicky and acted as though he was embarrassed that they had been caught.

Nicky scrambled to her feet and backed towards the door. "Sorry, Ben, Tina." she whispered. "Thanks for having me, but I have to go." Quickly she turned and fled up the steps.

Tina ran after her. "Nicky, are you okay?" she asked softly.

Nicky didn't stop till she was in the garage. Then turning to her friend she whispered, "Don't ever invite me to a party again, Tina." Tears ran down her cheeks and sounded in her voice.

Tina gripped her arm. "I'm sorry, Nicky. I didn't know he was going to try to do that to you. I thought you would be okay. I'm sorry." Tina put an arm around her. "Let me give you a ride home. I'll just go tell Ben."

"No, Tina." Nicky cried pushing her away. "I can't. I'm sorry." Turning she fled down the street.

By Monday morning Nicky dreaded going to school so much she was almost sick. "I don't want to have to see Andy or Tina ever again." she cried to herself as she walked down the road. "Or Ben for that matter. Who knows what he thinks of me." Tears ran down her cheeks. "I hate him. I will never go to a party again, but more important my parents must never find out." she determined.

Soon she heard a car pull up behind her. She trembled as she turned her head then relaxed a little when she saw it was Dustin. *Why don't I feel threatened by him?* she wondered. *Maybe I should. After all, daddy says that's all a boy wants.* But even as Dustin stopped she couldn't help but smile.

"Will you let me give you a ride to day?" he asked kindly.

"I suppose." she said as she slipped into his car. As she buckled in she felt herself tremble.

Dustin smiled at her. "You look tired." he watched her closely. Tired was an understatement. She looked as though she were about to collapse, and as though she had been crying, but he wasn't going to say that.

"A little." Nicky admitted. "I just haven't slept well the last few nights. Worried about finals I guess." she tried to smiled.

"I remember when mom was home schooling me last year. I was so worried that I was going to fail and not be able to go to collage." he laughed. "Then what a surprise when I told mom and dad I wasn't going to collage the next year. But was going to work instead. It surprised me as well. But I just felt it was right somehow."

Nicky smiled as she settled back in the seat. She liked listening to him talk. It made her feel calm and helped her forget her troubles. "Tell me about your family. Are you an only child?"

Dustin smiled. "Nope. There are seven others besides me. I'm the oldest then there is Sara, she's about seventeen. Then Caden, he's twelve. Olivia is ten, Josh, Jason, and Joy are three and Julia just turned one." He looked at her "What about you? You have any siblings?"

Nicky felt her stomach knot. "No. Just me." she tried to smile. "Mom and dad wanted more but after me mom miscarried they never tried again. It was really hard on her."

Dustin looked away. "I'm sorry, I didn't mean to upset you."

"No, it's okay." she smiled. "Really, you had no way of knowing."

Dustin pulled the car to a stop. "I'll see you after school, if I can." he smiled.

"Thanks." Nicky smiled back. "I think I would like that."

Nicky hurried into the school, hopping Andy wouldn't be there, but much to her dismay he was there, waiting for her as she walked in the door. Angrily he gripped her arm. "I want you to go out with me this weekend." he hissed. "And don't you dare breath a word about the other night. I mean it, Nicky."

Nicky trembled as she glanced at him. "Sorry, Andy, but I'm busy this weekend. Maybe some other time." Before she finished the bell rang. To her surprise he let her pull away and she hurried quickly down the hallway to class.

"Saved by the bell." she muttered as she pushed open the classroom door.

As soon as school was over that afternoon she was again approached by Andy. When she saw him coming she shot a quick look around and relaxed a little as she saw Tina and some of the other girls standing around at the lockers.

"You will go with me sometime soon." he growled in her ear. "Or I'll make sure you are very, very sorry." He stepped closer to her as if trying to make other people think something was going on between them.

Nicky trembled as she stepped back. "I don't know what you mean, Andy. I have to go." Her stomach knotted as she hurried out the door, she practically ran down the street. What if he tried to catch her on the way home? What would she do?

Her mind filled with dread as she hurried toward home. Tears ran down her cheeks. "I don't know what to do." she whispered to herself. "I'm scared, but I don't know what I should do." Once again lost in thought she jumped as a car pulled up behind her. Fear gripping her she started to run.

"Nicky!" called the driver.

Nicky turned quickly then smiled. She felt her whole body relax. It was Dustin. She felt sure he would protect her from Andy, but why did she feel that way? She couldn't answer that question even to herself. She just knew she felt safe with him. Should she, or should she feel scared? What if he was only out to hurt her? Quickly she pushed all those thoughts away.

Dustin smiled as he slowed. "Can I give you a lift home?"

Nicky shuttered. "I suppose you can at least a little way."

Dustin reached over and pushed open the door. "I'd be glad to." His eyes sparkled with his teasing. "I hope you don't think it's to weird, me offering you rides that is. I don't want to make you feel uncomfortable. I know we don't hardly know each other, but I -" he stopped.

Nicky smiled. "It's not. I mean you don't. I mean, I like the rides. Thank you for the offer." She flushed. Why did she suddenly feel so tongue tied?

Dustin glanced over at her as he drove to the corner. "I'm glad you like them. I had hoped-" he stopped.

Nicky looked at him quickly. What was he going to say?

Dustin flushed. "I hoped you liked them as much as I did." he finally said. His heart cramped. He wanted to say some much more. He wanted to know if this was God's will. He wanted to know if she was the one God had for him. He wanted to ask her out and have her say she would be delighted, but he hardly knew her. Maybe it would be better if he waited a while.

Nicky smiled weakly. "I have enjoyed them." Even as she spoke her stomach cramped. She could tell be his face he wanted to say more. Her heart flip-flopped. Did he have feelings for her? Was he going to ask her out?

Silently she rebuked the feelings and thoughts. *I can't go out with him. Daddy doesn't let me go out with anyone and even if he did he wouldn't let me go with someone who is almost a complete stranger. Besides that, I don't know that I would want to get involved with a boy. Daddy was right all they want is to hurt me.* Nicky trembled as she thought about Friday night.

Dustin pulled the car to a stop. The silence on the short ride was almost deafening. It seemed both had so much to say and both were afraid to speak.

Nervously Dustin cleared his throat. "Nicky," he almost whispered, in spite of his intentions not to be nervous. "Nicky, I wanted to ask you something."

Nicky trembled as she looked into his eyes. "Yes." she tried to keep her voice steady, though she could feel her whole body shaking.

Dustin looked away then back at her, "Nicky, I - that is to say - I wanted to - I just." Dustin stopped to scared to go on. What if she said no? His heart turned over. Her rejection would be worse then not asking at all. If she said no he would take that as his sign they were not meant to be together. And he didn't want to lose her. Again he took a deep breath determined to ask her out, but he just couldn't force out the words. "Will you wait for me in the morning if I'm not here waiting for you?" he finally asked.

Nicky trembled. "I'll try. It will all depend on the time." Nicky stomach tightened. She had to get home or she would be in trouble for being late again. Slowly she slid out of the car. "I'll see you tomorrow, Dustin." she said forcing a timid smile. "I need to get home now."

Dustin smiled. "Tomorrow." As soon as she was gone he wanted to kick himself. "Dustin, why didn't you ask her?" he muttered. "I will tomorrow." he finally promised himself as he drove home. "I have to, before more feelings develop." he sighed. "Help me, God." he pleaded. "I need your strength. I need you to show me what to do."

Chapter 4

The next morning Nicky hurried out the door hopping her father wouldn't be watching her. Fear raced through her, what if he found out that she was riding to school with a boy? As she rounded the corner her stomach muscles knotted. Dustin was waiting for her.

He smiled as she walked up. "I was beginning to worry. I thought you might be sick or something."

Nicky tensed as she slid in the car. "No, just running a little slow."

They drove to the high school in silence. When they pulled to a stop he looked at her. "Nicky." he whispered. His voice cracked and she looked at him in surprise. It wasn't like him to be so nervous, even though she had only known him a short time she knew that.

"Nicky." Dustin tried again. "Nicky, I - I wanted - what I mean to say-" he stopped and sighed.

"I'm listening." she assured him. "Go ahead and tell me what ever it is you want to say. Please, I don't want to be late." she glanced nervously around. Why was he acting so strange.

Dustin bit his lip. "I don't want this to be to weird, I mean we only met like last week, but, Nicky, I want - I wanted - to ask you something." his voice cracked again.

Nicky looked up at him and trembled. "I'm listening."

Dustin looked deep into her eyes and his heart fluttered. "Nicky, I wanted to ask you if you would go - if we could -" he took a deep breath. "Would you like to have dinner with me on Friday?"

Nicky gasped. "Dustin, I don't know - I mean I just -" She couldn't date. Her father would find out and it would make things even worse at home. "I can't." she finally whispered looking down.

Dustin tilted her chin up and looked at her closely. Fear ran through him as he saw the pain in her eyes. "Is there someone else, Nicky?" he whispered. He was afraid to ask but he had to know.

She trembled as she looked away. "No, there is no one else. I just - its just that - well, I don't have the time."

Dustin looked at her doubtfully. "How much time would one night take, Nicky?"

Nicky blinked hard as tears sprang to her eyes. She wanted nothing more than to say yes. She wished with all her might that she could, but she knew what would happen if her father found out. Slowly she looked up at him. "I don't want to." she whispered.

Dustin looked into her eyes. "You don't mean that, Nicky." he whispered. He sensed her hesitation, and wished he knew what she really wanted to say. "You want to go out as much as I do, or you wouldn't have been accepting rides from me so willingly, right?" He looked into her eyes as she turned to face him. "Please just give me a chance. If you still feel this way after a couple of dates, I'll leave you alone. I won't bother you again. Please, Nicky, please."

"I can't, Dustin. I'm sorry." she looked away fighting the tears that threatened to spill over at any moment.

"Can't or won't?" Dustin reached over and tilted her chin so she was looking at him. "Are you saying it will never happen. Or are you saying it's all to new right now?"

Nicky looked away.

"I'll wait if that is what you are saying. I didn't want to hurt you, I just wanted - I didn't want to -" he stopped unable to go on. He hadn't imagined the hurt of her saying no, he just thought that she would say yes. He looked into her eyes. "Are you saying no, Nicky?"

Nicky bit her lip and nodded.

Dustin turned away. "Then I guess this is goodbye." he whispered, trying to sound as if he didn't care that she had turned him down and failing miserably. His voice broke and he felt tears sting his eyes. He felt as though his heart was sick. He never dreamed it would hurt this much.

Nicky reached for the door as tears stung her own eyes. She glanced back at him, he was still looking away from her. Her heart broke, she couldn't let him leave like this. She couldn't walk away from the one person, though she had only known him a week, she felt cared about her, the one person who made her feel safe. She heard a voice inside whispering "Your father will find out. You can't keep it a secret." She bit her lip and pushed away the thought. "You weren't wrong." she whispered. "I do want to go out with you I just - I can't."

"Why?" Dustin looked at her closely. "Do I need to get your parents permission? Is that why you say you can't?"

Nicky trembled. Him asking her parents would be even worse then never seeing him again. No matter what happened between them she had to keep it a secret from her family. "I'm just scared. I never went out before." she quickly answered hopping to get his mind away from her parents.

Dustin smiled. "Me neither, but I wouldn't mind changing that if you were the one I went out with. If you will let me, I'll ask your dad when I take you home tonight to make sure it's alright with him."

"NO!" Nicky cried. Then stopped when she saw the surprised look in Dustin eyes. "I mean, he's not home. He'll be gone on a business trip this weekend. And he doesn't get home from work till really late at night."

Dustin looked at her pleadingly. "Please, Nicky. Just give it a chance. If you decide it won't work, I'll leave you alone. Just one date, please."

Nicky looked up at him with tears in her eyes. *If only it were that easy.* she thought. "Okay." she whispered. "Just one."

"Does Friday work? I could pick you up at seven if that's okay." Dustin smiled into her eyes. "Are you sure I don't need to at least talk to your dad first? I don't want to cause any trouble. And I would like to meet your family."

Nicky flushed. "No, you don't need to talk to him. I told you he's going to be gone. I'm going to be home alone this weekend. Why don't I just meet you somewhere on Friday?" Nicky trembled thinking of the consequences should her father ever find out. *I will not let him rule my life forever,* she thought rebelliously, *no matter what he says this is my life.*

Dustin looked at her closely. "I guess if you would rather. How does seven at Roper Café sound?"

Nicky smiled, glad he wasn't pressing the issue of meeting her parents. "Sounds good. I'll see you there. Is there-" suddenly she stopped. "What time is it?" she gasped.

Dustin looked down at his watch. "Oh, Nicky, I'm sorry it's nine forty-five."

Nicky jumped out of the car. "I'm sorry, I have to go. I don't want to be late to my next class also."

"See you this afternoon. Sorry I made you late." He smiled apologetically.

Nicky forced a smile back but her stomach knotted painfully knowing what she had just done to herself. "It's not you fault." she whispered. "I'll see you Friday if I can." She turned quickly and ran into the school.

As soon as school was out Nicky raced home. She was so afraid her father would find out about her being late to classes that morning that she didn't even think about meeting up with Dustin. She made it home in less time than she had ever been able to before, though because she was late to class she had received detention, she was still way later than she should be getting home. As she reached the door she stopped.

What if her father was already home and waiting for her? She groaned and slowly opened the door. Not seeing her father any where she relaxed a little and hurried into her room. Dropping her bag on the floor she turned to go back out and nearly jumped out of her skin. Her father was sitting on the edge of her bed.

He looked at her and sneered. "Worried about something, Nichol?"

Nicky trembled as she faced him. "I just didn't see you there." she tried not to let him see her fear as she stepped away from him.

"I hope you have a good explanation for why you were late to class this morning." he growled as he stood and stepped closer to her and pulled of his belt. "Will you ever learn." he grabbed her arm and slugged her in the stomach. "I've had all of this I'm going to stand for. You will never be late again understand."

Nicky trembled as she looked up at her father. "Yes, sir. I understand." She bit her lip as he whipped her trying to keep from crying out.

Chapter 5

Nicky groaned as she opened her eyes it was morning. She ached all over. She jumped as her door opened.

"Get up," her father growled, "you have five minutes to be ready for school. I'm taking you there on my way to work. That way I know you aren't late. Hurry it up! I don't have all morning." He grabbed her by her hair and pulled her out of bed. Then slammed the door as he went out.

Sighing she pulled on some clean clothes. Looking in the mirror she gasped. She had bruises on her face and arms, and her nose had dry blood under it, a large welt ran from her left ear to her chin. She felt a large bruise on her side from her father hitting her the night before.

Tears stinging her eyes she hurried to the bathroom and washed as good as she could. Looking in the mirror she felt like crying. "Why does he hate me so much? Why can't he just hit me where it won't show? I'm so scared other people will see. If I wasn't afraid of what would happen if I were caught I would run away from here and never come back."

When her father knocked on the door she jumped. "Nicky, hurry it up or you are going to make us both late, me for work and you for school. Now come on!"

She bit her lip. *If only I could get away.* She sighed as she opened the door.

Her father grabbed her arm as she came out. "I told you to hurry. You are the slowest girl I have ever met." Angrily he pushed her forward. "Now, get out to the car."

Nicky stumbled as he pushed her again. What would Dustin think when she didn't show. Would he think she was just hunting for him to ask her out and then she was going to ditch him. Tears weld in her eyes but she wouldn't let them fall. It would just be another reason for her father to hit her if he saw. Hopefully Dustin wouldn't be upset. She would just have to think up something to tell him, later.

As they neared the corner Nicky trembled. What if Dustin was there waiting? What would her father do if he suspected something?

When she saw Dustin's car she wanted to hide, so he wouldn't know she was there, but instead she looked straight ahead not daring to even glance his way for fear her father would notice.

Dustin glanced at the car as it came around the corner and his heart stopped. Was that Nicky? Who was with her, her dad? Why wasn't she letting him take her to school? His stomach knotted and he knew something had to be wrong. She wouldn't just get a ride from her father, if that was who it was, for no reason. He bit his lip. Was it because she had been late to class the day before? If it was her family abusing her, had he just made it worse?

"God, please help me know." he whispered. "Maybe I can talk with her this afternoon. I'll just have to get off early enough to pick her up." he determined. He drove on to work sadly, the whole morning seemed empty with out the early ride. He hoped Nicky wasn't upset with him. Maybe that was why she hadn't let him take her home yesterday. He sighed, and maybe not. He wouldn't know till he talked to her and he hoped he would have a chance before Friday.

As soon as the bell rang Nicky hurried outside. *Maybe Dustin will be able to give me a ride home.* she thought. She hadn't realized just how uplifting riding to school with Dustin was until that morning. It had made her feel safe and protected, even though she didn't know why. Yet as she walked out into the sunshine her heart sank. Her father was there to pick her up. Quietly she slipped in the car.

Her father looked at her. "Well?" he snapped. "What happened to make your day go so bad. You didn't want your father to pick you up for some reason. Thought maybe you would be able to flirt with the boys a little did you?"

Nicky trembled. Just hearing her father talk sent shivers up her spine. She felt jumpy, as though anything she did he was going to hit her for. "No, I just wasn't expecting you to be here. Thanks for coming to pick me up, dad." she tried to make her voice sound natural but must have failed, for her father laughed coldly.

"I'm sure you are so grateful." he scowled as he pulled to a stop in front of the house. "Now get in there and get ready to start supper. And don't even think of sneaking out. I have to get back to work for a few more hours. I want supper ready and the house clean when I get back. Do I make myself clear?"

"Yes sir." She tried not to whisper, but she felt her heart sinking. What was he going to do to her?

As her father drove off Nicky whimpered. "I want to run." she whispered. "I want to run away and never see him again. I can't stand being here." Turning she hurried into the house to do as her father asked.

About seven she heard her father stumble into the house. Trembling she stepped out of her room. "Daddy, I didn't think you would be gone so late. I kept dinner warm for you. I'll get it on the table." she turned toward the kitchen but her father stopped her.

"I don't want supper. Get over here." he growled.

Trembling she walked over to him. "Yes, sir?"

Grabbing her arm he slapped her. "I told you to clean the house. Do you call this place clean?" Angrily he slapped her again.

Nicky bit her lip. What did he mean, what had she forgotten?

"I asked you a question, you brat." he screamed as he twisted her arm. Suddenly he pushed her to the floor. "You didn't scrub the floor. You didn't dust the fan. What else didn't you do?" He pulled her back to her feet and pushed her into the middle of the living room. Grabbing up his whip he cracked her with it. "You are lazy, no good, worthless, trash!" Again he cracked the whip.

Nicky trembled. Her father suddenly stopped hitting her and pulled her into the kitchen. Laughing he tied her to a chair. She bit her lip. What was he going to do to her?

"You ready for your first drink, girl?" he laughed. "I know your mother wouldn't approve of this, but it's high time for you to have it." He laughed wickedly as he opened a bottle and forced it in her mouth.

Nicky wanted to scream, but instead she tightened her jaw trying to keep her father from getting the bottle in her mouth. *No, daddy. Please no! I don't want to drink, not ever.* she screamed silently in her thoughts. Her stomach turned as she tasted the liquor and she thought she was going to be sick.

Her father poured the bottle down her, most of it ran out of her mouth, when it was gone he pulled the bottle from her mouth and opened another one. Nicky dropped her head and groaned. She felt her stomach turn and tasted vomit in her mouth, but knew better then to throw up with her father watching.

He laughed and dumped the other bottle over her head. "Now get use to the smell and the taste." he laughed. "And you will learn to love it." Laughing wickedly he left the room. Leaving her tide to the chair.

Nicky blinked back tears. "Is there no one who can help me." she whimpered.

She woke to her father slapping her face. "Get up you worthless brat." he snapped. "Get your bag and get in the car. You're going to be late to school."

Nicky slowly opened her eyes, slowly she stood. Her father grabbed her arm and pushed her to her room.

"Get that bag and get out to the car. You don't have time to clean up now." he snapped. "You are going to make us both late."

Nicky trembled as she obeyed. She wanted nothing less than to go to school looking and smelling like she did, but she knew it would do no good to argue.

As her father pulled up at school he scowled at her. "I'm sure you remember I am leaving today for a business trip. I leave within the hour, but your mother should be back this afternoon or at the latest in the morning. Things are still the same. Our rules still apply, if you disobey you will pay for it. Do you understand?"

Nicky trembled at the hate in her father's voice. "Yes, sir. I will obey."

"Good. Then get out and don't be late." he snapped.

"Yes, sir." Nicky said again as she opened the door. Her stomach turned as she walked into the school. She could still smell the beer on her hair and skin. She wanted nothing less then to go to school. She didn't want people to think she drank, nor did she want anyone to see her in the state she was in. "I'll just have to try to freshen up in the bathroom before I see anyone." she muttered as she hurried into the school.

As soon as the last bell rang she ran out hoping the fresh air would keep anyone from noticing the way she smelled. She had done her best to stay away from everyone that day and Tina hadn't said a word. She started home in fear, then relaxed a little when she remembered her father wouldn't be there.

"Nicky, wait!" a voice called.

Nicky trembled. She knew the voice well, it was Andy. Slowly she turned wanting nothing less then to talk with him.

As he came up next to her he grabbed her arm. "I want you to go out with me tomorrow. Meet me at the 'Corner Café' at seven." he leaned close to her. "Got it. Do not be late or you will be very, very sorry."

Trembling she tried to pull away. "I'm not going out with you, Andy." She pulled again. "Let me go."

Andy smiled wickedly. "You don't and you just remember what I said. I will make you very sorry. You will be there. Got it!" he leaned closer as if he was going to kiss her.

Nicky trembled as she pulled away. "No!" she cried. She managed to pull her arm free and started running down the street. She wasn't even sure she was going in the direction of home, but she knew she had to get away. She ran as fast as she could. Then suddenly she stumbled and fell to the side walk.

"Nicky, let me help you." Someone said.

Nicky felt strong hands pull her to her feet. She gasped and tried to pull away. When she saw that it was Dustin she relaxed a little. "Thank you." she whispered as he let her go.

"You should slow down a bit." he chuckled. Then looking closer at her he asked, "You okay?"

She suddenly realized she was trembling. "I'm fine." She stepped back remembering her fathers threat and the beer that he had poured on her last night. She didn't want Dustin to smell her, nor did she want him to know just how scared she was.

He smiled. "Come on I'll give you a ride and you can tell me about it." he whispered as he led her to his car. He could tell by the look in her eye that she was scared.

As he opened the door for her she stepped back her mind searching for an excuse not to ride with him. "I really don't think you want to give me a ride today. I'm all sweaty from P.E. and I really don't think -"

"Nicky." Dustin whispered. But that was all he needed to say. Slowly she slid in the car and waited for him to say something. Fear knotted her stomach.

Climbing in he looked at her then drove to the corner. As he pulled the car to a stop Nicky grabbed the door handle franticly, she wanted to get away before he said something. She was so scared someone would find out about her father and she knew that would only make things worse.

"Thanks but I need to run." she tried to push the door open. Then looked at Dustin. He was watching her.

Fear ripped through her. "Dustin, unlock the door. This isn't funny. Let me out!" Tears stung her eyes, but she wouldn't let them fall. If he decided he wanted to do something to her she had walked right into his trap. But she had felt safe with him. Were her instincts just messed up?

Maybe she was wrong. Maybe guys were suppose to do that to girls and she just felt wrong for not wanting to do it.

"Nicky, calm down." he said softly. "I'll unlock the doors I just wanted to talk first."

Nicky bit her lip. "I don't want to talk." She pushed at the door again. "Let me out, Dustin, I mean it." she leaned away from him as he leaned closer to her. "NO! I mean it. Let me out." She cried out as her back touched the door. "Get away from me!"

Dustin leaned closer to her. "Nicky." he whispered. Suddenly he chocked. His heartbeat quickened. Had she been drinking? He suddenly felt sick. Was that what her problem was, she didn't want him to know she drank?

Nicky saw the look on his face and wanted to scream out the truth but didn't. "I really need to go." She trembled, what was he going to do or say to her. "I need to go home, Dustin. I'm in a hurry and don't have time to be messing around. Let me out!" She pushed her back into the door trying to force it open, but soon stopped. The pain was almost to much to bare.

Dustin turned back and unlocked the door. "Fine. I'll see you tomorrow Nicky." he said without looking at her. Pain ripped through him. *NO! This is not how things are suppose to be,* he thought. *I don't want a girl that drinks or smokes.*

Nicky looked at him. "Tomorrow?" Just who did he think he was to threaten her and then think she was going to let him give her a ride again?

He smiled at her. "I thought we had a date, unless you were planning on standing me up."

Nicky groaned inwardly. She had brought this on herself, but she didn't want him to think she would go back on her word. "I'll do my best," she said slowly. "What time did you say again?"

Dustin looked at her closely, had she really forgotten or was she just acting like it? "Seven, is that to late? We could make it earlier if we need to."

"Seven is fine." she whispered. "I'll see you then. I don't want to be rude but-" she wanted to explain to him what had happened. She wanted him to understand and help her, but she was to scared. She dropped her gaze and felt her fight drain out of her. "I really have to go. Mom was coming home today and she doesn't like it when I'm late, otherwise I would like to talk. Maybe it will work better tomorrow."

Dustin smiled. He could see the fear leave her eyes and sensed that she was telling the truth this time. "I'll see you then."

Nicky slowly walked down the street.

Dustin watched her for a few moments, a knot of fear in his stomach at the defeated slump of her body. As she turned to go up a house drive she lifted her chin and straightened her shoulders.

"Let me know, God, please. I thought you were giving me the go ahead. Now, now I'm just not sure. Can you please help me know what is going on?" he sighed again and drove home. "I want to love her." he groaned, "but should I? Am I just setting up myself for heartbreak?"

Nicky trembled as she opened the door. "Mom, mom, are you here." There was no answer and she smiled. "Am I going to be home alone?"

Glancing over she noticed the answering machine was blinking. Wondering who it could be she pushed the button. "Nichol, it's mom. I won't be home till at least Sunday. Your dad said he left a list of things for you to do on the table. Be sure you do everything. If you need anything call me, and be good. If you go out, no being around people, and don't be eating a lot. I don't want you putting on a lot of weight. Your father said the scales were reading over a hundred yesterday. You know what will happen if you are over a hundred and five. I mean it, Nichol."

Nicky smiled. "I'm home alone till Sunday, sweet. I can't hardly believe it. I hope all goes well. At least I don't have to worry about them finding out about my date." She smiled to herself. "I better stick to the time though, no telling what dad planted around here to be sure I'm obeying." she sighed. "Even when I'm alone, I'm not free."

The next morning she hurried off to school. She felt a quake in her stomach at the thought of how she had pushed Dustin away yesterday. It was the first time she had a chance to talk to him since Tuesday morning and she had pushed him away as though she was mad at him. She wouldn't blame him if he didn't pick her up today.

Still she hoped, but as she rounded the corner her heart sank. He wasn't there. Slowly she walked on toward school. She heard someone pull up behind her and her heartbeat quickened. She wanted to run, but wasn't sure if that would put her in more danger or less.

"Can I give you a ride?" someone called out.

Nicky turned quickly. "Dustin!" she cried as he stopped. She slid in and smiled. "I didn't think you would come for me today." she tried not to sound to surprised.

Dustin grinned. "Well, I was running a little late." he stopped then went on more seriously, "I'm not mad at you, Nicky. I just want some answers." He pulled the car to a stop outside of the school.

Nicky quickly cut him off. "I can't talk now. Maybe tonight, just not now. I'm sorry." Quickly she jumped out and ran to the school.

Chapter 6

As Nicky walked in the house that afternoon she smiled. All she had to do was get the things done her dad wanted her to do and she was on her own. It felt good to be home by herself. Not worrying about her dad hitting her, or worse. Quickly reading through the list her heart sank. How was she ever going to get all that done? With a sigh she started to clean the kitchen.

About six thirty Nicky looked at herself in the mirror. "At least I don't have to worry about fresh bruises." she muttered. "Maybe things will change soon. If only he would see I am an adult." Nicky looked in the mirror again. "Now would be the perfect time to run away. If only I knew they would never find me. I know what would happen if I tried and was caught." she shivered. It wasn't worth the risk, but if things got worse would it be? She glanced at the closet where her fathers gun was. "Maybe I should just end it all." she whispered. Then she shook her head stubbornly. "That is just what he wants me to do. Die." she flushed glad no one was around to hear what she had said.

Pushing the thoughts aside she hurried to the door. "At least I don't have to worry about them finding out about Dustin right now. If I try hard maybe I can keep it a secret. I'll probably have to keep it a secret from Dustin that they don't know." A tear rolled down her cheek. "I think I could love him. Is that possible? I know I would like the chance to find out, but I also know if daddy ever finds out I will wish I was dead." With a sigh she hurried to the restaurant where her and Dustin where to meet.

Dustin waited outside the café his heart beating rapidly. Would Nicky come or did she intend to stand him up. He looked down at his watch. Five till. What if she decided not to come.

"Just be patient, she'll be here." he whispered to himself. He was so nervous he felt like throwing up. He couldn't do this. "That's no way to think," he said to himself, "all I need to do is relax." Taking a deep breath he bowed his head. "God," he whispered. "God, I need your help tonight. Show me what your will is for my life. If you don't want me to be with her, show me. I don't want either one of us to get hurt because of a relationship that isn't your will. In Jesus name, Amen."

He looked up and saw Nicky coming up the side walk. His heart stopped then thundered loud enough for her to hear. Taking a deep breath he stepped out of the car.

Nicky smiled, "Sorry, I guess I'm a little late." She flushed.

"No, I don't believe you are." he smiled down at her. She was nervous also he could tell. "I'm just a little early." he glanced down at his watch. "You are also. It's three till." He smiled, "Shall we." he motioned toward the door. With a smile she nodded.

Soon after they sat down the waiter came over. "Can I take your order?"

Dustin looked at Nicky who nodded. "I'll take a cheese burger and chocolate shake. Please."

Turning toward Nicky the waiter asked, "and you?"

"I'll have a grilled cheese and water." Nicky's voice trembled slightly.

"Alright I'll bring that right out."

Dustin looked over at her. He desperately wanted to ask a dozen questions, but felt he wouldn't get honest answers. *I don't want to seem to pushy,* he thought. *After all it's really not my business. I just don't want her to be hurt. I just want to know what is going on.* "God, please help me know what to say." he prayed quietly.

Nicky caught his look and smiled. What was he thinking? The look on his face said it wasn't good. "You alright?" she asked a little concerned.

"Fine." he smiled. "Guess I have first date jitters."

Nicky flushed as relief flooded over her. She wasn't the only one who felt nervous. "Me too." she said softly, feeling need to respond. She would not consider the night at Ben's a date. She wouldn't consider it anything but a mistake.

He smiled, but concern washed over him, that confirmed his fear, the bruises were from her family. His stomach suddenly felt sick. Why had she not said any thing about it? Surely she knew that there was help. His mom and dad had been foster parents for many children in those situations. *Is that why I feel this way. Do I just feel sorry for her, or is there more. Do I love her?* he wondered. *Is it possible?* His heart fluttered. He knew it was more.

He felt love for this girl and had since the first day he saw her. Though he had tried to deny it, he knew he couldn't any more.

The waiter brought their food then. "Can I get you kids anything else?" he asked.

"No, I don't believe so. Thank you." Dustin answered looking at Nicky she smiled and nodded.

The waiter nodded and left.

Dustin smiled at Nicky. "Shall we pray."

Nicky looked confused. *What's that?* she wondered. In silence She sat there waiting to see what he would do next.

Dustin cleared his throat, then bowing his head he began, "Dear Heavenly Father we thank Thee for this food. Thank you for the time that we can share together. It is blessed in your name. Amen."

Nicky had watched him through the whole prayer and when he finished and raised his head she asked curiously, "What did you do that for?"

Dustin stared at her in surprised. Didn't Nicky know about God? Hadn't she ever seen someone pray before? "Because I'm thankful for the food and I want God to know that."

"God?" Nicky looked at him closely. Did God really exist? Her father had always told her God was a myth. Was he wrong? Did he send Dustin to teach her more about him. "Who is God, and how can you talk to someone who isn't even here?" She asked earnestly. She didn't want to miss this opportunity to find some answers. If Dustin could tell her more about God she wanted to learn even though her father had told her she was never aloud to listen to one word about God.

"God is every where. He lives in me, that's how I talk to him. He's my best friend." Dustin said with a smile.

Nicky looked lost she felt unsure what to say. "Where did you meat him?" She finally asked unsure of what to say. Her mind raced. *I don't want him to think I'm stupid, but if there is someone out there who could save me from my dad, I want to know.*

Dustin smiled. "At church."

"Oh." her voice came out a soft whisper. Fear washed over her. Her parents had told her about church. They said it was where a lot of bad people go, people who only wanted to hurt her. What had they called them? Christians. Yes, that was it. They had called them Christians.

Her mind whirled so fast she thought she would be sick. Dustin hadn't tried to hurt her. He had always been polite and friendly. Had her parents lied to her about Church to keep her away from it? Had they lied to her about Christians because that was what her grandparents were and they didn't want her to have anything to do with them?

Dustin looked at Nicky thoughtfully, "Do you go to church any where?" He could guess the answer, but felt the need to say something. He watched her curiously, *Surely she has at least heard of God,* he thought.

"No, never." was her abrupt answer.

"Would you like to?" his voice was soft yet pleading.

"Me?" Nicky gasped. Her pulse raced though her heart ached at the same time. "I don't think I can. That is, I don't think church is the place for me." she flushed not wanting to say more.

"Why not?"

"Because. There are-." suddenly Nicky stopped. "Can we talk about this later?" she asked softly, glancing around the room.

"Sure." Dustin smiled, "You sure you don't want any more to eat. Ice cream or anything?"

"No thanks." Her tenseness had taken away even the slightest hint of appetite.

They finished their meal in silence. As they walked out of the restaurant Dustin started walking her to his car.

Nicky trembled. *What if he's going to try something?* she thought to herself. *I can't stop him. Was Daddy right? Should I have stayed away from him, because all he wants out of me is sex.* Without warning a tear slid down her cheek.

Seeming to sense her discomfort Dustin looked at her. Seeing the tears in her eyes he was surprised. Softly he touched her arm hopping to relax her a little. "Let's go for a walk down by the lake." He suggested as he turned away from the car and headed back down toward the lake.

Shivering she nodded. "I'd like that." *I can't do this,* she thought. *I just want to go away.* Nicky felt her stomach turn over. *I think I'm going to be sick.* Another tear slid down her cheek. *What if he tries something?* she wondered. *Should I feel scared or should I feel safe?* She felt uneasy. She had always felt safe around Dustin before, yet she was afraid he was going to end up like Andy and try to hurt her, before he let her go home. Her thoughts refused to come out in order, and her mind refused to stop racing about.

Dustin watched her as they walked. "Nicky, are you okay?" he finally whispered.

Nicky dropped her head. "I'm fine." she answered trying to keep her voice steady.

"If that is the truth, why are you crying?" his voice was soft, but she heard the concern in it.

She trembled as she turned away. "I'm sorry."

Dustin reached out and took her arm, turning her to face him. "You don't have anything to be sorry about. There is nothing wrong with crying if there is a reason behind it."

Nicky looked away fear gripping her heart. She could never let anyone know the reason for her tears.

Dustin felt himself tremble. "Did I upset you, Nicky? Did I do something-"

"No, you didn't do it." Nicky broke him off as she pulled her arm away from him. "It has nothing to do with you." she looked down. "I really don't want to talk about it. If you don't mind. I much rather talk about something else."

"Okay." Dustin agreed as he motioned to a spot on the sand for them to sit.

Nicky cleared her throat uneasily. She wanted to ask about his beliefs but didn't know how to start. She didn't want to sound like an idiot, yet she did want to understand why this boy was so different from what her parents told her. They had told her boys would only hurt her. Her father had threatened to "Show her what boys wanted out of her" yet Dustin didn't seem like that at all. He seemed nice and comforting. When she was around him she felt safe, as though he wanted to protect her from harm. This was something new to her and she didn't understand it at all. She had never felt this way. No one had ever made her feel safe before.

Dustin looked at her, she seemed to be deep in thought, yet she was looking straight at him. "Nicky?" his voice was soft yet questioning.

She flushed, "I was just wondering, that is, I wondered if you could tell me-" she took a deep breath trying to swallow her fear of what he would think of her. "I don't want to sound like a complete idiot, but - well, who is God?"

Her question silenced him. Dustin felt his heart cry out in pain. Nicky didn't even know about God. How could that be? Surely she was joking. Yet one look at her upturned face said she was dead serious. "God, please show me what to say." he prayed quietly. "I don't want to turn her away because I say the wrong thing."

Finally he said, "God is the creator of the universe. He made all things. He made you and me. He loves us very much. He sent His only son to earth to die for us, because he loves us so much. He sent Him to save us from our sins. He rose again and lives forever. He saved me. He is my best friend. He is with me always and I know no matter what, he will always protect me. I love Him and He loves me. And as long as I walk in his footsteps and do all He wants me to do He will always be with me. He wants to love and protect you also." His last words came out a whisper.

Nicky was astounded. Was their really someone out there who loved her and wanted to protect her? Was it possible that this was true? She looked up into Dustin's eyes. They were shining, and she could tell that he was telling her the truth and also that he knew the God he was talking about. He wasn't just saying something from memory, or something he had made up, he believed it! She was so stunned for a minute she didn't know what to say.

"Is that why you are so different?" she asked after a moment. She felt herself shiver, as though she was afraid of what he would say.

"Different? What do you mean?" he looked at her questioningly.

"I mean most guys would not have kept their distance from a girl even on a first date, they would be trying to get all they could get. And go as far or farther than the girl would let them go, but you haven't. You seem to be trying to make me feel comfortable, like you wanted me to have a good time. Not just be here for your - well, for your pleasure, I guess." she looked away. *I've said to much.* She bit her lip.

Dustin looked at her quizzically, "I thought this was your first date, yet you speak as though you have had many experiences with guys." His heart hurt. *God, please don't let that be. I want a girl that is pure.*

She flushed, "This is my first date, but I have friends who talk and my parents, have said a lot of things." She stopped as she thought about all the things her father had said.

He smiled at her. "Not all guys are that way. Yes, there are a lot of them that are. And yes, God is a major reason I'm not like that. As I said before he's my best friend. He wants me to be pure for him. I don't want to do anything he doesn't want me to. If I were to try something with a girl I would not only be hurting me and her, I would be hurting God as well. God tells us to remain pure. I have no right to be with a girl till I am married to her. I have no plans of disobeying God, no matter how hard it is. I can't lose my best friend over my own foolishness and I don't plan to."

Nicky looked at him again quickly. "Where is he? If he is your best friend why don't I ever see him with you?"

"He isn't the kind of friend you see, he's the kind of friend you feel. He's in Heaven preparing a place for all Christians to go to be with him some day. Then we will be able to see him face to face." Dustin tried to explain.

Nicky thought for a moment. Something weld up inside her, a yearning she had never felt. "Can I meet him some day?"

Dustin smiled at her. "I'd like that very much." he whispered.

"When?" She burst out without thinking first. She wanted the peace that Dustin had. She could see it on his face and hear it in his voice. Was it possible that God could love her? She wanted that more than anything, to have someone who would love her and help her, someone who wouldn't hurt her or let her down.

Dustin looked at her surprised. He heard a hunger in her voice that he had never heard from anyone before. Was she serious? He wanted to pray with her right then, but felt, for some reason, it wouldn't be right. Why was he feeling the need to hold off from helping her become a Christian. Then he knew, she was not ready yet. She needed a little more knowledge before he rushed her into a relationship with God. Her heart was open yet not quite understanding. If he rushed her into a relationship with God it could do more damage then good at this moment.

"Tell you what," he finally said, after thinking and praying, "Why don't I come and take you to church on Sunday. Then you can hear some more. I don't think your quite ready to meet him yet. I want you to be, I just think you need to understand a little more. I don't want you to think something because I said something then feel disappointed because it's not what you thought."

"I'd like to go to church if it is like what you are telling me, but they wouldn't want me." she looked away.

"Give it a chance I think you will be surprised. I'll pick you up about nine-fifteen on Sunday and we can go together." he watched her closely. He couldn't believe she was serious. *God are you telling me something?* he wondered.

Nicky's heart stopped. Telling her parents she wanted to go to church would be bad enough, but going with a guy. She would never be aloud out of the house again if they found out. "Is the church far from here?" her voice trembled.

"No. It's the little one on first and main." He looked closely at her, "Why?"

She looked down. "I'll just walk to Church. That is if my parents let me go - I mean - They don't really like Church - it's just - they'll probably tell me I can't go. I don't want to be a bother to you." she bit her lip. *I shouldn't have said that, now he will wonder even more.*

"Why don't I pick you up. I don't want you to have to walk, especially by yourself. You can call me tomorrow night if you can come and I'll pick you up." He looked at her closely. "I'll call you if you don't call me, deal?"

Nicky laughed nervously, "You can't call me you don't know my number." Then fearing he would ask for it, she added, "I like to walk. I'll be just fine. What time does it start?"

"Nine-thirty." Dustin looked at her closely. "Are you hiding something from me?" his eyes twinkled and a teasing smiled played on his face.

Nicky trembled. "Why do you ask?" she snapped more then she meant and tensed.

Dustin saw her tears and his heart melted. He Hadn't meant to make her upset, he was only teasing. "You haven't let me drive you home in all the time I've been with you. You didn't even want me to pick you up tonight or to meet your parents before we went on a date. Do they not care who you go out with? Don't they want to meet the boys you date before you date them?"

"Oh, they care alright." she said under her breath. Then out loud she said, "I haven't met your family either."

"You're trying to evade my question," he smiled at her. "And you'll meet them Sunday if you come."

"I hope they are as nice as you. Do they not care that you are trying to date a girl that is not a Christian? I mean, don't you Christians have rules about that?"

"No, there are no rules." he smiled. "And as for you and I dating. They care and were a little concerned that I was dating a girl they had not met yet, but they were cool about it. How do your parents feel about you dating a guy they have not seen before?" he looked closer at her, "Or heard of?"

Nicky flushed. She couldn't tell him the truth. "I think I need to go now." She jumped up and turned away hoping he wouldn't ask any more. "I enjoyed the night, thank you. I'll see you on Sunday if I can." her voice broke slightly.

She started to walk away but he caught her arm, "Nicky, at least let me give you a ride home. Please. I didn't mean to make you upset. Don't leave angry." he pleaded.

"I can walk. I don't want to be a bother." As she tried to pull away a tear slid down her cheek. "Let me go, please."

"It's no bother." he replied then teasingly added, "it might be if you don't let me take you home."

His grin melted her heart and she turned to hide her tears.

His grin died as he saw her fear. "Nicky?" he whispered, releasing his hold. "What is it? Please tell me. Are you trying to keep it a secret for some reason?" His voice softened as he pleaded, "Please tell me, Nicky. Please. Why don't you want your parents to know about me."

"Dustin, please," her voice sounded of tears. "Please don't ask. I can't tell you and you wouldn't understand if I did."

He looked closely at her. "Why not let me be the judge of that?"

She looked up at him. Tears stood in her eyes. "Well I might as well." she whimpered. "But you won't want to talk to me ever again if I do."

Dustin laughed. "It couldn't be that bad, could it." Then as he looked into her face he caught his breath. Fear and pain blazed from her eyes. "What ever it is, Nicky, I'll still talk with you. I promise." He reached out and brushed his hand over her face. "Really, Nicky. You don't need to be afraid of me."

She looked up at him. "My parents don't want me to date. I didn't say anything before because, I really like you and I knew you wouldn't want anything to do with me if you knew. When you asked if you needed to ask them first I didn't know what to say. They don't want me to have any friends at all. My mom doesn't want me to have a boyfriend cause she doesn't want me to have the same trouble she did." Nicky's voice took on a sharp edge. And she quickly bit her lip. She had said to much again and she knew it. Now he would want more answers.

Dustin looked at her, "I know it's probably none of my business, but, what trouble?"

"Me." Nicky's eyes were once again about ready to spill with tears. "She got pregnant with me before they got married. I'm the reason they got married. My mom has resented my dad ever since, and I'm pretty sure he feels the same way. They're always fighting, that is when they're together. They try their hardest to make sure they aren't together more than just a few minutes. And that few minutes is spent comparing notes on me and making sure I'm not in any trouble."

Her voice was angry and full of hate. "Some day I'm going to run away and they will never find me. They won't be able to rule my life any longer. I hate them. Some day they will be sorry for-" Suddenly she stopped realizing that she was talking out loud. She flushed, "Sorry I shouldn't have said all that. Forget I did." she turned quickly to go, but once again he grabbed her arm, stopping her.

Dustin looked into her eyes, "That's alright. It sounds to me like you needed to talk to someone. You've never told anyone before have you?"

"Please lets stop talking about me." she whispered, looking away. "I can't-"

"Sorry I just-"

Nicky interrupted before he could finish. "My parents hate me. They didn't even want to have me. That is the reason they hate Christians, I think. My grandparents are Christians, at least that is what my parents say, I've never seen them. My parents moved here right before I was born. Someday I'm going to go find them and thank them for not letting my parents abort me." her voice rang with sarcasm. "If dad -" Nicky suddenly stopped. "Don't tell anyone what I just said." she pulled away a little trying to get him to release her arm. "I have to go. Really I do."

Dustin released his hold on her, "Nicky, do your parents know where you are? How did you get permission to be here to night if your mom doesn't want you around guys at all?"

Nicky trembled, "They - aren't - home." she tried to stop trembling. "Mom's been gone since Monday on a business trip and Dad left Thursday. Mom was suppose to be back yesterday before I got home from school but she called and said she wouldn't be home till Sunday probably." She smiled. "I still have curfew and rules, but at least -" she stopped.

Dustin turned her face to his. "Nicky, please tell me why you didn't let me give you ride the last few days. I need to know, please."

Nicky looked down. "Daddy was upset that I was late to school the other day. He took me to make sure I got there on time and picked me up to be sure I wasn't flirting with boys after school."

Dustin smiled, "And what if you were? Your almost and adult what could he do about it?" His teasing grin lit his eyes, but when he looked down at Nicky it died.

Nicky turned away. "I have to go, Dustin. I don't want to be late."

Dustin looked quizzical. "What time are you suppose to be home?"

Nicky trembled again. She felt sick. "Nine." she whispered, looking down.

Dustin looked down at his watch and then looked back up at her. "I'm sorry, Nicky. I wish I would have known. It's about Nine thirty."

Nicky turned pail. "I didn't realize it was so late. I really need to get going." She turned to leave.

"Nicky, wait," Dustin whispered as he grabbed her arm. "Could we try to meet early on Sunday. I really want to be able to talk with you for a little while before Church, please?"

Nicky looked down. "I'll try." she whispered. Then she looked up, "I really had a good time tonight. Thanks." she turned to go.

Dustin called after her, "Nicky, You're sure I can't give you a ride home?"

"Positive. Sorry but I have to go." she turned away and ran down the street before he could say any more.

Dustin watched her go. His heart began to ache, just what secrets did she hold? "Some day I will find out," he said to himself as he climbed in the car. "And if her father is hurting her he will regret it." he vowed. He desperately wanted to follow her. He wanted to see her parents and get there permission to date her. Then he shrugged. There was some reason she was trying to keep it a secret. "Please, God," he whispered. "Please lead Nicky to you. I love her. And, God, please, protect her from whoever it is that is hurting her." He sighed and headed home.

Chapter 7

Nicky bounded up the front steps to the house. *At least no one is home. I won't get beat for being late, unless they somehow find out when they get home. Then will I be in for it.*

Trembling at the thought of what her parents would do to her if they knew she was out this late she opened the door. She almost jumped out of her skin when a voice boomed out of the darkness.

"Where have you been Nichol!"

Nicky stumbled backwards. "Daddy!" she gasped. "I thought you were gone."

Her father gripped her arm and pushed her back against the door. "You thought just cause I was gone you could disobey the rules and stay out as long as you wanted to?"

"No, sir. I just lost track of -" her father's fist cut her off as he slugged her across the jaw then in the stomach. She groaned as he slugged her again and again trying to make her barf.

When she finally did she looked up at him with fear. Why did he always have to do this to her. Now he would know she had eaten.

"You are a worthless brat." her father scoffed. He pulled a whip off of the shelf in the closet and smacked her with it. "You answer me truthfully. You were with someone out there weren't you? You've been trying to flirt and see boys without me knowing it haven't you?"

His voice was so angry and full of hate Nicky almost cried. She knew all he wanted was reason to hit her more. She blinked hard to keep her tears back. "I was alone." she whispered. Fear pricked her as she thought of the consequences of his finding out that she was lying. Then she trembled knowing what they would be if he found out the truth.

He gripped her arm tighter as he struck her. "You are a liar and you are going to pay for it." he sneered. "When I get finished with you, you are going to clean this entire house, and you will do so before you eat or sleep again." He pushed her to the floor, "Am I clear." He smacked her again.

Nicky lowered her head. "Yes sir." she whispered. In her mind she thought, *I will accept my punishment, but I will hate you for it.* She groaned as her father struck her again. All the hope she had felt build in her as she had talked to Dustin seeped out of her.

All day Saturday Nicky cleaned the house, when her father got home that night, he once again beat her. She was in so much pain she didn't know how she was going to keep going, but he made her. He worked her all night to clean the house. Finally at about seven thirty Sunday morning he walked into the living room and glared at her.

Slowly Nicky stood up from polishing the end table.

Her father scowled at her. "It's about time you get done!" he snapped as he gripped her arm. "Now, you listen and you listen good. Your mother is going to be home soon and I want you out of the house. We are going to have some friends over and have a little party. I want you to stay out of the house all day. You will be back by nine tonight, if you are late you know what the consequences will be. Don't you dare come back early either.

Nicky bit her lip as she looked up at her father. "Yes, sir." she managed. She hurt so bad all she wanted to do was sleep, but she knew she had to obey. She also had a feeling her father was making her leave so she had to stay awake.

"Good, then get cleaned up and get out of the house." He father pushed her sharply backward and she fell over the end table. "And if I find out that you were with someone, you will be very sorry."

Nicky groaned again as she sat up. "Yes sir." She tried to answer calmly sure her dad would sense her nervousness, for she had just realized it was Sunday and she was suppose to go with Dustin to Church.

If her father noticed he didn't act like it. He merely grunted, "Get cleaned up and get out."

She hurried into the bathroom. At least she wouldn't have to be alone today. And it was raining of all things. One look in the bathroom mirror and her heart sank, she couldn't let Dustin see her looking like this. Her face was bruised and raw. Stripes marked places the whip had struck, other marks on her neck and face showed belt welts. Tears blurred her vision for a moment.

"Well I'll just have to make the most of it." she muttered. "I don't really have I choice. I just hope no one else notices." she looked at herself again. *How could they not!*

After a shower she looked and felt a little better, but still she didn't know how she would keep her face hidden. As she walked to the door her father called to her.

Slowly she walked towards him. He was standing by his chair at the far end of the room. Grabbing her arm he struck her across the face. "That's to remind you to keep your mouth shut." He said crossly then he grab his belt from the chair and stuck her across the back several times. "And that," he said crossly, "is to remind you to be home on time." he gave her a push towards the door. "Now Get out!" he stormed as he kicked her. "And remember what I said."

"Yes Sir." Slipping quietly out of the house she headed down the road. "I guess I better make the most of it." she muttered. "I don't think it's going to get any better."

As she neared the corner she slowed. The rain had soaked and chilled her clear through, but she hardly noticed. What was she going to say to Dustin if he noticed the marks and asked. She knew she couldn't keep the marks from being seen, no matter how hard she tried. Tears blinded her vision a moment. But as she reached the corner she quickly blinked them away for there was Dustin waiting for her.

"Nicky," Dustin called as she came around the corner. "You're getting soaked. Why didn't you get an umbrella." He jumped out and opened her door. The rain was chilly for early May. He felt the chill through his jacket and wondered that she wasn't even shivering.

Nicky slipped into the car welcoming the warmth. It wasn't till he climbed back in that she started to tremble.

Dustin looked at her. Quickly he took off his jacket and handed it to her. "It gets warmer if we drive so why don't we just drive a little."

Nicky bit her lip, but couldn't stop trembling. She understood he wanted to calm her and get her to realize he wasn't going to try anything. He only wanted to talk. She smiled, but looked away. "Thanks." her voice shivered and she flushed. She didn't want him to get upset, but he didn't say or do anything. Nicky's thoughts raced, her father hit her when she whispered. He had told her that no boy liked a girl that whispered or spoke to quiet to be heard, had he lied to her about that too?

After a while Dustin pulled the car to a stop. "Nicky, I need to know," he stopped as though not sure how to go on. He turned to her, "What did your dad do to you when you were late to class."

Nicky bit her lip and looked out the window. "What business is it to you?" she asked coldly. "I got in trouble and he took me to school the next few days, end of story. What would your dad have done if it had been you?"

Dustin smiled. "Told me not to let it happen again, and we would have talked about the reason I was late. Like we did because I was late to work and the boss called mom to be sure I was coming in. That was when I told them about you."

Nicky dropped her head. "I'm sorry, I forgot I made you late too. I can't keep from messing up anyone's life." she snapped. "Daddy's right I am worthless."

Dustin glanced over at her and felt tears sting his eyes. Why was she so mad? Slowly he reached out and touched her hand. "Nicky." he whispered. "Nicky, look at me." When she made no move to he sighed. "You are not worthless. You don't mess up peoples' lives. I was the one who made us late. I should have asked you the night before or waited till later. I'm sorry I got you into trouble, I didn't want to I just -" he stopped. "Nicky please look at me."

Nicky dropped her head. "I can't." she whispered. A sob escaped and she bit her lip. "I'm sorry, I need to get out."

Dustin grabbed her arm. "I'm going with you if you do so you might as well stay where it is dry. Just talk to me, Nicky. Please. You don't need to worry. I'm not going to hurt you."

Nicky bit her lip. "I can't talk about it. Please, just stop asking." she turned to look out the window.

Dustin reached over and touched her cheek as he did Nicky cried out in pain. Dustin pulled his hand back quickly. In surprise he looked at his fingers, blood ran down them.

Nicky glanced up at him then pulled as far away from him as she could. Her face was pail and her heart heavy. She had done what she should never do, she had screamed in pain. She knew her father would beat her hard for doing so and she was sure Dustin would too. In her fear she kept her eyes glued to him.

Dustin looked into her eyes startled by her outburst. "Nicky," he whispered shocked as he saw her face. Slowly he reached out his hand to her. He couldn't believe what he was seeing. Even in the dim light he could see the large bruises, blood and welts on her face. Slowly he touched it.

As he reached out Nicky tried to back away farther. Fear raced through her and she was trembling so hard she couldn't stop. "I'm sorry," she whimpered sure he was going to hit her. "Please don't. I'm sorry. I won't do it again. Please."

"Nicky!" Dustin said calmly. "What is wrong with you. Just calm down." He ran his hand down her other cheek, then rested it on her hand. He waited till she had calmed down a little then looked back up at her. "What happened?" He whispered.

Nicky dropped her head suddenly realizing her mistake in letting him see her fear. If he was going to hurt her that would only make it worse. "I just fell and bruised myself." she muttered.

Dustin waited till she looked in his eyes. "If that is true, why did you think I was going to hit you?"

Nicky trembled. "Please don't ask, Dustin. I'm not suppose to tell."

Dustin frowned. "And if you do?"

Nicky bit her lip. "You won't ever want to be seen with me again." she whispered.

Dustin laughed, "It -" he stopped seeing the look in her face. *Maybe it could be that bad.* Slowly he dropped back in to his seat and started the car. "We better get going." he muttered. "Don't want to be late or I'll be the one in trouble."

Nicky shivered as they drove to the church. How was she going to keep everything a secret.

As they drove to the church her thoughts turned to Dustin and his family. *Will they like me?* she wondered. *What if they don't and what if Dustin decides he doesn't want to see me any more, because I'm not a Christian like he is. I wish I had a friend like he was talking about the other night. It would be so nice to have someone to talk to sometimes. And to have someone who cares about me. Even if I can't see him. Dustin said God is a friend that you feel more than you see. Maybe I can meet him soon.* she sighed again. *No, he wouldn't want me. Like daddy says, I'm worthless.* A tear slid down her cheek. Brushing it quickly away, she blinked hard trying not to cry.

Dustin glanced over at her. "Are you okay?"

Turning so he couldn't see her face she bit her lip. "Fine." she finally answered trying to keep her voice steady. Her heart felt like it was braking. All she wanted was to get away from her father and not have to worry about people finding out. She wanted to tell Dustin the truth. She wanted him to turn her father in, but she also knew it would only get worse if that happened.

Dustin watched her a few more minutes. "It's okay if you need to cry. Sometimes it can make you feel a lot better."

Nicky blink hard. "No," she whispered. "I don't need to cry."

"Okay." he answered softly, "I hope you don't mind that I don't believe you. I think you do need to and I think it will make you feel better."

Nicky didn't say anything. She didn't know what to say and she couldn't speak without tears running down her cheeks.

Pulling into the parking lot Dustin looked over at Nicky. Were the marks on her face because she had been out with him to late? But she had said her parents were gone, if that was the case someone else was hurting her, unless her parents had come home and found out.

Dustin looked over at her. "Do you want to talk about it or not?"

Nicky shrugged, "Not really."

"Is it because of me? Is that why he hit you?"

Nicky trembled as she looked at him. "I don't know what you are talking about. I told you I fell. I did this to myself. Please don't ask any more, please."

Dustin saw the fear in her eyes and sighed. "All right. I'm sorry. I just wanted to help."

Nicky smiled up at him. "I know. I just can't talk about it right now. I'm sorry. Maybe someday, just not now."

Dustin smiled back. "That's fair enough." Getting out he walked around and opened her door. As they walked up to the church he stopped and looked down at her again. "Nicky, I'm sorry if I made you upset. I'm just worried about you."

She trembled slightly. "No need to be. I'm just fine." she whispered, but she shuddered in fear, of what her father might do to her if he found out about Dustin.

As they walked into the church Nicky felt surprised that even coming through the door you could feel the friendly atmosphere. After he introduced her to a few people he led her to a small room in the back of the church. The room was quiet in spite of a few teens sitting around a table.

A girl looked up as they came in and smiled. She rose when she saw Dustin and walked over. "You must be Nicky." she smiled. "I'm Sarah, Dustin's sister. He's told me a lot about you. It's good to meat you. Welcome to our Sunday school."

Nicky flushed. "Thank you."

Sara was warm and friendly. Her eyes sparkled like Dustin's, with a hint of orneriness in them. Her hair was dark brown and her eyes were an even darker brown, almost black. She was very outgoing and had a way of making people feel very comfortable around her. Nicky felt an immediate bond with her and the feeling seemed mutual.

They walked to the table and Dustin began making introductions all around, but Nicky felt to nervous to remember them all. Presently a tall dark eyed girl walked into the room. Sparks shot from her eyes when she saw Nicky and she immediately dropped into a seat beside Dustin. Dustin introduced her as Mary. For some reason Nicky felt uncomfortable and felt as though hate ran through the air as Mary looked at her.

What did I do? Nicky wondered as she nodded to Mary.

At that moment Mrs. Walm the Sunday school teacher came in. Walking up to the table she smiled. "Why don't we get started today? I seem to be running a little late. Dustin, will you please start us out with a prayer?"

Nicky glanced around and noticed all the other students with heads bowed and eyes closed. She trembled as she listened to Dustin.

"Dear Lord," he began slowly, "Please help us through the class today. Help Mrs. Walm as she teaches us, and be with the pastor in the after service. In Jesus name, Amen."

Dustin looked up at Nicky and smiled. She smiled back, but for some reason felt a little uneasy. The girl who was sitting on the other side of Dustin was still glaring at her and she still felt a tension in the air.

Mrs. Walm smiled at Dustin then looking from him to Sara she asked, "Would you please introduce your guest Sara?"

Nicky waited for Sara to tell her that she didn't even know her and she was Dustin's friend not Sara's, but to her complete surprise Sara looked over at Dustin grinned and said, "Sure." The way she spoke Nicky could tell she was up to something. "This is Nicky, Dustin's girl friend."

A gasp seemed to go around the room. Mrs. Walm looked startled. The girl sitting on the other side of Dustin froze.

"Sara!" Dustin hissed as he looked at Nicky.

Nicky flushed and looked down. She suddenly felt shy, but she also sensed that Mary felt angry. Dustin slipped his arm around her and she trembled. She felt some what safer, but his arm around her also made her feel afraid.

Mrs. Walm looked quickly from one to the other then, as if recovering from a great shock, she smiled at Nicky. "We are so glad to have you join us today." She looked disapprovingly at Dustin, and he quickly dropped his arm, Mrs. Walm smiled, then went on. "Now," she said in a loud clear voice, turning back to the class, "If you would all turn to Genesis chapter three our lesson to day is on the fall of man."

Nicky listened intently through class. She had never heard of such a story. It was so amazing to her. When Mrs. Walm began to explain the plan of redemptions brought because of the fall, and Jesus dieing on a cross for the sins of mankind she was even more amazed.

Without thinking she said her thought out loud. "How could it be possible?"

Mrs. Walm turned to Nicky. "How can what be possible?"

Nicky flushed she hadn't meant to speak, it had just come out. She glanced at Dustin, he was watching her. Slowly she looked back at Mrs. Walm, surprised the woman didn't reprimand her for speaking out of turn. "How could Jesus die for the sins of man? I mean, how could he just die for everyone? If we die because of sin then how could Jesus just do that for everyone?"

Mrs. Walm smiled. "Because he is God. He created the world, and mankind. He loves us very much. You see God didn't create us to sin. He created us to worship him and have fellowship with him. But Satan marred God's beautiful spotless creation. God knew when man sinned that he would have to give him a way of redemption, of coming back to God. But he also let man have a choice. God wants us to serve him because we love him, not because we have to, so he made us with a free will. Jesus is our mediator to God. He made it possible for man to have fellowship with God again."

Nicky smiled. She felt shy, but also eager. This was so amazing to her. She felt a strong desire to know this God. She looked at Dustin again as Mrs. Walm continued with the lesson.

He smiled at her then turned his attention back to the class.

Nicky looked back at Mrs. Walm, but her mind had a hard time focusing on the rest of the lesson. She just couldn't stop thinking about all that Jesus had done. "He must be a very great man." she thought.

When class dismissed Sara walked out with Nicky while Dustin stayed in to help Mrs. Walm set up the chairs for the children service. As they stood in the hall waiting Sara looked at Nicky and smiled. "I'll be right back I just need to do something a minute."

Nicky nodded and as Sara walked away Mary walked up to her.

"Stay away from Dustin." she hissed at Nicky. "He's mine and I mean it. If you tangle with me you will be sorry. Just stay away if you know what is good for you."

Nicky stared at her in shock. "What?" she gasped.

"You know what I mean. You just keep your sexy little paws off. That's is all you are is a little whore. I can tell that just by looking at you. You don't care about him the way I do, so just get away from him. He doesn't like you anyway. I can tell. He only wants to play hard to get for me." she leaned closer. "So don't get any idea's that he likes you because he doesn't. He likes me and that is that."

Suddenly Sara stepped up behind Nicky. "Give it a rest Mary. You've had a crush on Dustin since like the first grade, but it is very obvious he doesn't share your feelings. That is it would be obvious if you would ever open up your eyes."

Mary sniffed. "I wasn't talking to you Sara Davis." Then turning back to Nicky she said, "Just remember what I said." then she turned and walked away.

Nicky stood dumbfounded for a moment. Sara touched her arm. "I don't know what she said, but Dustin doesn't like her. He never has and he never will. Don't worry about it. He likes you and I can tell. Besides, he tells me things." Sara smiled warmly at Nicky. "He cares a great deal about you, Nicky."

Nicky flushed. "Thanks, Sara. I wondered how he really felt."

Sara looked at her closely. "How do you feel?"

At that moment Dustin came out of the Sunday school room followed by Mary and Mrs. Walm. Nicky stiffened as Mary walked by, but Mary sniffed and turned up her nose.

Dustin looked from Nicky to Sara. "What was that all about?"

Nicky bit her lip, but Sara shrugged and said, "You know Mary. She wants things her way, whether she can have them or not."

Dustin smiled at Nicky and they all walked into the sanctuary together. They stopped at a pew where a young woman and six children where already sitting. Nicky trembled. This must be Dustin's mom and siblings. Sara slid in then Nicky and Dustin sat at the end.

After they had sat there a few minutes a man walked up behind them, leaned down and whispered something to Dustin. Dustin frowned and whispered something back. The man frowned then turned to Nicky and smiled. "We are so glad you could come today."

Nicky knew immediately it was Dustin's father. For though he was twenty years older than his son the resemblance was strong, right down to the twinkle in there eyes. "Thank you." she smiled a little unsure of herself. "I'm glad I could come."

Mr. Davis smiled then walked over and said something to his wife before going up front.

Nicky glanced at Dustin a question in her eyes. Dustin smiled. "He is the preacher. We'll sing a few songs then he will teach us about God. Just wait, you will understand soon."

Nicky turned toward the front in time to see a look pass between Dustin and his father. She wasn't sure what it meant but for some reason she felt a little uneasy. Was she causing trouble by being there?

Nicky smiled as they sang the songs. She had always loved music, but she didn't think she had ever heard anything so beautiful. Everyone seemed to sing with their hearts. They seemed to understand what they were singing about. What was this "Amazing Grace"? It sounded so wonderful. And she wished she could feel all was well with her soul as the other song said.

After the singing they knelt to pray. Dustin leaned over and whispered to her. "I have to go out, but I'll be back in a few minutes. I just have to call the usual song leader and see if he wants to listen to the message by phone. I'll be right back."

After prayer Dustin's father read a scripture. As he talked Nicky felt astonished. The questions she had seemed to be being answered without her even having to ask. He spoke of God's love. He spoke of Jesus coming to the earth to die for the sins of man kind, and then of Jesus rising up from the dead. A hope rose inside her that she had never felt before. When he said that Jesus loved everyone despite the bad things we do. She was shocked.

Jesus loves me? she thought in amazement. *How can he love me when I don't even know him? Why would he love me? Daddy says no one will ever love me, but will God anyway?* Eagerly she listened as he explained about God's love and forgiveness. She felt her heart quake. Was it possible that this could be real? Had Dustin told his Dad about her and that was why he was speaking about all this, or was it just coincidence? She didn't care. As long as she could meet Jesus and know him as Dustin did, she didn't care.

Mr. Davis closed his Bible. "Now Friends," he said, his voice echoing throughout the sanctuary. "Won't you come. Jesus died for you, won't you come and live for him? Accept him into your life. Acknowledge him as your Lord and Savior. Won't you come? He is calling you."

Nicky felt her heart flutter. She turned to Dustin. "I want to Dustin, please. I want to accept him. Please."

Dustin smiled as he took her hand. "I was hopping you would." he whispered. "Come." he led her up to the front.

As they knelt there Nicky looked at Dustin. "What do I say. I don't know what to do."

Dustin smiled. "Just tell him what is on your heart. He'll understand. Tell him you are sorry for your sins and that you don't want to sin anymore. Just talk to him, it will come to you."

Slowly Nicky bowed her head. "Dear God," she whispered. "I need you to forgive me..." as Nicky prayed she felt a heavy weight lift from her heart. She felt clean and fresh. She didn't know how to explain what she felt, but she knew she liked it.

Dustin squeezed her hand. "When you are done asking just thank him." he whispered. "When you feel ready we will go sit back down."

Nicky smiled. She felt a strong love sweep over her. A love she couldn't explain. She had never felt so happy, nor had she ever felt so loved.

When service was over Dustin led Nicky over to his mom. "Mom," his voice sounded a little hesitant. "This is Nicky. Nicky, this is my mom. Lisa Davis." he turned as his dad walked up to him. "And this is my Dad, John Davis. Dad, this is Nicky."

Mrs. Davis smiled warmly at her. "Glad to meet you, Nicky. Our son has told us so much about you."

Mr. Davis also smiled, yet he seemed a little more reserved. "Glad to meet you." he finally said.

Nicky flushed. "I'm glad to meet you too." she said trying to sound calm. She felt Mr. Davis's hesitation, was there something he didn't like about her? She trembled. She wanted his family to like her.

Mr. Davis watched the two of them for a few minutes. He didn't want his son getting to involved with this girl. Dustin had already expressed his calling into the ministry and he felt that Dustin and Nicky getting involved would hinder his son from what God wanted. Finally he turned to Dustin. "What happen with the phone?"

Dustin shrugged. "He didn't answer. I tried a couple of times. I left him a message that we were trying to get a hold of him and to call us back, but I never heard the phone."

Mr. Davis frowned and turned to his wife, "We better stop by and make sure everything is okay before we head home."

Mrs. Davis nodded, "Sara, please go get the kids rounded up."

Sara grinned. "Yes, mama." quickly she hurried to the back of the Church.

Mrs. Davis turned to Dustin and Nicky and smiled. "We are so glad you could make it today, Nicky. I hope to see you here more often." Smiling knowingly she began to gather the children's things then turned back. "Would you care to join us for dinner? It would give us all a chance to get to know each other better."

Nicky smiled weakly. "Sorry, I wish I could, but -" she stopped as she glanced down at his mom then turned back to Dustin. "I don't want to impose. I mean I just don't think I should." Her heart fluttered. She knew if she went she would have to eat then when she got home her father would make her throw up and he would know she had been with someone.

He smiled back, as though understanding it had something to do with her family. "I'll give you a ride. Maybe you could ask your parents. They might not mind. You never know."

Nicky smiled weakly then turned away. As they walked toward his car she looked up at him. "I can't let you take me home."

Dustin stared at her in shock. "Why? Don't your parents know where you are? Didn't you tell them that you were with me? Didn't you tell them after Friday night? Where do they think you were?"

Nicky looked down. "You don't understand. It's different for you. My dad-" she stopped and looked away. "I really don't want to talk about it."

Dustin sighed. "Don't they know about us, Nicky?"

Nicky kept her head down.

Dustin turned her face so she was looking into his eyes. "You have to tell him, Nicky. We can't see each other and keep it a secret from your parents. Either you tell him or I will. Fair enough?"

Nicky trembled, finally she nodded then looking up into his eyes again she whispered. "Thank you for bringing me to church. I won't ever forget and I won't ever turn back. Thank you so much for giving me this opportunity."

Dustin smiled. "I'm glad, God is real to you now, Nicky. I really am."

Nicky smiled. "I don't hate dad now. I just wish I had a way of learning more about God."

Dustin smiled. "The Bible is full of things about God and laws on how God wants us to live."

Nicky looked away unsure of how to tell him she had never heard of a Bible before today.

As Dustin dropped her of that afternoon she resolved she would tell her family about Dustin, no matter what the consequences. She prayed for protection and help and wisdom to know when the time would be right to brake the news.

Chapter 8

Nicky trembled as she walked to school. "Monday." she told herself. "Only two more weeks. I can do it. I hope."

Soon she heard the familiar sound of a car slowing down. Quickly she turned and smiled. "Hi, Dustin." she called as she waved.

He smiled as he stopped the car. "Guess I don't have to ask today, huh?" he laughed as he opened the door for her.

Nicky flushed. "Sorry, I guess I was a little ahead of you this morning."

He shrugged, "I don't mind."

She smiled. "Will you tell me more about God?" she asked before he had a chance to ask if she had told her father about them.

With a smile he started telling her all he could think to.

To Nicky it seem the ride that morning was extremely short. As he pulled the car to a stop he looked at her. "Can I pray with you before we go?" he asked softly.

Nicky looked at him in surprise. "I'd like that." she finally said. "I - would you teach me how to pray better."

Dustin smiled. "Just talk to him." Slowly he bowed his head and cleared his throat nervously. "Dear God," he began. Then seemingly getting more courage continued. "Please help Nicky today. Lead her in the way she needs to go. Teach her your paths and help her remember you are always there for her. Amen."

Nicky smiled. "Thanks. It makes me feel better."

Dustin smiled. "I'll be praying for you throughout the day." he said. "And if you don't mind I'll pick you up this afternoon."

Nicky smiled, "I think I'd like that."

Suddenly she froze. "Oh, no!" she whispered.

Andy was walking straight towards her. He looked angry. Nicky trembled as he jerked open the door.

"What are you doing Nichol." he hissed. "Get out of this car." he gripped her arm and pulled her out. Looking at Dustin he scowled. "Stay away from my girlfriend." he snapped. Andy grabbed Nicky's arm and walked with her to the school.

Nicky glanced back at Dustin with tears in her eyes as Andy drug her along.

Dustin sat in his car stunned. "Girl friend." he thought. "I don't think so" Dustin had seen the look on Nicky's face and it was a look of terror. He sighed as he drove off. "I'll ask her about it later." he said to himself. "God, please show me what to say and do. I don't want it to be the wrong thing."

After school Andy, who had not let Nicky out of his sight all day, grabbed her arm and led her to the lockers. "What do you mean by two-timing?" he hissed.

Nicky looked at him shocked. "Andy I was not two-timing. I told you I won't go out with you. I don't like you. Now leave me alone, please."

Andy gripped her arm. "You owe me something." he snarled.

"What for?" she asked shocked.

Andy smiled wickedly. "For not saying anything about your dad."

Nicky trembled. "What about my dad?"

Andy leaned back on her locker. "Oh, come on, Nicky. That night at Ben's I saw a lot. Probably enough to put your dad behind bars for a long time."

Nicky turned away. "I don't know what your talking about." she whispered.

Andy grabbed her arm and turned her to face him. "Don't you?" he asked wickedly. "Suppose I explain it to the police. Then would you know."

Nicky looked at him. "What do you want from me?" she cried.

Dustin gripped her arm and led her outside to the parking lot. "I want to finish something I started at Ben's." he smiled at her. "And you are going to love it." he looked closely at her. "Or would you rather I tell your dad that you were getting rides to school with a boy."

Nicky trembled. "I won't sleep with you, Andy. Never. I'd rather rot."

Angrily her grabbed her and pushed her up against the building. "Don't make a peep or I'll tell the cops about your dad. Do you really want me to do that? And one more thing, you better make it good or I'll let your dad know that you are getting rides to school from some boy. I don't imagine he will be to happy about that will he?" he smiled wickedly at her as he leaned closer pushing his body up close to hers. "I told you, you would be sorry if you stood me up on Friday."

Nicky suddenly bolted. Running as fast as she could into the wood behind the school. Her thought was to get in there and hide, hopping he wouldn't be able to find her. As she ran she felt an arm grab her and bring her up short.

Nicky bit her lip, trying to keep from crying out in fear, as she struggled to fight him off.

Andy pushed her and kicked her then suddenly flung her to the ground and crawled on top of her. "I'll show you just what you missed out on." He grabbed hold of her shirt and jerked. Before she had time to scream she felt his mouth close over hers.

Her stomach turned over and she tried to pull away. Fear shot through her as she realized that this was, without a doubt, going to happen to her. She couldn't stop him. When he finally lifted his head she bit her lip and whispered, "Andy, please, don't do this."

Andy slugged her across the jaw. "I'll do what I want, when I want. You are mine and I'm going to make sure you know that."

He grabbed her up and pushed her against a tree. She squeezed her eyes shut as she felt him reach down to undress her. Suddenly something Dustin had said that morning popped into her head. "Help her to remember you are always there." Nicky bit her lip, *Please God.* she thought. *Help me!* out loud she cried. "Leave me alone, Andy. Leave me alone don't do this."

Some how she managed to break his grasp on her and raced away again. Fear weld up inside her as she heard footsteps behind her. She ran harder, but knew her strength wouldn't last long, suddenly her legs gave way and she fell to the ground. Tears streamed down her face. "God help me please!" she cried.

Andy grabbed her arm and pulled her to her feet.

Fear raced through her and she kept her eyes squeezed tight shut. She pulled away wishing she could disappear. Then she felt a hand on her shoulder. Panic raced through her and her mind whirled. *He has his friends here to help. Oh, God, please help me,* she thought. "No!" she screamed as she reached up and began clawing while at the same time turning her head and trying to bite the hand that held her captive. "Go away. Go away."

Instead of him hitting her back as she expected she only felt a little shake. "Nicky." someone said firmly but kindly.

Slowly she opened her eyes and found herself looking into the concerned eyes of Dustin, not Andy as she had feared. Quickly pulling away she turned to look and see where Andy was and found him just sitting up close to her side.

Dustin angrily grabbed Andy and turned him to face him. "She told you to leave her alone." he growled. He raised a fist and slugged letting him go at the same time. Andy fell to the ground in a heap. "Don't ever touch her again." Dustin kicked him. "Now get out."

Andy jumped up and ran back toward the school. "You'll be sorry!" he screamed as he raced off."

Nicky looked up at Dustin still in shock. "Dustin?" she whispered as though unable to believe it was true.

"It's me." he whispered back as he brushed his hand over her cheek. "Are you okay?"

Nicky trembled, "How did you, where did you come from?" she asked. Then she noticed blood running down his cheek and guessed it was from her clawing him. Tears slid down her cheeks as she back away. "I'm sorry." she whispered trying not to look frightened. He had every right to hit her. She had hurt him. What was he going to do to her?

Dustin smiled and shrugged. "You didn't know." Then he added. "I got here to pick you up and saw him leading you out here. I knew something was up so I followed. Sorry it took me so long to get here." he looked at her closely. "Are you sure you're okay?"

Nicky shuttered. "I'm sure." she whispered taking a deep breath to calm herself.

Dustin could tell she was scared. Her eyes were wide and wild looking. She trembled so bad her teeth chattered.

"It's okay." he whispered as he touched her cheek.

Nicky saw him reach out his hand and quickly turned her face away from him. When he touched her she jumped, sure he was going to hit her at the very least. When he didn't she was surprised.

"You're strong Nicky." he whispered.

Nicky trembled. "I don't think so." her voice caught in her throat.

Standing he offered her his hand to help her up. "We better get going it's later than we think. Do you need to go into the school for anything?"

Nicky trembled. "I have to go back and get my bag." she whispered taking a deep breath and trying to fight back more tears. "Then I'll be ready." Slowly she stood biting her lip as she fought back a cry of pain. She must have twisted her ankle when Andy stopped her.

Dustin watched her for a moment then unbuttoned his shirt and held it out to her. "He tore you up a bit didn't he?" He heard the anger in his own voice and hopped it wouldn't frighten her.

Nicky trembled. She knew Andy had torn her shirt, but she didn't feel right about taking Dustin's even though he had a t-shirt on also. "Just a little. I'll be fine." she stepped back.

Dustin looked at her closely. "It's okay. Besides I don't think your parents would like it if you were seen in public like that."

Nicky smiled finally taking the shirt. "Thanks." she whispered as she slipped it on. Her heart fluttered. She looked up at him, he was smiling at her. "Are you sure this is okay?" she asked.

"I'm sure." he smiled at her with that teasing gleam in his eye. He opened his mouth as if he were going to tease then stopped, now wasn't the time. "Let's get your things and go so your parents don't worry." He finally said.

Inside Nicky grabbed all her books out of her locker and pushed them into her bag. Making sure she had everything she picked up her bag and turned to Dustin. "Okay. I think I'm ready."

Dustin smiled at her and took her bag. "Then lets go." he looked into her eyes. "I'm taking you home."

Nicky trembled. She knew he meant it this time. He was not going to take any chances on Andy trying anything with her. Giving him a weak smile she nodded.

As Dustin slowly pulled the car up in front of her house she looked at him "How, did you know where I lived?"

Dustin flushed. "I've watched you." he whispered He got out and opened the door for her. "Do you need me to stay with you till you talk with your parents?"

Nicky smiled at him. "No. You've done more than I could have asked already." she glanced down at his shirt and started to take it off.

Dustin stopped her. "Keep it for now. You can give it to me some other time." Suddenly he reached back in the car. "I almost forgot." He pulled a book out of the glove box and handed it to her. "This will help you in your walk with God. I hope you don't mind that I got it for you."

Nicky smiled as she took it. On the front it said "Holy Bible." Her heart thundered. "Thank you. But, what is it?"

Dustin smiled. "God's word. He tells us what to do and how we are to act as Christians. Start in the New Testament. I think it will make a little more sense to you."

Nicky carefully placed it in her backpack then with Dustin beside her started up to the house. When they reached the door she turned to him. "Thanks for bringing me home, and thanks for everything." she looked down embarrassed.

Dustin smiled, "My pleasure, but I wish it wouldn't have happened at all. Do you want me to talk to your parents or will you be okay."

Nicky smiled. "They aren't home." She sounded hesitant. *Should I tell him that?* she wondered.

"Do you want me to stay here till they get back? I don't want anything to happen to you while you are alone." He wasn't sure if that was a good idea and he felt his stomach tighten, but he wasn't about to leave her and give Andy a chance to try anything.

Nicky trembled, she wanted nothing more than for him to stay with her, but she didn't want her parents to know about him, not yet anyway. "No." she finally answered. "That probably wouldn't make a very good first impression with my dad. He might think -" she stopped and looked up into his eyes. "Well, you know."

Dustin looked into her eyes. "I do. I'll see you tomorrow then?" His voice was soft and hesitant.

She smiled. "Tomorrow." she said softly as she turned to go in the house. Suddenly the door opened. Nicky stumbled back in surprise. "Dad, I thought you weren't going to be home till late."

Her father glared at her angrily. "Get in the house girl. I want a word with you." he growled.

Dustin trembled at the look in her fathers eye and the sound of his voice. What had happened to make him so upset, surely it wasn't just him bringing her home?

Nicky flushed, "Thanks again Dustin." she whispered as she hurried in the house.

Her father angrily turned to Dustin. "I think you need to leave now." He grunted "Thanks for bringing her home." Turning he slammed the door.

Dustin stood dumbfounded for a moment then turned to leave, his heart heavy. He couldn't figure out why, he just knew he didn't like the look in her fathers eye.

Nicky trembled as her father turned to her. She could tell by the look in his eyes that she was in more trouble than even she could imagine. "I thought you weren't going to be home till late tonight." she whispered.

"Is that any reason for bringing a boy home." he snapped as he moved closer to her. All of the sudden he stopped. "Where did you get that shirt from?"

Nicky trembled. "Dustin." she tried to sound calm but her voice shook with fear.

Her father suddenly grabbed her arm and started shaking her. "I told you what I would do if a boy ever tried to get close to you. Now you tell me what you were thinking." He shook her harder, "Did you lay with him?" He grabbed a hold of her with both arms and shook her so hard her head wobbled. "Answer me!"

"No." she finally managed.

"No! No, you won't answer or no, you haven't slept with him." her father drew back a little surprised.

Nicky trembled. "No, I haven't been with him."

Her father looked at her than gave her a sharp push, almost knocking her to the floor. Pulling off his belt he stepped closer to her. "I think you know what is coming." he laughed wickedly.

Nicky bit her lip as her father stepped closer to her. "I didn't do it!" she screamed surprising herself.

Her father pulled back then slapped her across the face. "Don't you dare lie to me!" he pushed her to the floor. "Get that shirt off. Now! You are going to get what you deserve you little whore!"

Chapter 9

The next morning her father pushed her into her room. "Get ready for school and don't you dare be late. You have ten minutes and you better have all your homework done. I would keep you home and finish punishing you, but you have a big test today I believe."

Nicky dropped her head. "Yes sir." she trembled as she walked into her room. As she changed she heard her father say something the he started shouting. She bit her lip and tried to keep from crying.

"Nichol!" her father sounded upset. "Hurry it up girl or you are going to be late."

With a sigh she looked herself over. Bruises were very evident, but maybe Dustin would think they were from Andy. She trembled as she stepped out.

"Don't be late." he growled at her. "And your grades better be perfect or I will take the points you missed out of your hide."

Nicky bit her lip. "Yes sir. I remember." she tried to sound calm yet her voice trembled.

"And don't let me ever catch you with that boy again. If you see him, you tell him you hate him and never want to see him again. You will not be a whore on my watch, you got that!"

"Yes Sir." she groaned.

Her father held up her school bag. Then he grabbed her arm. "Don't forget what I told you." he snarled. "I see you with that boy again and I will make sure you never go near him again."

She trembled. "I promise."

He released her some. "Good." he looked at her coldly. "Get the whip."

Nicky bit her lip and dropped her head, but made no move to obey.

"Get it." his voice was soft, but also threatening.

Slowly she walked over to the closet and pulled it out. Trembling she brought it to him.

He raised it angrily. Folding it over he struck her several times. Then he turned her to face him. He slugged her until she looked up at him and took a full punch without looking away. "Don't forget." he growled. He handed her the bag and pushed her out the door. "Now, get."

Trembling she ran to the corner where Dustin was waiting for her. As she slid in Dustin looked at her. He didn't say anything till they were on there way. "What happened?" he asked softly.

Nicky whimpered. "Nothing."

He glanced at her. "You really expect me to believe that."

She glanced away. Her mind raced. *How can I tell him what daddy wants me to?* she wondered. *How can I promise never to see him again?*

Dustin pulled the car to a stop. "Nicky?"

Slowly Nicky looked at him.

"Did he hit you?"

Tears burned her eyes. "Dustin please." she whispered trying to keep her tears back.

He reached over and touched her cheek. "Did he?"

Nicky bit her lip. "Why do you want to know?"

Dustin sat back in his seat and handed her a napkin. "Your lip is bleeding, your bruised, your scared. All I want is an honest answer. We can get you out of that house, you don't have to live like this. All you have to do is tell someone. I want to help you." He sighed as she took the napkin and dabbed her lip. "Just don't lie to me. Fair?"

Nicky nodded. "Fair." She winced as she pushed the napkin up to her mouth. "I'll just have to splash some water on it." she looked up at him. "Thanks for bringing me."

Dustin smiled. "My pleasure. Can we pray before you go?"

She nodded. They both bowed there heads as Dustin prayed for help and protection for Nicky.

Nicky smiled as she climbed out taking her bag with her. She decided not to tell Dustin what her father had said. She would just have to try hard to keep it a secret from them both. With a sigh she ran in to school, hoping she could stay away from Andy all day.

Nicky sighed as she walked out of school. "The week's almost over." she told herself. "Only three more days this week then only a week left till graduation." she groaned inwardly. *At least Andy wasn't at school today.* She smiled as she remembered how she felt when the science teacher announced he wouldn't be their because he was sick. Suddenly her smile died. She looked down at the paper in her hand for a few minutes then sighed. This was the worst thing that could of happened this week, or at all. If her father found out she would be in serious trouble.

All at once a car pulled up behind her. "Climb on in Nicky." called Dustin.

Slowly she opened the door. "Sorry, I didn't see you." she muttered sliding in.

He looked over at her and smiled. "No wonder. You looked like you were miles away. What's wrong? I thought I would get you from school."

She looked down at the paper in her hands. "Just history. I don't mind it, I'm just not good at it. It's been a hard subject ever since grade school."

"What's the matter, did you fail or something." he teased.

"I have never done this bad before. I just don't know what my parents will say." A tear slid down and splashed on the paper.

Without warning Dustin grabbed the test and flipped it over. He looked at it for a moment then up at her as he pulled the car over. He shifted into park then turned and looked at her. He seemed to tower over her. "Nicky." he said softly.

Nicky looked away. "I know it's awful. I'm so stupid."

Dustin stared at her. "Nicky, isn't it just a B."

"A low B. About the lowest I could get, in a B that is." She dropped her head. *What will daddy do to me,* she thought. She wanted to scream it but she knew she couldn't. Instead she snapped. "I'm so stupid."

"Nicky, stop! You are not stupid." Dustin looked as though he couldn't believe her. "I think that is awesome. I barley squeaked through history and you are upset because you got a B."

She looked up at him, "It's not that. It just that - well, I don't think my dad will be to thrilled. He thinks I have to be a straight A student."

Dustin looked at her strangely. "Would he really care that much about one test?"

Nicky look at him for a moment. "Maybe not." she muttered, knowing Dustin just wouldn't understand. She turned quickly to get out. "I have to go." She didn't want to give Dustin anymore reason to not trust her father or to think he was being abusive.

"Nicky, I thought-" he started.

"Dustin I mean it I really have to go. I'll see you tomorrow." Nicky jumped out of the car and ran down the street.

"Oh, Nicky. Why do you do this?" Dustin whispered as he watched her disappear. "If only you would let me help." he sighed. Would she ever open up to him?

Nicky slipped quietly in the door. Were her parents home yet. "Nicky!" It was her mom. "You are late again."

Nicky trembled as she looked at her mother. "I just walk a little slow that's all." she tried to sound calm. "I thought you weren't coming back till tomorrow." All of the sudden the door burst open slamming into her. She cried out in pain as she fell forward. Looking up she saw her father glairing at her. She trembled.

"Says she was just walking slow." her mother grunted as her father stepped into the room.

Nicky trembled as she coward away from him. He reached down and pulled her to her feet forcing her to look him in the eye. "Is that the truth or are you lying to me, like you lied about telling that boy what I said!" he growled.

Nicky bit her lip to keep her teeth from chattering. She didn't think she had ever been this scared in her whole life. "I-I-"

Her father flung her to the floor. "You worthless girl." Suddenly he reached down and snatched the paper out of her hand.

"Daddy I'm sorry." she cried. "I didn't mean to."

After looking at it a moment he passed it to her mother then turned back to Nicky. "What you been doing? Day dreaming during class about boys, no doubt. Well, I won't stand for it. You know better than to get a low grade on a test. And I'm going to make sure it doesn't happen again."

Nicky kept her eyes down, it wasn't out of shame; she didn't feel ashamed of what she did, she did it mostly to hide the flash of anger in her eyes. Her father gripped her arm tighter and tighter until she looked up at him. "You tell me the truth. You were daydreaming, that's why you got this bad grade. You let your mind get sidetracked by the boys, didn't you." it wasn't a question he would force her to give him that answer.

Nicky shuddered. *Please help me know what to do, God,* she bit her lip to keep her thoughts to herself.

She whimpered as her father struck her. "You answer me when I'm talking to you. It doesn't take any time to tell me the truth. You weren't thinking of lying to me were you?" his voice was cold and dangerous.

"No, sir." Nicky trembled. "I wasn't I just-"

Her father pulled off his belt.

Nicky trembled even more, but knew better than to back away.

Grabbing her arm he hit her across the back. "Don't ever even think about lying to me again. Do you understand."

Nicky trembled in pain. But before she could answer her father struck her across the legs. Nicky screamed before she even thought.

"Answer me." he hollered as he continued hitting her legs.

"Yes sir." her voice shook. What else was he going to do to her.

"Good. And just to be sure you don't forget." he grabbed her arm and drug her into the kitchen.

Nicky trembled what was he going to do. It didn't take her long to figure it out. Angrily he jerked the oven door open, then grabbing her arms he pulled her over to it. "Now," he said dryly, "You tell me why you where late."

Nicky trembled. "I was just walking slow that's all. I told you." she shook even more. She knew her father meant business.

Her father scowled at her, "Then whose car was it I saw you getting out of."

Nicky gasped. "It was-I was just-"

"Don't ever disobey or lie to me again." he said coldly. "And further more you can forget going back to school. You will never set foot there again. I don't intend to whip you so it can be hidden any more for a while, so you will just have to stay home. That will also keep you away from boys." he looked at her hatefully. "And don't think of sneaking about and going anywhere." He gripped her arms tighter, "Now, you answer me. Who's car were you getting out of?" He turned her so her back was to him and grabbed her hair.

Nicky bit her lip knowing what was coming.

Chapter 10

Her father, true to his word kept her home from school the rest of the week, beating her as often as he could.

She just didn't seem to be able to do things the way he wanted her to. About four o'clock Sunday morning he drug her once again into the kitchen. "This is a reminder to what I said before." He looked at her closely, "I'm going to be gone a few days. You will be good for your mother, any disobedience and you will get worse."

She whimpered. "I'll be good." she promised looking straight into her fathers eyes.

"Remember that." he said coldly. "And to make sure you don't forget anytime soon-" he pulled open the oven door.

Nicky jumped as she tried to pull away. "No!" she screamed before she thought.

Her father gripped her arm tighter. "Don't ever lift your voice around me. Especially when you deserve what you are getting." He struck her again, and again. "Understand!"

"Yes sir." she moaned.

"Maybe next time you will remember what happens when you disobey me."

Nicky trembled. "Yes sir." she dropped her gaze so her father would not see her anguish.

"Good. Now, don't be trouble for your mother. And leave her alone as much as possible, if you go out you don't see or speak to anyone, but don't stay out late either. Understand."

"Yes sir." she wanted to try to pull away from him, but knew it would only make things worse.

He hit her then pushed her to the floor. "Get cleaned up and get out of the house. I don't want you bothering her. And remember what I said."

"I won't bother her and I will remember." Nicky whispered as she went to her room. Tears filled her eyes as she looked in the mirror. "God," she whispered, "Why is he doing this to me. Please help me be a loving daughter, and even though it's not easy help me be respectful. Help me live through this till I'm old enough to leave."

Softly she slipped into the bathroom. As she shut the door she heard her father leave his room. A few minutes later he left the house. She breathed a sigh of relief. He would be gone three or four days. At last, maybe she could have a little bit of a brake. All her mom wanted was for Nicky to stay away from her so it shouldn't be to bad, till he got back anyway.

Walking back into her room she glanced at her book bag. Reaching inside it she felt the small book Dustin had given her. Sitting on her floor she smiled. *I wonder what this is anyway.*

Her hands trembled as she slowly opened it. On the first page she saw a hand written note. Tears ran down her cheeks. The note was from Dustin. Her heart skipped a beat as she read.

Dear Nicky,

I am so glad you have placed God first in your life. This book is God's word. It tells about God, His son Jesus, and all that he has done for us. It also tells us how we are to live as Christians. I hope this doesn't make you to embarrassed, but I want you to know, I love you, Nicky. I have from the first time I met you. You can trust me. I mean it. I'm not just saying it.

Dustin

Nicky bit her lip as she flipped through the pages. "You wouldn't say that if you knew me, Dustin. If you knew what daddy has done to me you would never love me." She closed the book and jumped up to get some clean clothes.

After cleaning up and getting dressed for church Nicky slipped quietly out of the house as she walked down the sidewalk her mother opened the door. "Just be home before dark." she called. "And call me if you won't be here for lunch."

Nicky turned, "I will." she called back.

Her mother grunted and shut the door.

Nicky trembled. Did her mother suspect something? Quickly she made her way toward Church, as she rounded the corner she smiled. Dustin's car was parked in their usual spot. The next moment she felt scared. What if he noticed the burns or the cuts on her face. Though she wore a long-sleeved lose shirt and long full skirt, in hopes that they wouldn't rub her skin, keeping the burns less painful, she felt scared. She slowed not wanting to meet him. What would he say, and what would he think about her not going to school the last few days? She couldn't let him know, he would hate her. She trembled as she walked up.

"Morning." he greeted her as she opened the door.

She smiled as she slid in being careful not to let her sleeves rub her arms or her back to touch the seat. "Good morning."

He watched her closely for a few minutes then drove to church. When they were almost there he reached over and touched her hand.

Biting her lip to keep back the cry of pain that threatened to escape she pulled her hand back.

Dustin parked and looked at her. "You don't want me to touch you?" his voice sounded hurt, yet his mind raced. Was he pushing her to much?

Nicky turned away not daring to see the look in his eyes. "It's not that." she whispered.

"Nicky." he said softly. "Nicky, look at me."

Slowly she turned her head to look at him.

"Why didn't you go to school any more last week?"

Nicky trembled. "My mom and dad needed me at home."

Dustin looked at her closely. "For what?" When she did not answer he said again, "Why did they need you at home, Nicky?"

She looked up at him. The sound in his voice frightened her. "They just did. I don't see how it's any of your business." She spoke a bit more sharply then she intended and Dustin turned away from her. Slowly he got out and went over to her side and opened the door. Offering her his hand he smiled.

Nicky trembled knowing she shouldn't have snapped. She also saw by the look on his face that their conversation was just beginning and he wouldn't let her go without some answers.

Her mind raced, *maybe he'll forget if I don't do anything to make him think anything is going on,* she thought. Then slowly she pushed the thought away. If he wanted a relationship with her he deserved to know the truth. She trembled. She wasn't ready for him to walk away, but why she really didn't know.

Chapter 11

As Nicky and Dustin walked out of church Dustin's mom stopped them. "Nicky, we have a splendid roast for dinner. How would you like to join us? I know you couldn't last week, but we really would like to get to know you better and give you the chance to get to know us better."

Nicky glanced at Dustin. "I-ah-I don't know, I mean I'd need to check with my parents and see that it was alright first. My mom kind of wanted me home for lunch today." she struggled to find an excuse. She didn't want to give Dustin more time to find out what her father had done to her.

"Why don't you call her and see." replied Mrs. Davis. "We really would love to have you."

Dustin cleared his throat as he looked at Nicky. She struggled with her decision. Quietly he held out his phone. "Why don't you call her and find out?" he said softly.

Nicky hesitated. If she went with Dustin that would only give him more time to talk with her. What if he found out everything? She knew she couldn't keep it all secret for long, but she didn't want him to know everything either. He would never want to speak to her again. Slowly Nicky reached for the phone not able to think of a good excuse. "Okay." she finally whispered.

Walking a short distance away she dialed the number. When her mother answered she trembled, but tried to keep her voice steady, "Mom, would it be alright if I didn't come home for lunch. No I don't have any particular plans I just thought I would hang out around the lake. Thanks."

She hit end then quickly deleted the number. Turning quickly she jumped to see Dustin was right behind her. "I can come." She said quickly as she handed him back his phone. She flushed as he looked into her eyes.

"I'm glad." he whispered. "We need to talk." He turned to his mom. "We'll meet you at home."

She smiled and nodded. "We'll be there soon."

Walking beside him back to the car Nicky's thoughts raced. What could she say to keep him from finding out the whole truth? What if she couldn't keep it secret from him? Tears burned her eyes. She didn't want to lose him, but why? She couldn't even answer her own questions.

Dustin climbed in the car and looked over at Nicky. "What are you trying to keep secret from me?"

She trembled in spite of herself. "What do you mean?"

"You know what I mean, Nicky." he looked at her closely. All threw church he had watched her. She had been careful of every move she made. She had a look of pain on her face about all morning, when she had bumped her arm on the pew she looked as though she would be sick. He felt sick not knowing what was going on.

Nicky looked away. The look in Dustin's eyes hurt almost as bad as the burns on her back. She bit her lip, what could she say?

"Nicky," Dustin tried again. "Please talk to me."

Nicky kept her head down knowing if she looked up now he would see her face and know how much she hurt. "I can't." she whispered.

"That is a lie." he growled. "You won't, you can you just don't want to. Why?" He dropped back in his seat and drove in silence to his home. He kept on watching her out of the corner of his eye hopping to get some kind of clue as to what was going on.

Nicky kept her eyes glued out the window the whole time. She didn't dare turn and look at him. Not even for a glance. Tears weld up in her eyes, yet she would not let them fall. Right now it was very hard to love her father, when it was hurting Dustin so much to keep her life secret from him.

Her whole body was tense and she felt tired, she sighed and turned her head to look out the front window. Without thinking she let her body drop back against the seat. She jumped then sat forward biting her lip to keep from crying. She glanced sideways at Dustin and flushed. He had seen, she knew he had.

Dustin saw her movement and looked away. If she didn't want to talk he didn't want her to look at him and see the hurt in his eyes. Slowly he pulled into the drive at his home.

Nicky trembled when the car stopped, not sure what they were going to do. She didn't want to talk, but she knew she was not escaping without telling him something.

She looked at him then quickly away. She could tell by the stiffness of his back he was still upset with her. "I'm sorry." she whispered. "I didn't want to make you upset.

Dustin shifted into park and turned the car off. Slowly he turned to her, "Nicky," his voice was soft yet full of pain. "This is bad timing but," he took a deep breath as though not wanting to say what he was going to say. "I don't think we can see each other anymore."

Nicky looked up at him in shock then dropped her head back down before he had a chance to get a good look at her.

Dustin kept his eyes on her so he could see her face when she glanced up at him. "I can't go out with you if you won't talk to me. I need you to trust me and if you won't talk that tells me that you don't trust me. I thought you cared for me like I did for you. Why can't you just be honest with me. I care a lot for you, Nicky, but-" he dropped his gaze, "I just can't date a girl I can't trust. All you've said to me today is a lie. Something is wrong, I can tell. Why don't you just tell me? I promise you can trust me. Would it be as hard as braking up?"

He reached out and cupped her face in his hands trying to force her to look at him. "Please, Nicky. I love you. What ever it is you need to tell me. It won't change the fact that I love you. I promise."

Nicky looked out the window. Tears slid down her cheeks, but she didn't want him to see. What if he thought like her father, that people aren't suppose to cry no matter how bad their hurting inside or out. Could she trust him? She had never had anyone she could trust before.

Dustin bit his lip, "Did I do something wrong?"

"No." she dropped her head as she started to sob.

Dustin sat quietly, waiting and praying. Why would God bring her into his life only to have them part this way. All she had to do was be honest and everything would be okay. He didn't want to lose her, but he couldn't stand her shutting him out when he felt she was in danger.

If it's her dad, he wouldn't let her talk without threatening to hurt her more. He would be afraid of being turned in. Dustin looked at her closely. "Nicky." he said softly. When she didn't answer he reached out and took her hand. *I have to know if I'm right. Please God don't let me be.* he thought. He took a deep breath and in one swift movement, before she could do anything, he jerked up her sleeve.

"Dustin please, don't." she jumped and tried to pull away from him, but as she looked into his eyes she knew it was to late. He knew. She bit her lip and dropped her gaze. "Please don't. You don't understand." she whispered.

Dustin felt sick all the way through. What had her father done to her. Now he knew why she had looked like she was in so much pain. Slowly he pulled her forward on the seat and touched her back.

Nicky cried out in pain, then quickly bit her lip, but this time made no move to get away. Slowly and carefully he pulled up her shirt just enough to see a little of her back, that was about all he could stand. "Nicky!" he cried out in pain for her. "What did he do to you?"

Nicky whimpered yet as Dustin pulled her around to face him he couldn't find any sign of pain on her face except the tear stains on her cheeks. Then he looked closer. As she looked at him steadily in the light of the sun he could see what he hadn't been able to before. Large welts covered the right side of her face, she had a small bruise under her left and right eye, the right side of her lip was a little swollen, and there were traces of dry blood on both cheeks.

Nicky looked into his eyes for a moment then quickly looked away biting her lip.

Dustin reached over and turned her to face him. "Nicky," he said softly. "Nicky, look at me." when she made no response he tried again. "Nicky, please! Just look at me."

Slowly she looked up at him. "I just fell, that's all. I fell." Tears once again started to run down her cheeks, she quickly turned away. "Please don't make me tell you."

"You fell? Onto what an oven door. You just happened to fall onto a hot oven door." He looked at her closely, "That's what burned you, it isn't it."

She bit her lip. Her heart hurt. What could she do, what should she do? Disobey her father and tell or lie to Dustin. As she looked once again into his eyes. She had her answer. If she lied it would be the last she would ever see of him. Then she trembled. If she told him the truth it probably would be also. "I just-" she started then looked away. *I can't tell.* she thought. *If I do he'll turn daddy in then it would be even worse.* The pain in Dustin's eyes was to great. It hurt her more then her father ever had to see him look at her that way. Tears burned her eyes.

"Nicky, please tell me. Maybe I can help. Please."

"No!" she burst out. "No, if I tell you, you must promise never to tell anyone. Not ever. Promise?"

Dustin looked at her in shock. "But Nicky, there's help out there. I can get him away from you so he will never hurt you again. Don't you understand-"

"No, You don't understand." Nicky interrupted almost screaming.

Dustin reached out a hand to calm her, but she thought he was going to hit her.

"No!" she screamed as she jerked her hands up and cowered away from him.

"Nicky!" he screamed. Forgetting about her arms and back he grabbed her wrists and pulled them down. "Nicky look at me." He shouted pinning her to the door.

"Don't shout at me." she screamed back. Suddenly the tears she fought flowed freely down her cheeks. "I put up with that enough at home. I won't put up with it when I don't have to!" she pushed on him trying to get away. Her back throbbed and she thought she was going to be sick. Suddenly she realized what she said.

"I didn't mean that." she whispered as she looked down. "Please let me go."

Dustin stopped and took a deep breath. "I'm sorry." he said softly as he let her go. "You are right I have no right to yell. I guess I just have a bad temper." He looked up at her. "Tell you what. Why don't we make a deal. I won't shout at you anymore if you promise never to cower away from me, like that."

Nicky bit her lip. "Okay." she whispered.

He brushed his hand over her cheek. Her whole body quivered in fear.

"Nicky, I promise I will never hit you. No matter how angry I get. I promise." he looked deep into her eyes.

Nicky could tell he meant it and she slowly nodded. "Okay." she whispered.

Dustin looked away. "Why does he hit you, Nicky?"

Biting her lip she turned away. "He made me promise not to tell. You don't understand." she whispered. "There is no way you could."

Dustin looked at her for a moment then whispered, "Make me understand, Nicky. I want to know. Why don't you want him turned in? He wouldn't be able to hurt you any more."

She looked at him sadly. "He's my father, Dustin. Besides I deserved everything I got."

Dustin reached over and turned her arm so he could see the burn marks again. "Everything Nicky?" he said softly as tears smarted his eyes. "You deserved everything? How can you say that? No one deserves to be hurt like this."

Nicky bit her lip in pain from his touch. "Yes," she whispered. "I deserved everything."

Dustin looked into her eyes. "What has he done to you? Please tell me, Nicky, please. Make me understand."

She looked away. "I can't." she whimpered. "I am forbidden. If I tell and he finds out that I told -" she shivered.

Dustin turned her face to look at him. "Nicky, tell me the truth, please." he reached over and gripped her shoulder. "Nicky!" he said loudly, shaking her a little.

Nicky trembled. What was he going to do. Her whole body was trembling so hard she couldn't stop. What if he told his parents or someone else, just because she wouldn't talk? It wasn't hard to guess. They would tell the cops and her father would kill her.

Suddenly she started to sob. Her whole body shook from anger and fear. "I hate him." she suddenly screamed. "I hate him. I've tried to do what God said and love him, but I can't. I will always hate him for what he has done to me." Suddenly she looked up into Dustin's face and gasped. "I didn't mean that." she said softly.

Dustin saw the fear in her eyes and suddenly realized he had been to sharp with her, before and now. She was in bad enough shape without having him scaring her also. He let go of her and dropped his face down near hers. "I sorry." he spoke softly hoping to calm her. "I'm just worried about you. I don't want to see you hurt."

Nicky looked up at him, "Then stop asking about my life."

"I can't." he said so quickly she knew he was serious. "I care about you to much."

Nicky bit her lip, "If you care about me then promise you won't tell anyone. If you do it will just make things worse." Nicky shivered, *how could things get any worse?* she wondered.

Dustin looked at her closely, "On one condition. You be honest with me from now on. If I ask something tell me the truth." he looked straight into her eyes. "If you talk to me I will not tell anyone else unless you tell me I can." As soon as he said the words his stomach knotted. Could he keep that secret, if he felt her life was in danger?

Nicky bit her lip but nodded. What else could she do? If she said she wouldn't, he'd tell what he did know and then she might as well have told everything anyway. She would get the same punishment whether she did or didn't. All that had to happen was for her father to think she told.

"What did he do to you and why? Is this why you weren't at school any more last weak, so he could beat you?"

Nicky dropped her gaze. "Well," she bit her lip. "You remember the test?"

He nodded.

"There's part of your why."

Dustin was shocked. "And the other part?"

Nicky trembled as she looked away. There was no way she was going to tell him it was because her father had seen them together.

Dustin looked at her closely. "And your back?"

Nicky shuddered but continued. "He beat's me a lot. He left this morning for a few days. This was my reminder to be good." She bit her lip, "If I get a low grade I get whipped. This time he thought it was because I was day dreaming about boys, when I should have been focusing on my school work. He wanted me to remember. I guess the pain of burns is suppose to last longer than the other pain."

Dustin stared at her in shock. He hadn't been spanked in years and he never remembered his father hitting him with a belt or anything else on the face, and he had never burned him. Didn't her father know she was a grownup. He looked down at her with tears in his eyes. "And your cheek and chin?" he whispered.

Nicky whimpered then bit her lip. "I cried out when he burned me. I was in shock it was the last thing I expected." she looked up into Dustin's eyes. "I'm not aloud to cry. He says it's a sign of being weak, and as long as he can help it he won't have a weak daughter."

Dustin didn't know what to think or do. He was in such shock all he could do was turn away.

Nicky trembled. Had she done the right thing? Did Dustin hate her now, like her father had told her everyone would if she ever told.

Finally he turned back to her. "Is that why you hate him?"

Nicky looked away not willing to give him the whole reason. "I - when I was praying last week I felt like - I don't know - just like I didn't hate him anymore. Like I still could love him no matter what -" she looked down and whispered hopping he wouldn't hear. "No matter what he did to me."

She looked up and continued in a hurry. "I keep on thinking of what your dad said last Sunday, about when Jesus died and the Romans beat him. I think about how he said that Jesus asked God to forgive them, because they didn't know what they were doing. I figure if Jesus, the savior of the world, could love them and forgive them he would want me to love my dad." She took a deep breath and her voice trembled, "But it's so hard."

Dustin smiled, "I can't even begin to imagine what it must be like for you. I wish I could do something to help. Why don't you want anyone to know what he does to you?"

Nicky bit her lip. "Like I said, I deserved everything he did to me. Please, Dustin, if my dad gets locked up he will just find another way to hurt me." She lowered her gaze. "I'd rather have it be him. He doesn't hurt me all the time, like someone else will if daddy knows I told."

Dustin looked at her questioningly, "What do you mean?"

Nicky bit her lip. Once more she knew she had said to much.

Dustin turned her face up to him. "Did you mean sexually, Nicky?"

His look burned into her heart. Fear shot through her. Slowly she nodded, "Yes, that is what I meant." she whispered.

"Has he ever-" he stopped as though afraid to go on.

Nicky whimpered as she looked away. "Not in the way someone else would."

"Nicky, please!" Dustin cried out in agony. "Talk to me. I want to know. Please."

Nicky looked up at him with tears in her eyes. "I can't talk about this now. Please, Dustin. I'm still a virgin if that is what you want to know, now can we please drop it."

Dustin looked at her, wanting to reach out and hold her. He felt angry and couldn't bring himself to, fearing if he did he would frighten her worse. He took a deep breath. "What did your parents say about what happened Monday?" he asked roughly.

Nicky lowered he head. "They don't know. I never told them." Tears choked her.

"Don't you think you should have told them." Dustin moaned. "Don't you think they would like to know."

Nicky shivered. "All Daddy would have done is say I deserved it. He would have said that he told me that's all boys wanted out of me and I should have listened and stayed away from them. He would have said it was all my fault. Then he would have raped me himself, for disobeying." When she finished her voice was angry. She looked at Dustin, "That's why you can never tell what daddy does to me. He has already made it very clear what he will do to me if I tell someone." She looked into his eyes. "I'm trusting you. And you better never tell another soul. Not ever!"

Dustin looked into her eyes and saw her fear. He smiled, "Thank you for telling me. I won't say anything until you say I can." He bit his lip, "I promise. Just try to be a little more open from now on please."

Nicky smiled. "I'll try, but - nothing never mind."

Dustin looked at her again. "Nicky?"

She looked down and bit her lip. "I'm sorry, Dustin, but, I really don't want to talk about it any more."

With a smiled Dustin got out and opened her door, helping her out of the car he whispered. "I won't say a word to anyone about him. I promise."

Nicky smiled, "Thanks. You don't know how much that means to me."

Slowly they walked toward the house.

"I think I should warn you before you go in," Dustin teased. "It is never quiet here."

Nicky smiled. *It's never quiet at my house either.* she thought. Out loud she replied. "That's okay. I don't think it will bother me."

Dustin laughed. "You will be surprised how mush noise a couple of kids can make."

Chapter 12

Nicky enjoyed being with Dustin's family. His mom seemed so happy. And she could tell by the way his parents looked at each other that they loved each other very much. They always seemed to enjoy being together, the whole family did.

After lunch Dustin suggested they should play Chess.

"I don't know how." Nicky said smiling.

Dustin grinned. "That's alright I'll teach you. It's not hard."

Sara walked up behind him. "I'll help you play, Nicky. If Dustin taught you how to play you'd never be able to win." she grinned at her brother. "Right, Dustin."

Dustin flushed. "Hay, I'm a good player."

"Yah, sure." Sara smiled. "So good you would tell Nicky how to move her players so you would win, yes?"

Nicky grinned at Dustin. "I don't think I would mind Sara helping me learn."

Dustin groaned. "Maybe Chess isn't such a good idea after all."

Sara smiled as she dropped down by Nicky. "He always looses when he play's me or Dad. The only reason he doesn't loose to mom is she never has the time to play a long game."

Nicky grinned as she looked at Dustin.

He smiled back and his eyes twinkled at her.

Sara and Nicky joined forces against Dustin and soon had the game won. After that Mrs. Davis suggested a Bible game, or something a little less noisy, while she put the kids down for a nap.

After that they had a little Bible study. Nicky was surprised to learn all the things the Bible said about things she had always questioned. Then they prayed and it was time to go back to Church.

Dustin turned to Nicky. "Are you coming tonight or not?"

Nicky bit her lip. "I want to but," she looked quickly around hopping his parents couldn't hear. "What time do you get out?"

Dustin shrugged. "Depends on how long dad talks. Sometimes it's eight other times it's nine."

Nicky bit her lip. "Maybe I better not. I don't want my parents to get upset."

His eyes softened. "I understand." he whispered. "I'll take you home then, if that's okay with you."

Nicky trembled. "Only part of the way this time." she whispered. "I don't want to bother mom. She might be sleeping."

Dustin looked at her closely. "Are you sure that is all?"

Nicky nodded. "Dad is going to be gone for a few days. Remember, I told you."

Dustin nodded. "I guess you'll be at school tomorrow then."

Nicky trembled. "I don't know. I'm not exactly suppose to be around people at all, and if Andy tries anything." she shuttered. "I just don't know. I might be, but don't wait on me."

Dustin smiled. "I'll wait if I want to."

Mrs. Davis turned as they walked into the kitchen. "Are you not going to church with us tonight, Nicky?"

"Not tonight." Nicky said with a weak smile. "I have to go home, but thanks for having me here. I really enjoyed the day."

Mrs. Davis smiled. "We enjoyed having you. Come back any time. If you want to you could come over on Friday and we could have another Bible study."

Nicky flushed. "I'd like that but I'll have to see."

Dustin caught his breath. He knew his mom had said Friday to keep them from actually dating. *Oh, well.* he thought. *It probably would be best for her since her parents don't even know about us.*

Dustin drove back to their usual meeting spot in silence. "You sure I can't take you home?" he asked softly.

"Not tonight, Dustin." she whispered. "One of these nights you can I promise. Just not tonight. I really don't want to make mom upset." she trembled.

Dustin smiled at her. "Do you really think it would bother her that much?" Dustin looked at her closer. "Are you not telling me something, Nicky?"

"What would make you think that?" she asked weakly.

"The way you are acting." he said coldly. "Come on, Nicky. What is it?"

Nicky trembled remembering her promise to be honest with him. "Daddy doesn't want us to date. He doesn't want me to see you any more. He kept me home from school because he saw me getting out of you car on Tuesday. He said if I can't obey him he'll whip me till I do."

Dustin bit his lip. "It was because of me?" he whispered.

Nicky looked away. "Not entirely. He doesn't want me to be around anyone. He's afraid if I am, I'll tell or they'll find out what he is doing to me. He wants the liberty to beat me without worrying about leaving scars. If a boy gets close to me he thinks-" Nicky stopped.

Dustin looked at her. "He thinks what, Nicky?" He reached out and tilted her face up so she was looking at him. "He thinks we'll have sex and I will find out and turn him in."

Nicky nodded as tears ran down her cheeks. "I'm sorry. I just -"

Dustin held up his hand.

Nicky jerked back and suddenly winced in pain.

Dustin sighed. "I wasn't going to strike you, Nicky. I was just going to tell you to stop I don't want to hear an apology for something that really isn't your fault. But one thing I would like to know, why didn't you tell me on Tuesday he didn't want us to be together?"

Nicky bit her lip and trembled. "I - I just didn't -"

Dustin looked at her closely. "You didn't want me to leave you, is that it?" his voice was soft and full of love.

Nicky looked down.

"Nicky, please." Dustin reached out to her. "Can't you tell me?"

Nicky whispered, "Yes, that is why. I didn't realize how much I had grown to care about you until then. I knew I liked you, but -" she stopped again. "This is crazy. I mean we have only known each other for a few weeks. Yet I can't imagine not seeing you." she ended on a whisper afraid of what he would say. She flushed at how outspoken she was.

Dustin smiled. "I know." he whispered. "Me to."

Nicky smiled. "Thank you for the day." she said looking into his eyes.

"Thank you for being honest with me and for trusting me. I know it was hard, I'll try harder to understand, I just wish you would tell someone."

Nicky reached to open the door. "I can't. I'm sorry. I'll see you soon?" she whispered.

Dustin nodded. "Tomorrow hopefully."

Nicky smiled, "I'll try."

Dustin smiled at her. Before she got out he reached for her hand. Looking at her closely he asked, "Nicky, do they know about us now?"

Nicky trembled. She had to tell him the truth. "No." her voice was barely audible.

Dustin looked into her eyes. "I don't think we should see each other until they do, and until they are fine with it. I really think if you would let me talk to your dad it would be fine."

Nicky bit her lip. "I'll tell them soon. Really I will."

Dustin nodded. "I want to know when you do."

Slowly she nodded. "Okay." she turned away. "I really need to go."

He smiled and nodded. "Okay." He squeezed her hand before letting her go. "Nicky, do you read your Bible."

She smiled. "A little. I haven't really been able to. I'll try harder." she promised.

Dustin reached out and touched her cheek, "I want this to work." he said softly. "I don't want to hurt you, but I do want this to work. Please don't make your parents mad by not telling them. I want your family to be okay with us going together."

Nicky looked away. "You don't understand." she whispered.

Dustin smiled. "Can I pray with you before you run off?"

She smiled. "I'd like that."

Together they bowed their heads.

"Oh, Lord." Dustin began, seaming to search for the right words. "Please be with Nicky. Give her strength for this week. Help her family to someday soon come to know you. And help them not to be upset about us dating. Amen."

Nicky smiled at him. "See you soon." she whispered as she opened the door.

"Be careful." he called as she ran down the street.

Chapter 13

The next morning Nicky slipped quietly out of her bedroom hopping to be able to get to school.

"Where are you sneaking off to?" her mother snapped.

Nicky jumped and turned to see her mother standing behind her in the hall. "I was - I was just -" Nicky stammered trying to find an excuse.

Her mother scowled at her. "You better be getting off to school. This is your last week and I want you to graduate. I know your father didn't want you going any last week, but I don't want you hovering around the house all day. I have to go to work and if you are in school I at least know you are out of trouble."

Nicky trembled. "Yes mama." quickly she stepped back into her room and grabbed up her bag. "Thank you, God." she whispered.

"Just keep out of trouble and don't be late coming home." her mother yelled as Nicky ran out the door.

"I won't." she called back. "I hope." she added to herself.

The rest of the week went much the same. Friday morning her father still wasn't back so once again she ran off to school. "I hope he's not back yet tonight." she muttered to herself.

Dustin was waiting for her at their usual spot. Nicky smiled as she climbed in. "Thanks for giving me a ride all week."

Dustin grinned. "My pleasure. I hope I will be able to tonight as well."

Nicky shivered. "So do I. Daddy's not back yet, but if he comes before tonight I won't be able to."

Dustin looked at her closely. "You don't think he will agree with us seeing each other even if it's at my parents?"

Nicky looked away, "Yes, I mean no. I mean - well, It's not that. It's just that - well it has been a week and -"

Dustin looked at her, concern in his eyes. "Nicky, please tell someone. I don't want you to get hurt.

"I can't tell. I told you that already." she cried.

"Then let me." he pleaded.

"I can't." she whispered. "I'm sorry. I told you because you promised not to tell, if you tell I will have to lie to the cops if I don't daddy will kill me. Please, Dustin, promise you won't say a word. I trusted you. That is the only reason I told."

Dustin sighed. "Then I will see you tonight?"

Nicky nodded. "I'll do my best. Remember its you that wants me to tell them."

Dustin nodded. "I remember. If I see you tonight, I'll take it that that means they are okay with it."

Nicky smiled. "I'll do my best."

Soon they stopped at the school, Dustin bowed his head and Nicky did likewise. "Dear Lord," he prayed. "Protect Nicky and give her strength for today. Amen."

As soon as he finished Nicky jumped out, "Last day, I better not be late." she grinned as she waved, then turned to walk into the school.

Dustin sighed. "Dear Lord, Please protect her. Help her father not to hit her any more."

After school Nicky ran home. She didn't see Dustin on the way and when she reached her house she was glad, for no sooner had she walked in then her father pulled up outside.

Gasping she ran into her room. "Thank you, Lord, for not letting Dustin get me today. If he would have Daddy would have seen me getting out of his car." Quickly she changed, as she was finishing she heard her father walk into the house.

Opening her door slowly she looked out. "Hi, daddy." she said softy.

Her father looked up at her in surprise. "You been behaving yourself, girl."

Nicky trembled. "Yes, sir." she said calmly.

"Good." he snapped. "I'll ask your mother later and she better say the same thing." he looked up at her. "I want you out of the house tonight, Nichol. Don't be out passed nine, but just get out of the house for a while."

Nicky looked at him in shock. "Yes, sir." she finally managed.

About five thirty she heard her mom coming in. stepping out of her bedroom she waited.

Her father looked up at her angrily. "You ready."

"Yes, sir." she said. Her voice quivered slightly, but her father must not have noticed.

"Well, get out of the house then." he snapped. "Just don't be late."

Nicky hurried to the door. "I won't." she promised as she hurried out.

Her mother smiled at her as she walked up the steps. "Is your father home?" she asked softly.

"Yes, mama." Nicky trembled as her mother stepped closer to her.

"Run along then." she said coldly.

Nicky hurried down the steps and to the road. Trying not to act in a hurry she headed toward her and Dustin's meeting place. She knew she was early but anywhere was better than home. "I can't believe he didn't hit me once." she said to herself as she walked down the road. "Is it possible he will stop." Her heart leaped at the thought of it. Then she sighed. "I guess I'll find out. I just need to remember and be home early."

As she rounded the corner she walked more quickly. *I hope I can have a good time at his house tonight*, she thought. *If only daddy will stop hitting me, then I wouldn't have to worry about bruises.* Deep in thought she nearly jumped out of her skin when a car pulled up behind her.

"Nicky!" called the drive.

Nicky turned quickly then laughed. "Dustin." she called as he stopped and opened the door for her to climb in. She slipped in the car quickly, and shut the door.

"Where you headed?" he asked softly as though afraid to ask.

"To meet you." she whispered.

Dustin cleared his throat. "Your dad not home yet?"

Nicky shrugged. "He's home. He got home right after I did."

Dustin looked at her and smiled. "See it wasn't that bad, was it?"

"I have to be home by nine." She didn't want to deceive him, but she also wanted to be with him. If her dad didn't hit her anymore, she would tell him about her and Dustin. If he did, she didn't think there would be much point in telling it would just make him worse. She would tell sometime but she didn't think Dustin needed to know she hadn't yet. She felt her heart give a little quake and a small voice say, "You know you should tell the truth."

Nicky bit her lip. She knew that was true, but she couldn't bring herself to do it.

Dustin smiled. "Sorry I didn't get you today. I'm actually on my way home from work right now. We had to stock today and then the truck came in and had to be unloaded. It was a mess."

Nicky smiled. "That's okay. At least you were able to get me now."

"That's one way to look at it I suppose. If I hadn't been on my way home you would have been waiting on me a while."

Nicky shivered. "I wouldn't have had to wait. I could have just walked to your house. It's not that far."

Dustin glanced at her. "Oh well, this way you'll just have to put up with me longer."

This time Nicky's grin reached her eyes. "I don't mind." she said softly.

When Dustin dropped her off that night he looked quizzical when she asked him to drop her of at the corner.

"Nicky, did you not tell them yet?"

Quickly she looked away.

Dustin looked out the front window and bit his lip. "Are your parents having a party or something?"

Biting her lip she shrugged. "It looks like it." She dropped her gaze not wanting him to know how much she dreaded going home.

He looked at her and slowly reached out and took her hand. "Will you be okay, or is he in there getting so drunk he's going to kill you when you walk in."

Tears sprang to her eyes as she pulled her hand away. "Don't! It's not like I want life to be this way." she turned and opened the door. "I'll see you next Friday." She wanted to get away before he said anything else.

Dustin nodded. "I guess you will. But hopefully you'll see me on Sunday."

Nicky looked at him. "I forgot. I'll see you Sunday at Church. That makes next Friday not seem quite so far away."

Dustin grinned. "I was actually meaning the graduation, but I guess I'll see you for church too." Dustin look down into her eyes, "Nicky, did he hit you?"

She blushed and looked down then back up meeting his gaze. "Nope, not even once." She saw him relax a little.

"I hope he doesn't any more."

Nicky nodded. "Me to, but - never mind. I need to go. Thanks for the ride."

He nodded. "Any time. See you Sunday."

Nicky climbed out and waved before heading home. Her heart raced. Slowly she opened the door to the house and ran to her room not wanting any of her fathers drunk friends to see her. Exhausted and relieved she colapsed in bed.

"Nichol!"

Nicky jumped as her father pushed open her bedroom door.

"Daddy." she said calmly. Fear washed over her, but not for anything would she let it show, she slowly stood as she glanced at the clock, it was two in the morning. She shivered.

"Where have did you go last night and what time did you get home." he asked coldly.

"I just went for a long walk." she trembled as he came closer. "I was home at nine."

"Don't you lie to me!" her father screamed as he grabbed her arm. "You've been out with that boy haven't you?"

Nicky shuttered. "Daddy, I only went out because you wanted me to. I went for a walk, I promise."

Her father pushed her to the floor. "Just like you walked every day this week?"

Nicky trembled, "What do you mean?" she ask hoarsely.

"You walked alright, you walked to school and back. Well, I won't have you disobeying me Nichol Varson. I told you before I wouldn't stand for any disobedience and as soon as I'm gone you disobey me." he screamed as he began to pull off his belt. "I guess I'll have to teach you what I mean."

Nicky shrank back as her father raised his belt. "I was only-" Her fathers belt cut her off as he struck it across her face.

"Don't you make any of your excuses. You know what I meant when I said it." he smacked her again. After a few more blows he grabbed her hair and pulled her to her feet. "You've got a week worth of punishment coming so you might as well deal with it." He angrily raised a whip and struck it across her back.

Nicky bit her lip as she tried to keep back her cry. *So much for hoping,* she thought.

After beating her he grabbed strips of leather, pushed her up against the back of her bed. "You will pay for everything you have done." he snarled. He slugged her in the stomach.

Nicky groaned as she sank to the floor. As he kicked her in the stomach again she threw up.

He grabbed a handful of hair and pulled her head up. "You know better than that girl." He slammed his fist into her jaw then pushed her against the bed. "Now, well see how soon you can get out and disobey me." he snarled as he forced a bandana between her lips and tied it behind her head, so she couldn't talk. Angrily he kicked her. "You will stay here till I let you go." he said coldly. He turned and left the room leaving her alone.

Nicky turned her head away from the door. *Help me God, please. I know you want me to be loving and respectful to him, but I don't know how.*

Chapter 14

Late Saturday afternoon Nicky woke to her father slapping her. "Get up you worthless brat." he snapped. "If you think you are going to that graduation of yours you are going to get this house cleaned first." He reached down and untied her.

Nicky trembled as she stood. Her father towered over her and smelled of whiskey. She felt her stomach turn. What was he going to do to her?

As if in answer her father grabbed her arm and flung her out in the hall. "I said get to work." he hollered. "I want this place spotless."

Nicky trembled as she stepped back. When she started to clean her father watched her like a hawk as if waiting for her to mess up. She felt stiff just waiting for him to strike her. As the night drug on she felt even more miserable. When at last morning came the house was fairly sparkling.

Her mind raced as she thought about how she could get out of the house. She trembled at the thought of what would probably happen to her if she asked. At nine thirty she finally worked up the corage. *He's going to beat me anyway I might as well do something to deserve it,* she thought as she turned to look at her father. "May I go?"

Her father scowled at her. "Graduation isn't till two. You don't need to leave till it's time."

Nicky trembled. She couldn't stay here, there was no telling what he would do to her between now and then. "Please Daddy. I just wanted to hang out with a few of the kids. This will be the last time we see each other."

Her father grunted again. "If you think you need to go then go." He caught her arm as she walked by. "But you will pay for it later. Do I make myself clear?"

Nicky shivered at the look in his eye. "I understand, daddy. Thank you." she hurried to her room to get ready whispering a prayer of thanks as she did.

As she walked out the door she trembled, she knew she would regret this later, but for now all she wanted was to get away. As she rounded the corner her heart stopped. Dustin wasn't there. Biting her lip she looked this way and that. Where was he? Then she noticed the sun, it was late, at least ten o'clock.

I guess I'll walk to church. Anything is better than home. At least daddy can't hurt me until I go back. A tear ran down her cheek. *I wish I didn't ever have to go back. I wish I could just run away.* She shivered knowing the consequences if she tried and was caught. Yet the thought still remained, and she couldn't push it away no matter how hard she tried.

Seeing the church Nicky suddenly felt her stomach quiver and she thought she was going to be sick. She had never been near the church alone and she had only been there a couple of time with Dustin. What would she do if it had already started? Taking a deep breath she prayed for courage and the knowledge of what to do. Slowly she made her way down the hill to the little church.

As she walked in she trembled even more. The classes were just getting out and kids were headed into the sanctuary. Her eyes quickly scanned the crowd for Dustin. Where was he? Did he not come this morning? Then all at once he was there, stepping out of their class room.

Nicky felt her heart stop. He was talking to a girl, the same one who had glared at her when she first started going to church with him. They laughed together and she leaned over and hugged him.

Nicky's heart stopped. Had Dustin been lying to her all this time? Was he really seeing Mary until he had met her, was he two timing. Tears sprang to her eyes and jealousy ripped through her like she had never felt before.

She bit her lip. Was she messing things up for Dustin. If he wanted to be with Mary she was sure his parents would rather he was. After all she had been a Christian for a lot longer than Nicky. Besides she probably didn't have any problems with her family that would end up hurting Dustin and possibly his family.

Tears burned her eyes. *What do I do? I don't want to mess up his life any more than I already have.*

Dustin suddenly looked up a saw Nicky standing by the door. He hurried over and smiled as though nothing had happened. "Nicky! I thought you weren't going to make it." he whispered as he reached out to her. He stopped and looked at her closer, "Is everything alright?"

She looked up at him her eyes wide and took step back. "I'm sorry, I didn't mean to -" suddenly she knew she couldn't handle it any more. Her heart broke and she turned and ran out of the church. "I can't believe I was so stupid!" she screamed to herself as she ran down the street blindly.

"Nicky!" he called startled as the door slammed shut behind her. He ran outside and looked up the hill, seeing her disappearing. "Nicky, wait!"

Suddenly Dustin felt a hand grip his shoulder and spin him around.

"Dustin Davis." his father hissed. "I will not tolerate this kind of behavior from you. You are suppose to be setting an example here." He gripped his arm tighter. "Get back in the church and I don't want to hear of any more of this kind of behavior from you, do I make myself clear?" his father frowned at him. "I don't know how to begin to say how disappointed I am. I thought we raised you better than that."

"But dad it -" he started to explain. His fathers look silenced him.

"You will not talk back to me, Dustin Andrew Davis. I thought I raised you better than that also. Is this what hanging around with that girl has got you?" his father gripped his arm and turned back to the church. "You get back in there and sit with your mother. I will not have you behaving like a five year old. But if that is how you behave then I will treat you like one, and you will be punished like one."

Dustin pulled away, not liking the tone in his father's voice when he had spoke of Nicky. "She is not 'that girl.'" he snapped. "Dad I love her and I am not sitting here while she needs my help. Something is wrong and I have to find her."

His father frowned even deeper. "You heard what I said."

Dustin pulled away from his father. "And you heard what I said. You can do whatever you want to me, but I am going to find her." he turned and ran to his car.

Dustin's father stood dumbfounded for a moment then turned back to go into the church.

Nicky ran blindly till she could run no more, she didn't even know where she was running. She knew she didn't want to go home, but there was no other place to go. "How could I have been so stupid," she rebuked herself, "to think that he actually cared about me? Daddy was right. I am worthless and no one will ever love me. I can't believe I fell for everything he said. All he really wanted was to be close. Why did I ever even try?"

Out of breath and strength she collapsed under a large shade tree. "God, I really need you now. The only person who I had to talk to me about you has betrayed me. I thought he really cared, but I was wrong. Am I wrong about you also, God? Do you not love me either? Is there someone else out there that you would rather have in my place?" She then burst into uncontrollable sobs. Exhausted she fell asleep.

Dustin drove silently as he watched for any sign of Nicky. "Where would she go?" he wondered out loud. "I don't think she would go home, not if her father hit her, but where else might she be. Please, God, help me to find her." Sighing he pulled to a stop in front of his house. *This is the only other place she would go,* he thought. Slowly he looked around then his heart stopped. Was that her laying in the yard? He felt his pulse race as he jumped out of the car. "Nicky!" he called as he ran towards her.

Hearing her name Nicky groaned and opened her eyes. Pain ran through her as she tried to sit up and then remembering everything that had happened, she laid her head back down and whimpered. *How could I have been so stupid. And now I have to pay for it when I get home anyway. I wish I had never met Dustin.*

"Nicky!" Dustin called again as he ran up to her.

Nicky jumped, looking up at Dustin she trembled unsure of what to do. What was he going to do to her? She wanted to scream all the anger she had at him at that moment. She wanted to hurt him, but she felt to scared to move. Why had he followed her? Why wouldn't he leave her alone? *What is he going to do to me. If he is really dating that other girl and now he knows I know it, will he rape me to get what he wants then leave me?*

Dustin dropped to the ground beside her. "Nicky." he whispered as he reached out to her.

Seeing him reach for her she suddenly jumped and bolted. "Get away!" she screamed.

Dustin ran after her. "Nicky please stop. I just want to talk to you." Dustin forced more speed and soon grabbed her arm pulling her to a stop. Turning her to face him he took a deep breath trying to control his temper as he looked into her eyes.

Nicky felt her stomach turn as she looked back at him and tried to pull away. "Let me go." she whimpered as she pulled again.

Dustin felt her body tremble and saw fear in her eyes. What was wrong? "Nicky," he whispered as he reached out and touched her cheek.

Nicky jumped, ducking her head. "NO!" she cried sure he was going to strike her. Pulling again she broke free from his grasp and dropped to the ground. "Get away from me!" she screamed dropping her eyes so he couldn't see her pain. As he knelt down beside her she scooted back. "Go away! I hate you!" she screamed again.

"Nicky!" Dustin whispered. "Nicky, stop! Please."

Trembling she backed away from him more. "Just go!" she screamed as she turned away. "Get away from me. I don't want to talk to you." Anger rushed through her and as he reached out to touch her she jumped up pushing him back.

Dustin jumped up and gripped her arm hard. "What is wrong with you!" he screamed. "All I wanted to do was talk to you! Talk to me, Nicky, what is wrong? Why did you run away from me at church?"

Nicky dropped her gaze so he wouldn't see her cry. "I'm sorry. I made a mess of things. Why didn't you tell me you didn't want to be with me instead of lying? Did you think I was stupid, that I wouldn't figure it out." she pulled away. "Just go away, Dustin. Live your life and good luck to you and your girlfriend. You don't need to lie to me."

Dustin stared at her as he released his grip on her arms. "What?" he whispered shocked. "Nicky, I don't know what you are talking about."

"You and that girl, hugging. I can't believe I was so stupid. All you wanted was to get me to talk so you could tell your parents and turn my dad in, isn't it? You only wanted to be physical with me, but you put on some nice Christian act. I can't believe I was stupid enough to fall for it." she backed away. "My dad was right all you want to do is hurt me." she looked up into his face. "So, are you on his payroll now or what?"

"Nicky, I don't know what-"

"You know very well what I'm talking about. He just wanted another reason to beat me, so he hired you to act like you liked me so I would get into more trouble. I can't believe I fell for it! He's right I am a stupid whore!"

"Nicky!" Dustin screamed as he grabbed her arm. "You are not stupid and you are not a whore."

She pulled away. "You don't need to pretend anymore!" she screamed back.

"What am I pretending!"

"Oh, don't act as if you don't know. What do you want from me, Dustin? Sex is that it, or just to get me to talk. Well go on tell everyone about my father. That's all you care about is turning him in, so go ahead. He can't hurt me anymore than he already has. The only thing left is to kill me and I wish he would!"

Dustin suddenly slapped her. "Stop that talk!" he screamed. Suddenly he realized what he did. In shock he released her.

Nicky dropped to the ground with her hand over her mouth.

Dustin sank down in front of her. "Nicky." he whispered as he reached out to her.

Nicky pulled back. "Just go away, Dustin." she whispered as all the fight drained out of her. "Please just go away." Fear suddenly overcame her and she started to cry. Why did life have to turn like this. She thought she could trust him, but he had lied about loving her. He was just like everyone else in her life. All he wanted to do was hit her and hurt her any way he could.

Suddenly the anger she had built inside of her all through the years welled up and she didn't even try to pull her temper under control. She was tired of being under her fathers power. She was tired of being controlled and she wasn't going to do it any more.

She jumped up her eyes blazing as she looked down at him. "I hate you." her voice was deathly quiet, and she trembled as she heard what she had just said. "I have to put up with that at home but I don't have to from you and I'm not going to. If you want to have your fun you can just go have it with your girlfriend. Don't ever talk to me again!" Her voice rose with ever word and by the time she was done she was screaming loud enough the whole street could hear.

Dustin stood and looked down into her eyes. It took his breath away to see the hate raging inside her. His temper flared, but he tried to keep it under control. He reached out to touch her and she jumped back.

"Don't!" she screamed. Suddenly she pushed him away from her. "Get away!" She struck out hitting, biting, and scratching anything she could think of to get him away from her. The hate her father had fed into her was bursting out and, though she wouldn't ever admit it to anyone, she didn't want to control herself.

At that moment Dustin also losing control of his temper grabbed her arm and back handed her. Just that fast the whole ugly moment was over. Nicky stared at him and he at her. Both breathing hard and not sure what to say.

"Nicky," Dustin whispered stepping closer to her.

"Dustin Andrew Davis!" The voice was hard yet strangely quiet.

Both Nicky and Dustin jumped. Dustin whirled around. Then bit his lip. It was his father. The family had pulled in just in time to witness the last scene.

Nicky trembled as he turned back to her sure he would hit her more now because his family had seen. She backed away. "Don't, Dustin, please." she whimpered. "Please just get away." Her anger and fight had died like a fire that is suddenly quenched.

Dustin could feel the tears in his eyes. Now his parents were here and he and Nicky wouldn't have the time to talk. He had wasted the time that they had together, screaming instead of trying to figure out why she was so upset. Suddenly, with a sick feeling in his stomach, he realized something else; he had become the same as everyone else in her life by striking her.

Tears stung his eyes. He could have at least tried to be calm. Before his parents came closer he looked down at her. "I'm sorry, Nicky." he whispered. "I shouldn't have hit you. I just wanted -"

"What is going on here!" Mr. Davis was almost screaming as he walked up to them.

Dustin glanced sideways at Nicky but couldn't tell who was more scared him or her.

Mr. Davis gripped Dustin's arm. "I asked a question and I want an answer now!"

Mrs. Davis stepped up to Nicky. "Are you alright dear?" her voice was soft and seamed to relaxed them all a little.

"I'm fine." she whispered as she backed away. Yet she felt anything but fine. She was so scared and her heart was aching from what she had seen and from Dustin striking her. The ache from her heart seemed equal to the ache of her body.

She kept her head down which surprised Dustin. *She's never looked away from momma before.* he thought. *Why would she now? Surely I didn't leave a mark I didn't hit her that hard.*

Mrs. Davis turned to Sara and the kids who stood not far away. "Take the kids in the house, Sara, and feed them lunch. We don't have long before we have to leave."

"Ah, momma." Sara began to protest.

"Sara, do as your mother says." Mr. Davis scolded not once taking his eyes of Dustin.

"Yes, sir." she muttered as she led the kids in the house.

"Well," he scowled, "You have set quite the example today. I thought you two were old enough to work through a problem without resorting to fighting."

"Dad I just-" Dustin started.

"Do not interrupt me, son." Mr. Davis snapped. "You are never to hit anyone, a girl especially, let alone your girlfriend. What are you thinking? I don't know what has come over you today. It doesn't really matter, because I want it to stop and I want it to stop here and now. You two are old enough to have a rational discussion without violence. However, if you insist on acting like children I will treat you as such. Now, apologize to each other for what you were screaming about and Dustin you apologize for hitting her. Then I want to know what is going on." He looked at them both sternly.

Nicky trembled but still kept her head down. "I'm sorry." she whispered.

Dustin looked at Nicky and didn't say anything.

"Dustin!" his father's voice held a warning.

He took a deep breath. "Dad this is between me and Nicky. I really don't see how it -"

"Dustin do not argue with me. Just do as I say." His father angrily interrupted.

"But Dad -"

"Do as I say, Dustin." His father scowled at him. "Or I would be of a clear mind to give you a sound thrashing for hitting her."

Nicky trembled at hearing Mr. Davis. Were all fathers just abusive. Was that how it was suppose to be. *Now I'm just causing more trouble.* Her mind raced at the thought of Dustin getting hurt because of her.

Dustin could tell his father was not going to let them talk about anything alone, for a while anyway, and he could also tell his father was serious about thrashing him. He turned and looked at Nicky. An embarrassed flush creped to his face, "I'm sorry." he whispered.

Nicky turned away. "I have to go." she whispered.

Dustin reached out to stop her but his father grabbed him before he could touch her. "Nicky, please -" Dustin whispered. "Don't go."

"I have to. I need to get to school. I don't want to be late." she pulled away from his mother, who had gently laid an arm on her shoulder to stop her. "I'm sorry I messed things up for you so badly. I didn't know he was already seeing someone of your faith. I won't bother your family again."

"Nicky." Mrs. Davis whispered as she touched her arm. "Please, let's talk. I'm sure he has a good reason for not talking about it before. I'm sure he has a good reason for not telling you," She looked at Dustin. "Or us."

Dustin looked at Nicky. "What do you mean?" he whispered. He felt choked. What would make her say something like that. He had never even thought of dating anyone else and he never would, especially when he was dating her.

Suddenly forgetting his parents and the welts and bruises on her face she turned on him. "You know very well what I mean. I can't believe I actually believed you when you said you loved me. I can't believe I was so stupid. I can't believe I trusted you. Why did you ever talk to me? Have you been seeing her the whole time we've been going together? Is that why she looked at me the way she did when I first came to your church? Did you think I was stupid that I wouldn't figure it out, or did you just not care? Is that it?" Angrily she pushed him away from her. "All you wanted to do was hurt me, so why didn't you do it right away. Instead you have to make it hurt worse by actually acting like you care. I can't believe she never left you or ratted you out!" Angrily she pushed him again.

"Nicky." Dustin cried shocked as he saw the welts and bruises on her face.

She saw his hand coming toward her and jumped back stumbling as she did. She fell to the ground. Looking up at him as he started to lean down to her she backed away. "NO! Dustin, don't please. No!" She jerked back striking him. She gasped as her hand fell to her side. "Please don't. I'm sorry, I'll do what ever it is you want just leave me alone. Please, don't - " Tears streamed down her cheeks as he knelt down beside her. "I'm sorry." she whimpered her whole body trembling in fear.

Dustin looked up at his parents who stood idly by watching the whole scene. Wishing they would leave, he looked down at Nicky. Tears stung his eyes as he brushed his hand over her cheek. Her father had hit her again, he was sure. "Nicky." he whispered. "What are you talking about. I haven't been cheating on you. I didn't mean to hurt you. I'm sorry I hit you. I shouldn't have. My temper just ran away with me. I am sorry. I didn't mean to strike you. Can you just please look at me and tell me why you are so upset?" He touched her arm gently. "Please, Nicky, just calm down. I'm not going to hurt you. Just talk to me, please just tell me-"

Nicky pulled away. "As if you don't know." she snapped. She felt her eyes burning as her tears threatened to fall. Quickly she turned her head so he wouldn't see. "I have to go." she whispered.

Dustin grabbed her arm stopping her from standing. "Nicky, please, don't leave like this. At least talk to me. I don't know what you mean, truly I don't. I haven't been with anyone else. Please, at least talk about it."

"Go away Dustin. Go hang out with your girlfriend. I'm sure she'll never let you down." Nicky pushed him back trying to get him away from her. "All you want is to further my pain. I don't want to talk about it, when you already know what is going on."

"That's not true, Nicky. You know it's not. At least let me give you a ride to the school." Dustin looked down at her and gently cupped her chin in his hand forcing her to look at him. When he saw the marks and bruises he felt sick. What was going on in her home? Did that have something to do with why she was so upset.

Nicky bit her lip as she tried to look away. Fear knotted in her stomach. If she told him she wouldn't ride with him, he would no doubt tell his parents about her father. She felt as though she had no choice, she had to at least try to get him not to tell. "You may give me a ride to school." she whispered.

Dustin looked at his parents. His father nodded then turned to Dustin mother. "Go on in Lisa I'll be in shortly."

She smiled hesitantly at Nicky and Dustin and headed in to the house.

Dustin caught the look in his fathers eye and turned to Nicky, "Will you wait for me in the car a minute?" he whispered. He looked down into her eyes. "It's going to be alright." he whispered for her ears alone.

Nicky trembled as she looked from Dustin to his father, then quickly went to the car, from there she could see them talking, but couldn't hear what they were saying.

After Nicky left, Dustin's father turned to him with a frown. "It sounds like you have a lot of explaining to do." he muttered. "I guess we'll meet you at the school in a little bit." he started to turn away then turned back. "But I think you better get all your facts straight boy. She has obviously seen something that made her think you where seeing someone else. What made her think that?" His frown darkened his eyes. "Just what have you been up to?"

Dustin bit his lip in thought. "I really don't know dad. I don't know what could make her think that, but I'll do my best to find out. And also straighten out this whole mess."

His father grunted. "Well think about it, and talk about it, because you and I are going to have a long talk tonight after we get back. And you better have some good answers." He started toward the house then turned back. "You better plan on bringing her home with you so we can talk and maybe her parents also." He looked at Dustin strangely.

Dustin groaned but nodded. "Yes sir." The last thing he wanted to do was have any kind of private conversation with his father around.

As he started to the car his father called after him, "And don't you ever strike her again. Do you understand?"

Dustin's temper flared. "I won't!" he snapped. Dustin smiled as he climbed in the car, yet he felt his stomach knot. Nicky wouldn't even look at him, and he didn't blame her. That was the worst part, He felt so awful for hitting her. He didn't blame her for hating him, but he wanted to know why she was so mad.

Nicky rode in silence, unwilling to give Dustin any more reason to hit her, or any reason to find out anything about her family. Her heart felt heavy. She felt as though she had lost her best and closest friend, as though she had been sold out. All the anger and fight she had was gone. She felt numb. Why did this have to happen? She wished she had never met him. She was able to bear her life before, but now she didn't feel as though she could. A tear slid down her cheek and she quietly brushed it away. Fear knotted her stomach as she thought about the beating she was going to get at home, especially if her father saw her with Dustin.

Dustin pulled the car to a stop and turned to look at her. "What made you think I was cheating on you, Nicky?"

Nicky looked out the window and refused to answer. A picture of him and that girl hugging flashed through her mind and she quickly pushed it away. "I have to go in." she said coldly trying to hide her hurt.

"Nicky, please." Dustin begged as he grabbed her arm. "Won't you at least talk to me?"

Nicky bit her lip trying to keep back her tears.

"I thought you said your father didn't hit you." he said coldly as he released her arm. "Where did the marks come from then? Are you cheating on me with someone who is hurting you."

Nicky turned on him. "That is none of your business. And just incase you wanted to know. He hit me because I was with you. I got home a little to late. He beat me for all that night and worked me to death Saturday and this morning, at least the time he didn't have me tied up or worse. And further more, I'm only here because I agreed I would pay for it later." Anger surged through her and she jumped out of the car. "I have to go." she snapped and slamming the door left him sitting there speechless.

After a few minutes he walked to the school. "You could at least give me a chance to talk." he murmured as he went in and tried to find a place to sit. Her words rang in his head, her father was hitting her because she was with him. He felt sick. If that was the case she had sacrificed a lot to be with him. Tears filled his eyes.

He had to talk to her as soon as this was over, he was afraid if he didn't she might do something drastic, or just give up on living. He wasn't sure which was worse right now. If her father hit her as bad as he appeared to, every day in her life was a battle to survive. What was she really going through and what did he do to her that she had called worse?

Chapter 15

After the graduation Dustin slowly filed out with the rest of the crowd. He saw Nicky's father standing on the other side of the room, but he didn't see Nicky anywhere. Was she hiding from him? He started toward her father then stopped. If her father was hitting her because of him, wouldn't his talking to her father at her graduation make it worse instead of better? He sighed. Slowly he glanced around again hopping to see Nicky. They still needed to talk.

Dustin felt his heart quake. If she was feeling as down as she looked in the car, there was no telling what she might do. She looked as though she had almost given up. He but his lip. Did he do that to her?

A tall gray woman stepped up to him. "Are you looking for someone?" she asked kindly.

Dustin smiled. "Yes, actually I am. Have you seen Nicky Varson?

"Hum, Nicky Varson. Oh, Nichol. I saw her come in here not to long ago. Oh, I think she went with Andy. I thought I saw them head for the lockers. Guess they needed to get the rest of their stuff." She smiled. "I'm sure she'll be back soon."

Dustin smiled weakly. "Thanks." he muttered as he hurried in that direction.

Looking up Nicky's father saw Dustin hurrying out and frowned. This looked a little odd. Quietly he followed sure Dustin and Nicky where up to something.

Dustin's blood roared in his ears as he stopped to think. Where was he going? He had no idea "Please God, lead me to where I need to go. And God, please let me get there before it's to late." He looked up and down the hall. "Think, Dustin, think." he muttered to himself. "If you were Andy where would you take her." As he glanced up and down the halls again his eyes stopped on the bathroom door. "That's it." he thought. Taking a deep breath he pushed open the door.

As soon as he stepped in he felt sick for he could hear Nicky's voice and also Andy.

"No, Andy, please." Nicky sounded close to tears.

"Aw, Nicky. You will love it." Andy laughed. "Tell me you love me and come on have some fun, or would you rather I tell someone." He laughed. "Come on it will be a lot better than that boyfriend of yours could ever do."

"I don't have a boyfriend." Nicky murmured, her voice sounded hopeless.

Andy's laugh sounded harsh. "Yah, sure you don't."

Nicky took a deep breath. She tried to pull away from Andy. "Just do your thing Andy and get out of my life. If this is what you want, then do it."

Andy looked at her and laughed. Dustin heard the sound of hitting and his blood ran cold. "And what about your little boy friend."

Nicky groaned as she tried to sit up. "What about him?"

Andy grabbed her. "You will be mine forever and I mean it. I don't want you running off with some other guy and telling him I did anything to you. I wouldn't want it to get around."

Andy hit her in the gut then in the face. "Tell me you will never see him again. Tell me, Nichol. Tell me now!" Andy was screaming and hitting at the same time.

"I won't." she whimpered.

Andy laughed. "Good. Then get over here. You know what to do."

Dustin could take it no more. In anger he slammed up against the stall door bursting it open. It rammed into Nicky and Andy both.

Andy jumped up. "You!" He kicked Nicky sharply. "You liar."

Suddenly all three young people jumped Nicky's father spoke from behind them. "What is going on in here."

Dustin looked down at Nicky she trembled as she looked up at her father. Her lip and nose were bloody and she had a large bruise now covering the right side of her face. Her shirt was ripped and he could see welts on her arms and stomach.

Dustin felt sick, but as her father pushed past both boys he felt even sicker. He had made thing worse instead of better, he knew. Her father grabbed her arm and pulled her to her feet. "Just what are you trying to pull?" he snapped.

To Dustin's surprise Nicky just dropped her head. Dustin saw her defeat and his heart stopped. "Nicky, please." he whispered as her father grabbed her.

Nicky bit her lip as her father half drug her out the door then turned back to the boys. "I don't ever want to see either one of you near my daughter again!" he screamed. "And if I do, both you and she will be sorry."

Turning he pushed Nicky out of the room. Dustin followed quickly, but was only in time to see her father leading her out of the school and force her into the back of the car.

As he slammed the door she trembled. Now she would pay for everything she knew. She should have just let Andy rape her right off, but for some reason she couldn't.

To her surprise her father drove home almost in silence. When they got there he turned to her mother. "Your daughter was in the bathroom with two boys. They were trying to have sex." he snapped.

Nicky opened her mouth to say different but thought better of it and instead sat in the back and let her father scream.

"I guess you better take that out of her right now." her mother finally answered. "I think a good sound beating will do, but you know best. I need to go to work." she smiled at him as she slipped out of the car.

Nicky's heart dropped. Her mom was leaving and her father would do as he pleased till she came back. Fear gripped her stomach and she thought she would throw up, just from her panic.

Her father grabbed her and pulled her out, practically dragging her up to the house. When he opened the door he turned her around to face him and slammed his fist into her face.

Nicky, stunned by the sudden movement, fell backward into the house.

Her father stepped in and grabbing her hair drug her in and slammed the door. "You are going to pay for all this." he snapped.

Chapter 16

Early the next morning her father untied her and pulled her to her feet. "Get to work girl. This place is a wreck." he snapped as he pushed her into the living room.

Even though the sun was barely up she could smell the alcohol on her fathers breath. Tears burned her eyes as he slapped her.

"I told you to get to work!" he screamed. "Do as you are told."

"Yes sir." she managed. As fast as she could she tried to clean, but instead of just letting her work and watching her, her father stood over her and beat her the whole time.

Finally about two he left for a few minutes. "Bring me in a drink, Nichol." he hollered from the living room.

Nicky slowly went to the fridge. Her heart stopped as she searched. Trembling she walked into her father. "There isn't any." she said calmly, trying to hide the fear in her voice.

"Get cleaned up then and go down to the market and get me some and some cigarettes." he snapped as he looked up at her. "And you better be back here in half an hour. That is more than enough time to walk there and back. Hurry up!" he scowled as she stumbled into her room.

"What am I suppose to do?" she muttered. "I know I'm not old enough, but he'll beat me if I say no, and he'll beat me if I go and come back empty handed." her heart lurched they had been through this before. The owner of the market was a friend of her fathers and he knew that he sent Nicky after his stuff, but if anyone else was working it didn't work, unless of coarse the owner was there.

Trembling she stepped out of her room. "I'm ready to go." she said calmly.

"Good," he snapped. "And you know what I said, don't you dare be late and be sure to get the right kind."

Still trembling Nicky nodded and hurried out the door. She ran most of the way to the market. When she rounded the corner she stopped. "Oh, no." she muttered as she saw Dustin's car sitting there. "Why does he have to work today?"

Quickly she went into the store hopping she wouldn't see him, but as she walked up to the check out she froze, he was the cashier. Trembling she placed the beer on the counter.

Dustin looked up and froze as he saw Nicky standing there. What was she doing here, buying beer of all things. She wasn't old enough!

Nicky kept her head down as tears burned her eyes. She was sure he hated her now and she didn't blame him.

"Nicky," Dustin whispered in surprise, "What are you doing? Your not old enough to buy this stuff and I can't sell it to you even if you were. Don't you know Christians don't drink or smoke?"

Nicky felt tears flood her eyes and start to run down her cheeks. "There for daddy." she whimpered.

Dustin frowned. "Looks like he's been drunk to often lately."

Nicky bit her lip. She wanted to snap, but couldn't. All the pain she felt from him yesterday was gone. She wanted to hate him, but couldn't. Instead she found herself wanting to talk to him, wanting to be with him. Slowly she turned enough so he wouldn't see her tears.

"Hi there, Nicky!" a big friendly man appeared behind Dustin. He looked down at the counter. "Here for you dad again I see. He want a whole box of cigs this time too?"

"Yes sir." Nicky said dryly.

He pulled out what she needed and smiled. "You tell him I hope he gets better soon."

Nicky smiled weakly as she looked at the man. "I will."

Dustin looked at Nicky. "Better?" he whispered.

Mr. Bates smiled, "Yes, poor man, fell and broke both legs in a construction accident, he's handicapped till he can walk again. Messed up his back to didn't it?" he turned to Nicky.

"Yes sir." Nicky answered numbly. "Thank you for your help." turning she hurried to the door.

"Nicky, wait!" Dustin called. Turning to the man he asked, "May I take my lunch now?"

The man smiled at the two of them. "I don't see what it would hurt. Don't look like we'll be to busy the rest of today, why don't you just take the rest of it off."

Dustin smiled. "Thank you sir." hurried to clock out.

Nicky trembled. She didn't have time to talk to him now. But as he came out of the backroom she knew she didn't have a choice.

As she hurried out he motioned to the car. "We need to talk." he said softly. "Please."

Nicky nodded as she followed him and he drove to the corner. When he stopped he turned to her. "Nicky, I'm really sorry about yesterday. The whole day was messed up. I'm sorry for hitting you and I don't blame you for not trusting me. But I hope you can still talk to me and forgive me." he looked at her till she looked into his eyes. "I love you, Nicky. I'm not just saying it. I love you. I'm not cheating on you I promise."

Nicky looked away as tears filled her eyes. "Why do you delight in hurting me?" she whimpered.

Dustin bit his lip, what did she mean. "I don't, Nicky, really I don't." He was quiet for a few minutes then looked down at her again. "What did I do yesterday that made you think I was with someone else?"

Nicky bit her lip as the memory of yesterday flooded over you. "I saw you Dustin." she whispered.

"Saw me what?" He was at a loss. What had he done that made her think he was cheating on her.

Nicky looked up at him with pain in her eyes. "I saw you hugging that girl. Did you think just cause I wasn't there I wouldn't find out?" she looked away as her tears began to fall. "If you didn't want me to know why did you ever invite me to church?" she looked out the window as she tried to stop her tears.

"What girl?" Dustin felt as though he was choking as he tried to think of anytime on Sunday he had even been close to a girl besides her.

"Mary. The one who threatened me the first time I was there with you." she snapped.

Dustin looked at her, "Nicky, I promise I don't know - oh," he stopped as though remembering, "when we had just come out of class?"

Nicky nodded but still wouldn't look at him.

Dustin smiled, "Nicky, Nicky, look at me." he waited looking down at her.

Slowly she looked up at him. Tears where running down her cheeks and suddenly he realized this wasn't funny no matter what the mix up was. His eyes softened. "Nicky, I wasn't hugging her. When we came out of the classroom she asked me if I thought she would make a good nurse. I told her no and she laughed. Sara pushed me and I stumbled when I caught myself I was very close to Mary. She smiled at me and whispered 'I can make that girlfriend of yours float right out of your head, you'll enjoy the rest of your day if you forget about her. Just focus on me for a while. I'll make you happier than she ever could.' Then she leaned over and hugged me. I tried to pull away from her, then I looked up and saw you. Then you took off. I didn't know what had happened, because I hadn't done anything. I didn't think about what it looked like to you."

Dustin smiled down at Nicky. "Nicky, I don't have any feelings for her. I love you and I always will. I'm sorry for the way things looked and I don't blame you for being upset. I just wish you would have told me then what was bothering you. I couldn't make any sense of what you were trying to say. I'm sorry. I get it now."

Nicky dropped her head. "I'm sorry." she said softly. She felt stupid. She knew she should have trusted him more. What had she been thinking? "I don't blame you for hitting me. I was stupid and selfish and I deserved it."

Dustin gripped her shoulder. "Nicky, look at me." He waited till she looked up at him then went on, "You didn't deserve to be hit. I should never have struck you. That was very wrong of me. I hurt you and you didn't deserve any of it. You don't deserve to be hit by me or your father or Andy, for that matter. I'm sorry I hit you. I don't blame you for hating me. You weren't the one who was selfish, I was. I was angry and I took it out on you. That is not my right. I never should have and with God's help I never will again." he smiled into her eyes. "Can we try to start over?"

Nicky bit her lip, what would her father do if he found out. "I don't -" Suddenly she stopped the thought of her father suddenly reminded her she was suppose to be home a long time ago. "Oh, no! I have to go." she cried.

Dustin grasped her hand. "Nicky, please wait."

"Let me go." she whimpered. "I forgot I was - I need to -" she bit her lip.

Dustin let go. "Is your handicap father waiting for his alcohol?" he growled looking up into eyes.

Nicky flushed as she dropped her head. "Please don't." she whimpered.

Dustin frowned. "Why do you say that, Nicky? Talk to me, please. You said you would tell me the truth."

Nicky bit her lip. "He's friends with the shop owner. I'm to young to buy stuff. He asked the man if he were injured would I be able to get things for him. The man said they might could work something out. So Daddy told him he was hurt and I needed to get some things for him."

Dustin's frown deepened. "And you just went along with it."

Nicky whimpered then ashamed dropped her head. "He beats me if I come home without it. It's just a lot easier to do what he wants." she was practically screaming when she finished. "You don't know what it's like."

Dustin grunted his disapproval, but didn't say any more about it as he turned away. "I'll see you Friday if you can."

Nicky nodded slowly. "I'll do my best." glancing down at the time again she trembled. "I really have to go. Thanks for the ride." Quickly she grabbed the stuff out of the back and ran down the street.

Arriving at the front door out of breath Nicky stopped. Gasping she tried to calm her racing heart. Suddenly someone grabbed her from behind and pushed her in the house.

"You lazy no good fool!" her father screamed as he pushed her to the floor. "I told you to hurry, I sent you on an errand for me and what do you do, you sneak off and try to spend time with that boy - a boy I told you, you are never to see again - and waist time." Angrily he grabbed the whip. "If we have to go through this one more time you won't live to regret it." he growled.

Nicky trembled but bit her lip and quietly bore her beating.

Chapter 17

The weeks passed. Nicky tried to learn more about being a Christian. She found herself wanting to spend more and more time with Dustin and his family. They tried to meet at his place every Friday and have a Bible study.

Nicky knew she needed to tell her parents about being with Dustin, but couldn't bring herself to. Then in mid August, when Dustin found out that she hadn't told them they were dating yet he gave her one more week to tell them. She had tried hard all week, but just couldn't find the right time.

"I want you out of the house tonight. Don't come back till late. I'm having a party and I don't want you interfering. When you come home come in the backdoor and go straight to your room. I will deal with you when it is over." her father growled as he pushed her to the door. "If you do come back you will be in big trouble."

Slowly she nodded. "Yes sir." She trembled. If her father was having a party she would wait to come home till it was over. There was no way she wanted to be in the house when him and his friends got drunk and wild, without any other women there.

As Dustin pulled up to get her that night he looked down the street. "Your parents having a party again?"

Nicky bit her lip. "My dad is. Mom's gone again and he and his friends needed a place to drink."

Dustin looked at her closely, he could sense her fear. "Then I'm glad you got out of there." he whispered.

"Me to. I just hope they are gone before I have to be home." she looked down ashamed.

Dustin looked over at her and bit his lip, just what was life like for her? What all did she live through at home? "Nicky," he whispered. "You haven't told him about us have you?"

Nicky trembled as she looked up at him. "I just can't, Dustin. I keep trying, but I'm just not ready to take the punishment I know I will get for it." she bit her lip. *I shouldn't have said that,* she thought.

"We can't go on deceiving them, either you tell them or I will. Fair?" He watched her closely.

Nicky dropped her head. "Okay." she whispered.

Dustin smiled. "I'll give you till next week. If you haven't told him by Friday, then I am taking you home and we will talk to him."

She kept her head down so Dustin couldn't see her tears as she slowly nodded. "Okay."

All the next week she tried to find a way to tell her dad. She was to scared. When Friday finally came and he sent her out she sighed. *I just have to keep him from knowing.* she thought. *I can't let Dustin know that they still don't know.*

She walked a little ways then stopped. "What do I do? I can't go on like this. God," she prayed, "I need help. Please. I can't let daddy know."

Just then Dustin pulled up. "You running a little early today?" he asked jokingly.

Nicky smiled. "Just a little Dad wanted me out of the house early."

Dustin nodded. "You tell them?" He had a feeling she hadn't, but wanted to see if she would talk.

Nicky shrugged as she turned to look out the window.

Dustin took a deep breath to control his temper. There was obviously a reason she wasn't telling them, but why was she trying to keep it a secret from him? "I guess I'm taking you home then." he said softly.

Nicky didn't budge, but he saw her bite her lip.

He looked at her and frowned. She sat with her back stiff looking out the window. "Nicky?" he said kindly.

Slowly she turned to face him. Tears were running down her cheeks. "He's going to kill me, Dustin. I just know it and I don't want you to get hurt. Why can't we just keep going like we have been? It doesn't hurt anyone. Why do we have to tell?"

Dustin pulled up in the driveway. "Is that why you didn't tell them?"

Nicky bit her lip.

Dustin looked at her closely. "Then I am telling someone. I mean it, Nicky. If it's that bad I'm telling someone and getting you out of that house."

She gasped. "No, Dustin. You can't, you promised. You said I could trust you."

Dustin sighed. "Then I am taking you home tonight."

Nicky whimpered but nodded. "Alright. But I should warn you, things will get ugly."

Dustin shrugged. "We can't go on deceiving them, Nicky, and you know it. They are your parents and they need to know."

Nicky dropped her gaze, she didn't say anything, but he could tell she was scared. Finally she whispered. "If we have to, then I guess we have to."

Dustin smiled and squeezed her hand. "It's going to be fine." he whispered.

Chapter 18

"Okay," Mrs. Davis smiled later that evening as they all sat around on the living room floor. "Where did we leave off last week. Oh, yes, studding the ten commandments. Nicky, why don't you read a little for us. Just start at verse twelve in chapter twenty."

Nicky looked down and cleared her throat. "Honor thy father and thy mother: that thy -" Nicky stopped and looked up. "What does honor consist of. Does that mean to respect or does it mean to obey them too."

Dustin glanced up at Nicky and was startled to see fear in her eyes. What was she hiding?

Mr. Davis smiled. "In a way it means both. You do need to obey your parents, but you also need to respect them enough to trust that they have your best interest at heart. When they tell you to do or not to do certain things there is usually a reason, like, you could get hurt or, someone else could get hurt, or maybe it's just dangerous."

Nicky shivered, "But what if-"

She was interrupted as a loud knock sounded at the door. Mr. Davis smiled. "Hold that thought just a minute." he stood and slowly made his way to answer the door.

"I hope nothing is wrong." Sara spoke up. "Who ever that is hasn't stopped pounding since they started. They must just be impatient or it is an emergency."

Dustin grinned, "Probably, Miss Webster's cat's lost again."

Mrs. Davis smiled. "I'm sure it's not that at this hour of the night."

Dustin shrugged. "Wasn't it ten thirty the last time sparkles got lost and she sent Jennifer over here to see if we had seen it." Dustin laughed as he looked at Nicky. "You should have seen poor Jenny, she was so embarrassed to be knocking on all the doors around the neighborhood that night. She only works for Miss Webster, but she would be a good example of honoring someone, if Miss Webster was her mother. She does every blessed thing that woman asks."

"Is that what this verse means?" Nicky questioned. "I mean is that what honor really means. I'm confused."

"It means obey you little brat, and you would do well to listen to it!"

Nicky jumped up and whirled around to face her father. "Dad I - what did- what are you doing here." she stammered. Fear washed over her like she had never felt before as her father glared at her.

Mr. Davis smiled. "Now, Nicky, there's no need to be upset. Your father was just coming to get you."

Nicky took a step back as her father stepped toward her. "How did you-"

"Shut up!" her father struck her. "Get in the car. You are going home."

Dustin glanced quickly at Nicky as she stepped back again. "Dad I just -"

Her father's look silenced her as he reached out and grabbed her arm. "You will pay for all your lies and deceit, Nichol Deanne Varson. Now you are coming home with me."

Gripping her arm tighter he turned to go. Then he turned back. "I'll thank you to keep your son away from my daughter." he growled at Mr. Davis. "They were both told they were not to see each other." He then turned to Dustin, "And if I do catch you with her again, both you and she will be very sorry."

Dustin glanced from Mr. Varson to Nicky. She had her head down and he thought she was crying. "Mr. Varson-"

"Stay away from her." he screamed. "Or she will regret it." he turned and went out the door dragging Nicky with him.

"Keep your hands off of her!" Dustin screamed as the door slammed shut.

He started after them, but his father grabbed his arm. "You will only make things worse for her, Dustin. Let them go." he said softly.

Dustin pulled away. "Dad, please I have to go. Please."

Mr. Davis turned to Sara. "Go to your room." he said softly.

"Oh, dad." Sara objected.

"Now, Sara." He said stiffly not taking his eyes off Dustin. As Sara left the room he led Dustin into the kitchen where the kids were less likely to hear if they were to wake up. "What is all this about? Did you not get their permission to be with her."

Dustin felt his temper rise. He was not a child anymore. His father did not need to treat him like one. "Dad, I asked her if I needed to. She didn't think I should. I have talked to him, and that is about all. He never said I couldn't date her, but he never said I could." he pulled away. "I'm going to talk to him, now."

"I think you should let things calm down a bit. You will just stir up the hornets nest if you bother him tonight. My rules stand, Dustin. As long as you live under my roof you will obey me."

Dustin stepped back. "Then I might just have to move. I'm going over there. I have to make sure she is okay."

His father sighed. "Don't make him any more upset, or you will probably never be aloud to date her."

Nicky's father slammed the car door. Looking at Nicky he scowled. "You've been seeing that boy since before school let out haven't you? Tell me truthfully. You've been lying to me these past few months. You've been coming here every week. I suppose you've went and got religion, since you've been hanging around that bunch of hypocrites." he looked at her closely. "It was his car I saw you getting out of that night wasn't it? Answer me!"

Nicky trembled. She had known ever since she was little that her father hated church and wanted nothing to do with it or God, but she had never understood why. She still didn't understand, yet she knew that telling her father the truth about her belief in God would cost a lot more than being with Dustin. She took a deep shuttering breath. "Yes." she said calmly. "I believe in God. And yes, I have been with him since before school let out, he's the one who brought me home that day. And yes it was his car you saw me getting out of before school was out."

Her father looked over at her, then to her surprise drove home in silence. Stopping the car in front of the house he got out, slammed the door, and went around to her side. Before she could even get the door open he jerked it open and, grabbing her arm, pulled her from the vehicle. He shoved her towards the house knocking her to the ground a few times. "Get up there. Your not escaping your punishment now." He gave her another hard push. Nicky fell into the house.

Grabbing her arm her father hauled her to her feet. Just then her mother walked in. "What's going on?" she asked sharply.

"I've been telling you she's been lying to us. And tonight I caught her in the act. She's been seeing that Davis boy since before school let out, and now she thinks she wants religion."

An expression came over her mothers face that Nicky hadn't seen before, then was gone so fast she thought she must have imagined it. "You better get that idea out of your head right now, girl. All them people do is lie and hurt." She gave one wicked chuckle, turned to Nicky's father and snapped, "I just knew this would happen. You better do what needs done." Turning she left the house.

Nicky trembled. She could almost guess what was coming.

Her father left the room and soon came back with a beer bottle. He walked over to Nicky and held out the bottle and his face shone with anger and hate. "Take a drink." he ordered.

"No." Nicky stated flatly without hesitation.

Her father grabbed her arm and struck her face several times causing her to cry out. "Drink it." came the order again.

"I won't." she whimpered.

This time he grabbed the whip he had hanging on the wall and began striking it a crossed her back till blood streamed from her body. Finally he stopped long enough to grab her and push her back into the entertainment center.

She sunk to the floor as he came closer. And with every step struck her till he was standing directly over her. She whimpered as she coward from him.

He handed her the bottle. "Now Drink it." he ordered in a dead voice as he flicked the whip.

Dustin pulled to a stop in front of the house. "Please, God," he whispered. "Let her be all right." He slipped quietly up to the first window he saw and from there saw Nicky lying on the floor before her father and him giving her a beer bottle. His heart stopped. What was going on? He couldn't hear anything being said. But Nicky looked scared to death. "Don't, Nicky," he whispered to himself, "Please Don't."

Nicky felt ice hot. What should she do, what could she do? She hesitated only a minute, knowing the beating she would get for disobeying, and knowing she probably wouldn't live through it. "Please, God, give me strength." she prayed quietly, then swung the bottle against the center shattering it.

Her father grabbed her arm and nearly screamed in her face, "You're a dead Girl."

Nicky trembled. He lifted the whip and let it strike it's prey. Nicky cried out. This however only made her father's hits harder. After a while he grabbed her and hauled her to her feet only to throw her body against the wall.

Dustin watched in horror as her father grabbed her again. "Don't you ever let me catch you with that boy again you understand me." he screamed in her face. Nicky whimpered.

Her father smacked her across the face. "Look at me when I'm talking to you and answer when asked a question." he smacked her again.

Nicky tried to look up at her father but was again struck down to the floor as his fist met her face. "I want you to get one thing straight right now," he said dryly. "You ever see that Davis boy again, or set foot near a Church again, and I'll see to it that you live to regret it." He reached down and grabbed her. "Do I make my self clear." he asked his eyes boring straight into hers.

Nicky trembled and tried to pull away. "I Promise." she finally whispered.

He threw her body against the wall. As she slid down the wall to the floor he pulled her up again. Then reaching for her he stepped up closer. "I told you what would happen. Did you think I would lie?"

Nicky felt sick. "No. I - just-" Nicky trembled to scared to tell him the truth.

"Let me tell you right now, you ever try anything like that again and you will be sorry. You and him both will be very, very sorry, and I will make sure he wants nothing to do with you, right now! Do you understand what I'm saying?"

"Yes, sir." Nicky managed. She understood perfectly what he meant.

Dustin saw Nicky's father grab her and an anger that he'd never felt before ripped threw him. As her father pulled her into the bed room Dustin felt sick. What were his plans for Nicky. Would Nicky be okay? Should he tell someone or not, would she want him to? Would he see her again?

"What do I do, God, please show me." he cried not thinking that they could probably hear him. All of the sudden he felt a hand on his shoulder. He jumped and tried to turn but then hand held him firm.

"What are you doing here?" someone hissed.

Turning his head slightly he saw Nicky's mother and his blood ran cold.

She pulled him up to the front of the house and pushed him in. "Rich!" she called. "I think you have another problem to deal with."

Dustin shuttered at the sound of her voice. He knew immediately he had made things worse by being caught.

Mr. Varson opened the bedroom door far enough to step out and closed it quickly. Angrily he grabbed Dustin's arm and his wife slipped back out the door. The smell of alcohol radiated out of him and his eyes blazed.

"What are you doing here boy?" he snapped. "You think you could still have your fun with my daughter after I got through with her!" He shook him a little and laughed. "When I get through with her she won't want anything to do with you, and-" he leaned closer and almost hollered in his face, "If I ever find out that you have been with her, it will be a lot worse for her. You stay away from my daughter and if you tell anyone what you have seen I will kill her, make no mistake of that. I will kill her, I'm not like you Christians. I keep my word. Stay away from her!"

Dustin pulled back. "You will not ever find out I have been close to your daughter. That is not my place." Dustin stared straight into her fathers eyes. "But it's not yours either and I will turn you in if you don't stay away from her. You know as well as I do that you can't do anything to her when you are in prison, no matter what you tell her."

Her father laughed wickedly. "You have no idea what I am capable of." He grabbed Dustin's arm and pushed him out the door. "You tell and she will pay for it. Now get out!" He stopped and laughed, "And if I see you with her again, she will end up the party girl. I think you understand."

Dustin stepped back, unsure of what to do. Slowly he turned and walked back to his car. *Why did I have to let myself get caught? I probably just made it even worse for her.*

Inside Nicky trembled as she heard Dustin leave. Tears stung her eyes. She knew her father meant every word he said. "Oh, God," she whispered. "Please help me." Hearing the door open she looked up, trembling at the hate in her father's eyes.

"I told you never to tell anyone." he scowled. "Now, what do you think I should do with you." He took a step closer to her.

Nicky trembled but held her ground, biting her lip to keep from snapping back as she felt her temper rise. Knowing that if she let it get away from her, her father would be sure that it was cooled off very soon.

He raised his hand and struck her across the face. "You worthless brat." he snapped. "You just couldn't keep quiet could you. You just had to open your big mouth and tell someone. Or were you two close and that's why he found out?" he reached out to strike her. "Tell me the Truth!"

Nicky trembled again. "I haven't been close to him." she said coolly.

Her father laughed bitterly. "Is that a fact. Well we might just have to make sure about that." he smiled as he stepped closer and gripped her arm.

Nicky bit her lip as she tried to pull away. "Please, Daddy, please don't do this. I promise nothing has happed, and nothing will."

Her father laughed again as he pushed her.

Chapter 19

When Nicky woke it was Sunday. She groaned and slowly sat up. She could hear her parents talking and knew it had to be morning, before her father went to work, if they were both home.

"I'm not staying home just to be sure she stays put." her mother was speaking shrilly. "You locked the door and it's not likely she's going to get out anyway."

"Have it your way." her father answered. "I'll let her out tonight."

"Fine. I'll be home around six."

"You know I won't be home till almost Seven this is my late day to work."

"That's right. Well I guess I'll see you tonight then."

Nicky heard the door slam then after about five minutes she heard the door again. She was alone. Locked up, but still alone. She looked at the clock. It was ten till nine. Then she looked out the window. "Do I dare?" she whispered to herself, feeling surprised that she had spoken out loud. "No one will know." she thought. Then softly she prayed. "Dear Lord, Keep me safe. I know I probably shouldn't be doing this. But I'm going to anyway. I need to speak with Dustin. Even if only for a few minutes. To explain about Friday." She took a deep breath, "And to tell him I am sorry, not only for what happened but because I deceived him and made him think my parents knew and were okay with it." she sighed. "It's now or never." she said to herself.

Quickly she brushed her hair. Her stomach hurt and her head ached. As she looked at herself in the mirror she almost froze. One side of her face was swollen and bruised. A large piece of glass had sliced her face from her ear to her mouth. The other side was bad, but not that bad. Upon another look she changed her mind. She would not go to church. She would just go down by the river and wash. At least she would be out in the sun that way. Giving the room a quick glance she opened the window slipped out and dropped it back down all but a sliver so she would be able to open it again and get back in. Her parents were going to be gone all day so they should never find out. But what did it matter, her father would beat her any way. She might as well do something to deserve it this time. She shuttered at the thought of the consequences if she were caught.

Going the long way to avoid seeing anyone, like Dustin incase he decided to wait for her, she made her way to the river. As she sat by the waters edge she prayed some more for guidance and protection from her father.

What am I going to do? She muttered as she splashed water on her face and arms, then looked into the water. *Well at least I don't look quite so bad. Most of the blood washed off.* She didn't want to live the rest of her life this way but what could she do? "Please God, help me. Show me what to do." she whispered.

Deep in thought she didn't hear someone walk up behind her. Suddenly a hand touched her shoulder and a friendly voice said, "I hoped I get to see you today, Nicky."

Nicky jumped, partly from the startle and partly from the pain when he touched her shoulder. She glanced up then quickly back down. "Hi, Dustin." she muttered.

"I missed you, Nicky." He said softly, then looking closely at her he asked, "You okay?"

"Yes, why do you ask?" she answered stiffly, sure he knew what had happened the other night.

"If your okay then why won't you look at me?" his voice had a teasing sound to it but she could tell he was very serious.

Nicky, tears in her eyes, slowly turned and looked up at him.

He gasped when he saw her. "Oh, Nicky." he cried out in pain as he reached to touch her cheek.

She pulled away. "Please, don't."

"Did he do this to you?" Dustin asked his voice full of anger.

Nicky dropped her eyes. "He was drunk. It was not as bad as it could have been and he did warn me."

"Why, Nicky? Why does he do this?" Dustin's voice was softer now but his eyes were full of pain. "Please tell someone, before he hurts you worse." he looked at her closely. "Or, is it already to late?"

Nicky pulled away not wanting to answer his questions. "He made me promise not to. He swears he'll kill me if I ever do. And besides I told you before he would just find someone else to hurt me."

"Nicky," Dustin's voice sounded hesitant. "Did he - do - did -" he looked down unsure of how to ask. Then finally he looked back into her eyes. "What all happened Friday night."

Nicky trembled. Tears suddenly weld up inside her and she couldn't keep them back. "It could have been worse." she cried.

Dustin pulled her to him and held her. "I'm so sorry, Nicky."

Nicky trembled as she tried to pull away. She had never felt as safe as she did in his arms, but the thought of her father raping her if he saw them together made her pull away. "No, Dustin. We can't. If he were to see us together it couldn't be any worse. He promised he would rape me if he saw us together again." She stepped back and looked fearfully into his eyes.

Dustin felt somewhat relieved to hear her admit that her father hadn't raped her, but what had he done? He was sure it wasn't just a beating. "Talk to me, Nicky." he pleaded. "Please don't turn me away." He looked at her. "Did you tell him about us, is that how he found out?"

"I don't know how he found out. I didn't tell him. If I would of it would have been even worse then I want to imagine." she looked into his eyes. "It's over. He has made that very clear. I'm not even suppose to be out of my room right now. And I'm sure not suppose to be seeing you. You shouldn't have come to the house Friday." she looked into his eyes and smiled. "I heard you talking to him. He might not have - Promise me you'll never say anything to anyone. You must never tell your parent or anyone. Promise me, Dustin. You'll never tell a living soul what you've seen or what I have said, Promise!" her voice was full of fear. "I deserved everything I got. I had disobeyed and I needed punished for it."

"Is that what he's told you?" Dustin shot back.

"Dustin, please. You don't understand." A tear spilled down her cheek, quickly she brushed it away. "Try to understand that. Please don't tell. It's the liquor that makes him do things. He didn't use to be that way."

"If you don't want me to tell then tell me what he did to you. He had to of done something besides beat you. Tell me, Nicky. What did he do to you, or make you do?"

Nicky bit her lip. "I don't want to talk about it." she whimpered.

Dustin gripped her shoulders and waited till she looked up at him. "Please, Nicky. Please tell me." his voice was full of pain, and fear knotted his stomach as he saw her anguish.

She looked up into his eyes and anger suddenly shot through her. She felt so angry at her father for hurting her and Dustin she couldn't stand it. "He made me do him oral!" she cried. Then she pulled away. "Leave me alone, just go away." Dropping to the ground she buried her face in her knees and her body shook with sobs.

Anger surged through Dustin as he saw Nicky's pain. Slowly he dropped to the ground and put his arm around her. "I'm sorry." he whispered. "Is it because of me?"

Nicky pulled away and didn't answer.

Dustin pulled her close again, "Don't, Nicky. Please don't pull away. This is not your fault. Nothing you have done deserves this."

She trembled in his arms. "I thought you would hate me and never want to see me again."

"Why?" he whispered.

"Daddy said-" she stopped unable to go on.

Dustin held her tight. "He's wrong. Nothing he can do to you would make me hate you. I mean it, Nicky. I love you."

She looked up at him and suddenly pulled back. "Dustin, I have to go!" Fear shot through her. She couldn't let herself talk to him any more. The longer they were together the harder it would be to say goodbye. "I can't see you anymore. I mean it. I have to go."

Dustin looked into her eyes and held her arm to keep her from running. "Nicky, do you want to go home?"

Nicky shuttered as she looked away from him. "I don't have a choice."

"Yes, you do." he said softly.

She looked up at him in surprise. "If daddy finds me gone -" she stopped.

Dustin stood and pulled her up with him. He looked down into her eyes and she trembled feeling his love. He waited till she looked him in the eye, then slowly he lowered his lips to hers.

Nicky felt the jolt through her whole body. Tears sprang to her eyes as she kissed him back.

Finally he lifted his head and looked into her eyes. "Marry me, Nicky." he whispered. "Let me protect you from your father. I can't bear life without you."

Nicky stared at him in shock. "Dustin, I -" she trembled as she thought about the consequences if her father found out. "But my dad." she whispered.

Dustin pulled her to him. "I'll take care of it. Please, Nicky, please. If you go back what will he do to you? Do you really want that to happen?" He slowly traced her lips with his finger. Then kissed her again.

Nicky trembled as she felt his love for her. She didn't want to leave. She wanted to be with him, that was all she wanted. But what if her father found out?

Dustin lifted his head and looked into her eyes. "What do you say. We can do it right now if you want. I talked to Judge Nile and he said he'd pull some strings and get me a license today. If you'll say yes, he has agreed to marry us. We can do it today and you don't ever have to go back home."

Nicky stared at him in silence. Then for the fist time she felt herself relax. "Okay." she whispered. "I will."

Dustin smiled and led her to the car. "Are you sure." he whispered as he looked down at her. "You look scared."

Nicky laughed softly. "Only because I am. Dustin, what if my dad - he'll know right where I am when he gets home and I'm not there."

Dustin shrugged. "We'll be there before he gets home. It will all be said and done by then and he will have nothing to say about it. It will be fine."

Nicky shuttered. "I hope you are right."

Dustin hugged her again. "It will be fine." he whispered. Then he opened the door. "Shall we."

Nicky smiled as she slid in the car. Her heart skipped. She felt nervous, but happy.

After a brief ceremony Dustin drove them to his parents home. As they walked in the door he smiled down at her, "I'll find us a place of our own soon. In the meantime it may not be so bad living here. That way you won't ever be alone." He led her down the stairs to the basement which was basically his apartments except for his mothers washroom.

Nicky trembled as they went inside and he shut the door. Fear knotted at the pit of her stomach.

He looked closely at her. "Are you scared?"

"A little. Why? Can you see me shaking?" she laughed.

Dustin had not noticed her shaking until that moment. He pulled her close and looked into her eyes, "We don't have to if you'd rather not. We can wait until you're ready. I don't want to hurt you or scare you. If you need to wait that is fine."

Nicky looked into his eyes and could see he was serious. "I'm just a little nervous." she looked into his eyes. "I think I should wash up first."

she whispered. "I haven't had a chance really since-" she dropped her eyes. "Well, you know.

He smiled. "I wont get grossed out I promise, but if it will make you feel better the bathroom is just down this way." he led her to a small room off the bedroom and showed her where everything was. "If you need anything else just holler." he flushed as he looked down at her. "Nicky,"

She looked up at him. "What?"

"You don't need to worry about being good enough for me. I love you no matter what. If you are to scared it really is okay. Just tell me."

She smiled. "Thanks. But I think it will be - I think I'll be okay." her voice shook but she tried not to look as scared as she felt.

Dustin smiled. "I'll be in the other room."

Chapter 20

Dustin woke with a start. What had awakened him. His arm started to tingle and he looked down at Nicky asleep beside him. He smiled. This was probably the first time she'd let herself sleep soundly in a long time. His arm tightened around her. Her father would never touch her again if he had any thing to say about it.

Nicky stirred and opened her eyes. She looked over at him and he smiled at her. She smiled back, but still felt scared. Now that there was no going back what would her father do to her if he found her?

Dustin smiled at her. "It's going to be fine." he whispered.

Nicky shuttered but nodded.

Just as he was starting to relax again he heard the door open. "Dustin." his mom called. "Dustin, are you here?"

Dustin's stomach suddenly knotted. What was he going to tell his parents. He had never been afraid to tell them anything before, but what would they say when he told them he was married. His mom would most likely be fine with it. He was more worried about his dad. Especially since his dad had told him to stay away from Nicky for a while. And not to attempt seeing her again unless her family agreed.

He looked quickly at Nicky. She was pail from fear. "Is it going to be alright with them." she whispered. She could sense his fear.

Dustin shrugged. "It will have to be." He tried to sound calm, but butterflies fluttered so hard in his stomach he felt sick. He smiled trying to calm her and slipped out of bed.

Nicky trembled but followed. "Dustin." she whispered.

He looked at her and pulled her close. "It's going to be fine." he said again. "You are going to be fine."

Suddenly his door opened. "Dustin, didn't you hear us calling you. Did you have a -" suddenly his mom stopped seeing Nicky. "What is going on!"

Dustin and Nicky jumped, then turned and looked at his mom. "Mom, I can explain." Dustin began but his mom stopped him.

"Nicky," she whispered as she reached out a hand to touch the girls face. "What happened?"

Nicky pulled away and glanced at Dustin as though she was afraid to answer. "I - I just-" she stopped as though unable to continue.

"Well we can talk about it later for now we must get it cleaned out." she turned to Dustin. "And we will talk about this later. But after lunch. Come on." she spoke cheerfully, but Dustin could tell she was upset.

Dustin nodded to his mom and smiled a reassuring smile at Nicky. "Hungry?"

Nicky trembled and finally nodded to scared to answer.

When they got to the table Dustin's father gave him a hard look then turned to Nicky with a smile. "Glad to see you again Nicky. How are your parents?"

Nicky trembled at the look in his eye. "Fine." she finally answered. She understood he was asking if they were fine that she was here, but didn't think it would go over very well if she told him they weren't fine with it. She had caught the look he had given Dustin. What did it mean? Was she causing trouble? Tears burned her eyes. The last person she wanted to cause trouble with was Dustin.

After lunch Mrs. Davis asked Sara to put the kids down for there naps so they could talk with Dustin and Nicky. Sara groaned but obeyed. As the kids left the table Mr. Davis turned to his son.

"Did you talk with Nicky's parents or not?" he scowled at his son fiercely.

Dustin bit his lip as he glanced at Nicky. "No, sir." he finally said. "But - "

His father cut him off. "I don't want to hear anymore. Take her back to her parents house and talk to them. We are not going to cause trouble in her family. When they give you two permission to be together she can come back. Until then neither of you are to see each other. Am I clear?"

Dustin stared at his father, "Dad we need - "

"I don't want to hear any more Dustin. Do as I say. This conversation is over." he stood up. "I think now is as good a time as any. I want you to go to her parents and talk to them. Do not come back together unless they give you permission to be together." He looked at both of them. "This is not an option, Dustin." He headed for the door then stopped and turned back. "Come outside, son. I need to talk to you."

Nicky trembled as Dustin stood.

"Everything is going to be fine." he whispered as he left her. "I'll be back in a few."

Mr. Davis led Dustin out to the yard. "I don't think I need to tell you how disappointed I am in you, Dustin. You know you are not to be alone here with a girl. What is going on?"

Dustin cleared his throat nervously. "Dad, I need to tell you something."

Mr. Davis looked at him. "Is she pregnant?"

"No! It's not like that. We just, well, we got married." Dustin watched his dad closely to see his reaction.

He surprised him, however, by simply turning away. "I have to go, but you will do as I say, Dustin Davis. Don't disobey me again. This is not a funny joke and I can not believe you are treating it as one. Now, you will go to her parents house and talk to them and you will do it before church tonight. Am I -"

"Dad," Dustin interrupted, "this is not a joke. We are married."

Mr. Davis looked deep into his son's eyes. "I had better see you in church tonight, and you had better have her fathers approval before then." He turned and walked off. "I won't be back in time for church, tell your mom I'll meet you all there."

Dustin slowly walked back in the house. He turned and looked at his mom. "Now, what?"

She sighed. "Your father is a stubborn man. That is probably where you get it from. Maybe you should talk with her parents then try to talk with him again. I think it will be alright. He just wants everyone to be on the same page."

Dustin looked at his mom. "You know?"

She smiled. "I assumed something like this would happen. I'm just sorry things can't workout better. This should be a happy day."

Dustin looked at Nicky, "I guess we'll tell your parents then."

Nicky trembled but didn't say anything and Dustin wondered if she was scared or just upset by his fathers behavior.

Dustin took Nicky outside where they could talk privately. "I'm sorry Dad acted that way."

Nicky shrugged. "Don't be or I will have to apologize a million times for what my dad will act like.

Dustin smiled at her and hugged her close. "It's going to be fine." he whispered.

Nicky looked at Dustin. "We don't have to tell them at all. We could just act like it never happened." She looked quickly away so he wouldn't see the pain in her eyes.

"No we can't." was Dustin's quick reply. "I am not sending you back to your parents home. And definitely not now that it is my responsibility to take care of you. Dad's just going to have to get over it."

Nicky trembled.

Dustin looked at her. "You can't tell me you would rather go back home?"

Nicky bit her lip. "I don't want to cause you trouble, or get you hurt." she whimpered. "I didn't want to cause a problem with your dad. One dad mad at a time is bad enough. I don't think -" she stopped not willing to go on.

Dustin pulled her close. "Everything is going to be fine."

Nicky turned and walked down into the yard. "I don't know what I was thinking. I never should have done this."

Dustin reached out and stopped her. "What has you so frightened, Nicky? I need to know why you are so scared. Do I need to leave you here while I go and talk to him?"

Nicky jumped. "No possible way. That will make it even worse. I just don't want him - " she stopped unsure how to tell him what her father would do to her. "I guess we may as well go now. I don't think it will be pretty."

"Are you sure?" Dustin turned her to face him and looked into her eyes. "If you won't be safe at home, you need to stay here. I don't mind doing this on my own to keep you safe."

Her heart fluttered as she looked into his eyes. She wanted to stay away from her father. She didn't ever want to see him again, but she was not going to make Dustin face that all alone. "I have to go with you." Slowly she looked away. "I can't make you do this alone. I made this choice and I know I have to face the consequences."

Dustin took a deep breath, "Well, now is as good a time as any." Then he looked down into her eyes. "There are no consequences to face Nicky. I love you. It's done. He can't take this away from us so don't let him."

Nicky shuttered, but turned to get in the car. "You will soon see." she whispered. "Just wait. You will see."

Dustin turned to the car then turned back. "I'm going to tell mom where we are going. That way if we don't show up for church at least dad won't be to upset. I hope."

Nicky shuttered. *She might need him to come and save us if there is anything left to save by then.* Immediately she tried to push the thoughts aside. "Help us, Jesus." she whispered as Dustin ran in.

Chapter 21

As he pulled the car to a stop in front of the house he looked at her. "Are you scared?"

"A little. I wasn't even suppose to be out of my room. You know a little bit what my family is like, I guess, I'm just afraid of how my dad will react. I don't want you to get hurt and I wouldn't put any thing passed him, especially if he's drunk, which he is more often then not anymore." she bit her lip and looked down. "I shouldn't have said that."

Dustin took a deep breath. "It's the truth and your body bares the scares of it." he sighed as he stood. "I'm sorry, Nicky. I shouldn't have said that either." he squeezed her hand. "Well, shall we get this over with?"

Nicky realized she had been almost holding her breath. Now she trembled. What would her parents say? What if her father flew off with Dustin there? Taking a deep breath she looked into his eyes. She had never felt so scared in all her life. She felt like throwing up.

"Nicky," he whispered. "Please don't be afraid. I'll take care of you."

She bit her lip. If only he knew what was coming. "You can't promise that. You have no idea what he is capable of. I don't want you to get hurt, so just be careful what you say and how you say it. This news will not be accepted well."

Dustin looked straight back into her eyes. "I can't promise anything, you are right, but I do want to protect you. Just relax." he whispered putting his arm around her. "I'll try to protect you and when I can't God will."

She bit her lip and blinked back tears as they walked up to the house. "Please be sober." she muttered. As she reached to open the door it opened and her father stepped out. Stepping back a moment in surprise he looked at her then at Dustin. Then regaining his composer her looked back at Nicky. Anger showed in his face. "I was just setting out to look for you, girl. Your mother called me and said you weren't home." he grabbed her arm, "Where have you been, answer me at once!"

Nicky trembled. "I was just-" she started.

Before she had a chance to finish her father pushed her and Dustin both in the house and closed the door. "And what are you doing out of your room. I thought I made it clear you were to stay in there until I let you out. Your mother has been worried sick. She couldn't find you anywhere. And here you are walking up to the door as though you hadn't done anything wrong, and to top things off your doing it with a boy I told you never to see again." he gripped her arm tighter as though not willing, or yet still sober enough, to not strike her in front of someone. "Speak up young lady. Or you'll wish you had."

Dustin took a step closer to her as if ready to protect her at the first sign of danger. Putting his arm around her, he pulled her away from her father. "It's all my fault sir. She had nothing to do with it." he said bravely. "It was my idea." he stopped a took a deep breath. "We have something we need to tell you."

Mr. Varson looked quickly from Dustin to Nicky. Grabbing her arm he slugged her in the stomach. "You worthless little brat!" he screamed as she slugged her again and again. "I was not lying about what I would do to you if you ever got close to a boy. You tell me the truth and tell me now! Have you two been close." His words ended on a growl.

Nicky was shaking so bad she could hardly talk. When she tried her teeth chattered. She could smell the beer on her fathers breath and knew he had been drinking. "Daddy we- I - it's not what you -" Nicky groaned as her father slugged her in the gut again. Then without warning she threw up.

Her father glared at her then removed his belt. "I told you not to be eating." he stepped closer to her.

Nicky trembled as she back away. She could tell by the look in his eye he didn't care if Dustin saw what happened. "Daddy, please-"

Her father slapped his belt across her face cutting off her words. "You've been with him all day haven't you? Haven't you!" he hit her several times and with each strike again screamed "Haven't you!" He pushed her to the floor. "Don't you dare lie to me. It doesn't take all night to come up with the truth." He grabbed her hair and pulled her to her feet. "Answer me!"

"Yes, sir, I have." She answered trying to keep her voice steady.

Dustin stared at her in surprise. She was scared, he could tell, but her voice didn't even shake.

Her father grabbed her and pushed her towards the bed room; seeming to have forgotten Dustin was even there, or not caring what he saw. Nicky wasn't sure what Dustin was thinking but she had a feeling she knew what her dad was going to do.

"Get in there. Did you think I was joking about what I would do to you if you ever saw him again?" her father stormed.

Nicky trembled. "No daddy, I didn't think that. I just-"

Her father's fist cut her off mid sentence. "Don't you ever talk back to me, young lady. You don't want to be in your room?" his voice sounded mocking. He reached down and grabbed her arm pulling her close to him he whispered dryly, "you can let him see everything then."

Nicky trembled even more and tried to pull away. She felt the wall against her back and whimpered before she could stop herself. Dustin had protected her against Andy, but he couldn't against her father. *I shouldn't have ever let myself love,* she thought as she tried again to pull away, squeezing her eyes shut so she wouldn't see what Dustin was thinking of her.

She felt her father close in on her and reached down for her.

"No!" the cry came from deep inside surprising even her as she tried to turn away. "Daddy please! I won't ever again disobey you. Please!" Suddenly her father was no longer in front of her. She looked up to see Dustin grab her father and pull him away from her.

"Keep your hands off of her!" he screamed. How could Nicky live with this fear? Was this the first time her father had tried this or was this something she lived with day in and day out. Tears burned his eyes as he thought about what her father had most likely already done to her before today. *Scares that don't heal,* he thought as he pushed her father away from her.

"You think you can tell me how to discipline my daughter!" her father screamed. Pushing Dustin away he grabbed Nicky's arm and flung her to the middle of the room. Nicky stumbled falling to the floor.

She burst in to tears unable to handle her fear. What did Dustin think of her now. "Please, God, help me." she whispered. "We need your help."

Her father grabbed her and struck her face. "Stop them tears." he pushed her back to the floor. "Get on your knees." he ordered her.

Nicky trembled. She knew what was coming. As she dropped to her knees her father walked toward her. "You know why you are getting this don't you?" he taunted her.

Nicky turned away from her father. Tears blurred her vision. *I won't!* she cried quietly to herself. *I can't.*

Her father raised the whip. "I told you never to cry. You did it once to often. This is what that bunch of Bible goers has done to you, turned you into a blubbering child." he cracked the whip down and Nicky bit her lip. Suddenly he stopped and stepped closer to her. "Do it." he ordered stepping up in front of her face.

Nicky turned away. "Never." she said dryly.

Her father grabbed her hair. "Do it now."

Nicky trembled. "No." her voice was stronger than she thought it could be. Her mind raced. *I can't fight him forever. Wouldn't it be better to do it this way than to have him rape me? What am I suppose to do?* "Please God," she whispered, "show me what to do. I need your help."

Her father slugged her across the jaw. "You will do it, but if you would rather be beat first, that's your choice." He pulled her to her feet then kneed her in the stomach.

Nicky groaned as she dropped back to the floor. *Where are you, Dustin, and what are you thinking now?*

Her father raised the whip and snaked it a crossed her back. After a few lashes he stopped. "Go get the other one Nichol." he ordered pulling her to her feet.

Nicky trembled. With all her might she wanted to refuse, but she knew she couldn't it would just make matters worse. Slowly she walked to the closet. Trembling she shot a look at Dustin then slowly pulled out the whip.

When Dustin saw it he almost cried out. It wasn't a whip it was a chain.

Biting her lip Nicky slowly walked back to her father and held it out.

Her father took it and waited. Slowly Nicky dropped to her knees. He had done this only once before. Why did he have to be drunk tonight? Dropping her head she waited. When the first blow came she gasped trying to keep from crying out. With the next blow she did scream.

At the sound of ripping cloth Dustin wanted to cry out. He looked at Nicky on the floor and saw her shirt stained with fresh blood. Then he realized he had to stop her father. He was the only one that knew and he was the only one that could. He bit his lip. What could he do? Her father didn't give him time to do anything.

After a few blows he lowered the whip and pulled Nicky to her feet. "Are you ready to obey and answer my questions without hesitation." he growled.

Nicky looked away to hide the flash of anger in her eyes.

"Answer me!" he screamed as he pushed her to the floor. Then he turned to Dustin. "You answer." he took a step closer to Dustin. "Were you and my daughter close. Is that what you are going to tell me. You got her pregnant didn't you!" he grabbed Dustin and pushed him to the floor beside Nicky.

Turning his head slightly he looked at her.

Nicky trembled as she backed away from him.

Dustin reached out to her. "Nicky." he started.

Suddenly her father pushed Dustin back. Nicky bowed her head as her father pulled her to her knees. "If you don't you'll wish you had." he growled. Her father struck again. "Now!" he screamed as he repeatedly struck her.

Nicky whimpered as she fell to the floor. "I won't." she finely managed which only made her father strike her harder. Nicky bit her lip to keep back her cries of pain. Did Dustin understand why she was frightened or did he think it was all her fault? Tears pricked her eyes.

Dustin watched in horror as Nicky's father struck her repeatedly. No wonder she had not wanted to come home. She had told him he didn't understand what it was like and she was right. He flung his body over hers, protecting her from her father. "Has he done this before, Nicky. Or is it just because of me."

Nicky trembled. "It doesn't matter." she whimpered. "Please don't let him hurt you to. He'll let you go later."

Dustin felt his back begin to throb from the whip, yet his heart throbbed worse. "What do you mean?" he whispered. How could she bear this all the time? His arms began to shake from the pain. Suddenly the whip struck his neck. He cried out in pain.

Nicky heard the cry and burst into tears. "Get off me, Dustin. It me he wants to hurt. You have no part in this. Let him do as he wants to me. Don't let him hurt you, please."

Dustin's body trembled even more with pain, but he knew how weak she was and there was no way he was going to let her father strike her again if he could stop it. "It is because of me isn't it?"

"I - " Nicky started.

Suddenly Dustin felt strong hands on his shoulders. "Get off my daughter! And get out of this house. I don't want to ever see you or your family again. And you stay away from my daughter! Understood!" He pushed Dustin toward the door still screaming.

Dustin looked him squarely in the eye. "No Sir. I mean no disrespect but I will not stay away from your daughter."

Her father smiled as though that was what he expected Dustin to say.

Nicky trembled at the look in her fathers eye.

"You want to be with her?" he sneered. He grabbed Dustin's arm and pushed him to the floor. In one quick movement he pulled chains of the wall and more out of the floor.

Before Dustin even had time to put up a struggle he found himself chained to the floor.

Mr. Varson then turned back to Nicky, "You want to be with her you better learn how to handle her." he growled.

Nicky trembled as she backed away, but her father closed in on her. "Please Daddy, let him go, please!" she cried.

Her father laughed wickedly. "I won't hurt him unless he gets in my way. Don't you worry." He pushed her against the wall. "But I will kill you! You worthless piece of trash." he spat at her. "I wish I would have killed you when I had the chance."

Nicky trembled at her fathers words. What was he going to do to her? Fear pricked her skin and she felt as though she was going to be sick. Never before had his anger been so strong. Nicky struggled to keep back tears.

Her father pulled down chains from the wall.

Nicky stepped back, but her father held her tight. "You know what this is for." he said crossly. "Now get up here." he pushed her to the wall as though in mockery.

Dustin caught one look at Nicky's face and he felt sick. She was deathly white with fear. And though she was trying hard not to show it her eyes where full of pain.

Her father pushed her to the wall then grabbed her arm. Putting her face to the wall he locked the chains around her wrists. Then reaching into the other room he pulled out a hot iron. Looking at Dustin he smiled. "Watch and learn boy. If you are ever going to be with her you need to know how to discipline her." he laughed wickedly and pushed the iron into Nicky's back.

As the hot iron touched her Nicky gasped. Trying to keep from crying out she clenched her fists and bit her lip till she tasted blood. In agony she dropped her head against the wall.

Dustin turned his face away and once again tried to get lose. The smell of burning flesh turned his stomach as it filled the room. How could Nicky keep from crying out?

Nicky's father removed the iron from her back then quickly placed it in another spot. This he did several times before finally putting it back on the counter.

Nicky's body trembled in pain. As her father released the chain from her wrists she crumbled to the ground to weak to move.

Angrily he pulled her back to her feet and turned her to face him. "Are you ready to obey me?" His voice was cold.

Nicky dropped her gaze. "No." Her voice shook only a little.

He flung her to the floor beside Dustin. Then quickly reached down and unlocked Dustin wrists.

Looking from one to the other angrily her father grabbed her up again. Pulling out a pistol from his belt he smacked the barrel across her face. She fell backwards from the force as much as the pain. Dustin caught her before she hit the floor. Her father again grabbed her and pushed her against the wall. "Are you going to obey me?" he growled as he pushed the gun up to her head.

Nicky trembled.

Dustin suddenly jumped up and slammed into her father. "Get away from my wife!" he screamed.

"What!" screamed her father.

Nicky trembled as her father looked at her then at Dustin. He stepped closer to Dustin. "I told you to stay away from my daughter. Now you tell me the truth. You got her pregnant and because you are a Christian you are telling me you are married. Is that it? You are not married, but you've been close haven't you!" he screamed. Then turning to Nicky he cracked the whip across her face. "And you better tell me the truth. Answer me now! Have you been close!"

Nicky trembled and looked away from her father as she squeezed Dustin's hand.

Dustin looked up at her father and his temper rose out of control. "Maybe I should ask you the same question!" he hollered back.

Nicky bit her lip. She felt her father's stair burn into her. "You good for nothing little brat!" he growled. He gripped her arm tighter then suddenly pushed her sharply. "Who else have you told!" he snapped the whip across her back. "Answer me!"

Dustin jumped knocking her father to the floor. "Stay away from her!" he screamed. "Don't ever touch or threaten to touch her again! We are telling you the truth."

Mr. Varson jumped to his feet and gripped Dustin's arm. "Then you and she will pay for your disobedience and disrespect. He laughed dryly.

Both Nicky and Dustin trembled, but it was Dustin who spoke. "We are married. That is all we came to tell you. And if you kill us we will die married. You can not change what happened today."

Her father snapped the whip across Dustin's face. "You want to bet."

Nicky trembled as she saw a line of blood on Dustin's cheek.

A loud knock sounded at the door.

Mr. Varson gripped her arm harder. "You are one dead girl." he growled. "You know what is going to happen if I am turned in."

Nicky trembled and nodded. "Yes, sir." she whimpered.

He turned to Dustin. "You tell anyone I will kill her, make no mistake in that. I will kill her."

Dustin bit his lip as Mr. Varson walked by him to answer the door. Quietly he stepped up to Nicky. "You okay." he whispered.

Nicky bit her lip. "I'm so sorry." she whispered. "I didn't want you to see any of this."

Dustin bowed his head. "No, I am the one who is sorry. Sorry I didn't get you out of here sooner and sorry I made you come back to talk to him.

Nicky smiled. "You didn't know."

Dustin smiled into her eyes.

"Well I am so glad to see that everything is not happening as I said!" Nicky's father growled.

Nicky and Dustin jumped. "Dad!" Dustin cried as he saw his father standing there.

"Dustin," Mr. Davis' voice was hard. "I think you need to go home now. Mr. Varson has made it clear you are not to be with his daughter and I don't want there to be any more discussions about it."

Dustin stepped back. "Dad, you don't understand."

"Dustin." Mr. Davis broke him off. "Get out to your car and go home. You will not see her for at least a month is that understood. At the end of that time Mr. Varson has agreed to let you two see one another if you have done as you are told."

"Dad, she's not just my girlfriend anymore. We-"

"Not another word." interrupted Mr. Davis "Get out to your car and get home. We will discuss this there. Say goodnight. We will meet at the courthouse tomorrow after you are off work and this wedding, such as it was, will be annulled. It is not legal unless her father signs for her and he has already said he is not going to do that."

Nicky whimpered then quickly bit her lip. They couldn't stand against both of there parents. Trembling she looked into Dustin's eyes. She wanted to go with him. She wanted to beg him not to leave her. *What will daddy do to me when I am here alone!* she wanted to scream.

Dustin blinked back tears. He looked into Nicky's eyes. "I'll stay." he whispered.

"You can't." she whispered back. "I -" she stopped.

Dustin pulled her into his arms and held her.

"Let's go, Dustin. Now!" Mr. Davis' voice seemed loud in the quiet room.

Nicky looked into Dustin's eyes as he stepped away from her. "Don't let them know what happened here." she whispered. "I can't live through what he will do to me if he is turned in."

Dustin looked down at her and slowly nodded. "I love you. Will you-"

"I'll be fine." she answered quickly. "You better go, your father doesn't need to be upset also."

Dustin turned away and ran from the house. "God, save her." he cried as he started his car. "Is this what we are suppose to do?"

Dustin sighed as he pulled into the drive. His father pulled in behind him. Quietly he climbed into Dustin's car.

"I know you didn't want to leave her." he began, "But you can't be with her all the time. You had no right to try to run off and get married. You have held no respect for me or for her father. I am so disappointed in you I don't know where to begin."

Dustin dropped his head, his fathers words barely got passed his misery. What was happening to Nicky right now. What was her father doing to her? His heart turned over. Would she even be alive by morning?

Mr. Davis cleared his throat. "Just be thankful you didn't do anything. The last thing you need right now is a burden."

Dustin's head shot up. "Nicky is not a burden and what we do is up to us. If we were to get pregnant it wouldn't be a burden. It will probably be the only way you will ever see that we are serious about each other."

His father looked at him hard. "You listen to me, boy. You are going to continue on with your life. You will be leaving for collage in two weeks and you will go on with your plans. You are not going to see her again, do I make myself clear. After tomorrow this is over."

Dustin felt his jaw tighten. "You are not my parent any more." he growled as he jumped out of the car. Running into the house he slammed the door.

His mother looked up quickly. "Dustin," she stood up and walked toward him, "Where is Nicky?"

Quickly he turned away. "Ask him!" he snapped, motioning toward his father. He bit his lip and raced down the stairs not willing to let parents see what had happened to him at Nicky's.

Back at home Nicky's father turned on her. "I told you what would happen did you think I was lying!" he grabbed her and pushed her against the wall. "You will pay for what you have done."

Nicky trembled as her father lifted the whip. Slowly she bowed her head knowing she had no choice but to accept her punishment.

After several lashes he stepped up to her. "Do it." he growled.

"No." her voice was week, but her father heard.

Angrily he whipped her more. "You will do as you are told. If I have to whip all the fight out of you I will!"

Nicky groaned. Just how much more could she take?

Chapter 22

"Hay, Dustin. Where is you mind at." his boss asked him.

"Oh, I'm sorry Mr. Benton." he replied as he turned from stocking the shelves. "Did I stock something wrong?" It was Monday morning and he couldn't get yesterday or last night out of his mind. Was Nicky all right or had her father done something worse to her?

"No, you can relax. You've just been walking around here like a zombie today. Is going to collage really worrying you that much? Or are there other things on your mind? You are usually very talkative, but I don't think you've even said ten words today that I haven't pride out of you."

"Sorry, I just, I have a lot on my mind." Dustin turned back to the shelves. He couldn't look his boss in the eye fearing he would see the marks from Mr. Varson. "Please God, let me know that Nicky's okay. Somehow, please let me know." he muttered.

"Listen, Dustin," his boss began, pulling him back to reality for a few minutes. "Why don't you take the rest of the day off. You've only got a few weeks left to get ready to go to collage and I think you'll function better on the job if you have some time to do things to get ready. Why don't you go home and relax. Do something, just take the rest of the day and come back tomorrow more like your old self.

Dustin shook his head. "I'd rather work if that's okay. Going home is not going to make things any better. Trust me."

Mr. Benton shrugged. "Have it your way. How are things going with the Varson girl?"

Dustin's head shot up. "What do you mean?"

"I just wondered if you were still together." Mr. Benton chuckled. "I saw her father Friday and said something to him about it. He acted as if he didn't know a thing. Just like him, he never would admit that he had a soft spot for that little girl." Mr. Benton chuckled again.

Dustin felt his pulse race. So that's how her father found out! No wonder he had been so upset.

"Nichole." her mom called.

Nicky trembled as she stepped out of the kitchen. Now what had she done wrong? "Yes mama." she tried to sound calm.

Her mom scowled at her. "I need some things from the market." she held out her list. "Just don't take to long. I want to have plenty on hand. Your father wants to have a party tonight and you haven't cleaned in here yet." her mom pushed her toward the door. "Hurry up. And don't you dare see or speak to that boy. I'm timing you. You aren't back in half an hour and your father will come and get you."

Nicky slowly took the list even as her hands trembled. "Yes mama." She bit her lip. She wouldn't be aloud to leave for this party and she had a feeling she was the reason he wanted to have one. Tears stung her eyes as she turned to her room to change.

"Where do you think you are going?" her mother snapped.

Nicky dropped her head. "I was just going to change."

Her mother frowned. "You look fine. You don't need to worry about looking Christian. You are not permitted to look that way in this house, do you understand. If anyone asks about the marks just don't answer. Now, go! And you better get everything on that list."

Nicky bit her lip, but slowly walked out the door. *What am I going to do. I can't be seen like this.* Tears ran down her cheeks. "God, please help me." she whimpered. "If Dustin sees me like this he will hate me forever, and if anyone else does they will know what daddy does to me. What do I do?"

As Nicky neared the market she slowed slightly wishing she could disappear. Looking up her heartbeat quickened in fear. There were three men sitting in a truck in front of the market. One looked her way then smiled and said something to the others. Quickly they all got out.

She trembled. For some reason she felt uneasy. What was going on?

They all started towards her.

Quickly she started to back away. As they reached her one of the men grabbed her arm. "Well, well, well." he chuckled. "What have we here."

Nicky trembled, "Let me go." she whispered.

One of the other men laughed. "Sure, sure. After a few rounds maybe. The skinnier the better, hu, Chad?" he laughed again. The others joined him as they closed in on her.

"Let me go!" Nicky cried. Her heart roared. What was going to happen to her? These men would take what they wanted she felt sure of it. She also felt sure of one more thing, these men had been hired by her dad and she had walked right into his trap. She struggled trying to free herself.

One after another they laughed. Then as one of them reached for her she screamed. The door to the market swung open.

"Let her go!" came a voice.

Her heart leaped it was Dustin. To her shock the men released her and started running. At the same moment police sirens started going off and cops were suddenly every where.

Dustin stepped up close to her. "You okay." he whispered as he reached out to touch her.

Nicky dropped her head, unwilling to let Dustin what her father had done to her. Turning quickly she pulled away. She couldn't let the police talk to her, if they did they would know everything.

"Nicky," Dustin whispered. Pain sounded in his voice.

She felt shame run through her, though if it was from what had almost happened or from the way she was dressed she wasn't sure. He had seen those men grab her. He had heard her scream in fear. He had seen her almost humiliated right there on the square. She bolted, running as fast as she could through her blinding tears towards home.

"Nicky!" Dustin called again.

Hearing him she lost her footing and fell to the side walk. In no time she was up and running again. "No! No! No!" Fighting tears she ran with all her might, though she knew when she got home it would only be worse.

Dustin ran after her as fast as he could.

Nicky dropped down on the front step and buried her face in her hands. "I can't do this any more. Help me, God. I need you!"

Dustin dropped down in front of her. "Nicky." he whispered as he rapped his arms around her.

Pulling away she whimpered.

"Nicky, please don't -"

"Please don't touch me." she whispered. "I can't - it - just don't." more tears ran down her cheeks.

"I'm so sorry. Did they -"

"No none of them had a chance, but I'm sure they will later." she bit her lip as she turned away from him even more. "You aren't suppose to be here. What if dad comes home."

Dustin sat down beside her. "I'll take your beating for you." he whispered.

Nicky looked up at him then quickly looked away, but in that moment he had seen almost more than he could bear. He cupped her face in his hands and tilted her head up.

She tried to keep her eyes down, but couldn't.

"What did he do to you?" his voice broke as he saw all the marks on her face. He released her face and pulled her to him trying again to hold her.

Nicky pushed him back. "Dustin, please don't. If he sees -"

Dustin looked into her eyes. "That's not the only reason is it."

She looked away, but Dustin wouldn't let it rest. "I can't believe he let you wear a tank top and cut offs. Doesn't he know people will see." Slowly her started to pull up her shirt to see her back.

She jumped away. "Don't! Trust me, you don't want to see."

"I'm so sorry. I should never have left you. I should have stayed. It's all my fault."

"No it's not." she whimpered. "He would have found another reason, you were just the easiest one. You didn't make me do anything. I was the one who snuck out. I was the one who said yes."

"I want to protect you." he whispered as he turned her to face him.

"He won't let us be together. Today was a warning to stay apart."

Dustin looked down into her eyes. "You don't mean that what happen to day was because of him!"

"He hired them I am sure. Just to remind me that no matter where I go he is in control of me." she burst into tears. Suddenly someone grabbed her from behind and she screamed.

"You are right girl, I have control over you and you will pay for what you just did." Her father grabbed her arm and pushed her in the house then pushed Dustin in. "I told you never to see each other again!"

He grabbed Nicky and tied her hands behind her then tied her feet. "You will pay later!" he slugged her in the stomach.

Groaning she turned away unable to watch what her father would do to Dustin.

Grabbing Dustin, he pushed him to the floor then snaked the whip across his back. "If your parents are not going to make you mind, I will! Stay away from her unless you want more of the same."

Nicky bit her lip as she heard the whip crack.

Dustin bit his lip. How could Nicky endure this all her life?

After a few more strikes her father stopped and pulled Dustin to his feet. "Now you get out of here and don't you dare breathe a word about any of this. If you do I will do so to her that you will never want to look at her again. Am I understood."

Dustin held his father's gaze. "Hit me instead of her. If you want to hurt someone hurt me. Just leave her alone. This is not her fault. None of it. Everything that happened yesterday was my fault. And everything that has happened between us has been my fault."

Her father smiled. "You want punishment fine." He pushed Dustin to the floor and bound him, then untied Nicky and pulled her to her feet. Turning her so she was facing him and Dustin he grabbed her shirt and pulled it up.

Dustin cried out in pain as he saw Nicky's stomach. Laced across her were rose bushes.

Her father grabbed them and ripped them off of her.

Nicky screamed in pain. Her father slugged her in the jaw and she dropped to the floor. Whimpering she backed away from him.

He stepped toward her and snapped the whip striking her shoulder, again and he struck her cheek. Nicky moaned as her mother stepped into the room.

Dustin stiffened. He had seen her mom many times in the market and never known it was Nicky's mother.

"You sure the boy won't tell?" she snapped as she look at Dustin through narrowed eyes.

Mr. Varson laughed. "He won't tell if he wants her to stay alive." He turned to Dustin. "And believe me if I get turned in I won't just kill her, she will know every step of the way."

Grabbing Nicky he beat her into a corner, then repeatedly kneed her in the stomach. When she started to slump over he slammed his fist into her face instead.

Nicky wanted to barf. She tried to pull away, but there was no where to go. When her father finally let her go, she moaned and dropped to the floor.

Mr. Varson turned back to Dustin and cutting his ropes pulled him to his feet. "You so much as breath a word boy and I will make your whole family pay, you understand me."

Dustin shuttered as he looked at Nicky huddled up in the corner. "Please don't do this." he pleaded.

Nicky heard and tensed. That was the worst thing to say to her father. Now it would just get worse.

"Get out!" her father snapped as he spit tobacco juice at Nicky. "and don't you dare breathe one word."

Dustin stumbled as Mr. Varson pushed him out of the house. "You will never see my daughter again or I will make your entire family sorry you ever met her."

Dustin groaned. *What am I suppose to do, leave her or stay? Am I making it worse for her being here?* Tears filled his eyes as he heard her father raving, then the snap of the whip. Not one sound did he hear from Nicky as he turned to walk slowly away. No matter how much he wanted to protect her he couldn't put his family in danger. Her father knew he had them both.

Dustin groaned. What more would he do?

Nicky whimpered as she saw Dustin leave. She wanted to run out and go with him. She wanted to beg him not to leave her, but instead she turned away as her father came up to her.

"You were smart to figure I was the one who hired them girl, but you are still going to pay for what you did. You got my message, and you will remember it for the rest of your life."

Then he scowled as he looked at her. "I see only one problem. No matter what I do to you, it seems you and he are bound and determined to be together. So your mother and I have come up with a plan."

Nicky shuttered as she looked up at him. What was he going to do to her? Trembling she waited.

Her father gripped her arm. "I will see to it that you never see him again. Do you understand me." he growled.

Nicky dropped her gaze.

"I am sending you off to collage. You will not have a room mate and you will still be under my control. You are leaving this town and you are to never see or talk to Dustin Davis again. Am I clear?" he looked into her eyes and pushed his face close to hers. "If you behave, you have nothing to worry about. But if you don't you will pay for it when you come home on brake, or if necessary I will come and take care of it myself before, that is why you will not have a roommate."

Nicky shuttered as she looked into her fathers face. "Yes sir." she groaned. Tears stung her eyes. Now what were her and Dustin to do?

Her father glared at her. "No communication with that boy ever again. You are not to see him, you are not to call him, you are not to write to him. Any of these violations and I will make sure you are very sorry. I don't have to hurt you to make you pay for what you have done." He pushed his face down close to hers. "Do I make myself clear?"

Nicky groaned inwardly. "Yes sir." she tried to sound calm, but she trembled so bad that her voice shook. She knew what he would say next so she wasn't surprised when he pushed her to the floor.

"You have a lot of disobedience to get out of you before you go."

Nicky bit her lip as she whip snapped on her back. *Please God, show me a way out.* She bit her lip harder to keep the words from spilling out.

Pulling her to her feet her father threw her against a wall. "I should have killed you when I had the chance."

Nicky trembled. As he came closer she cowered away from him. Biting her lips to keep back her cries of fear.

After her beating her father pushed her to her room. "Get packed. We will leave by the end of the week, until then you are not to leave the house under any circumstances. Am I clear?"

"Yes sir." Nicky shuttered at the thought of what he would do to her if she tried to get out and was caught. "I won't."

Her father smiled and turned away then swung back around driving his elbow into her side. "Believe me girl, if you and he where close or ever attempt to be close and you end up pregnant I will see to it that that child dies.

Nicky shuttered as she turned away. She knew he was serious, but a fear was already in her heart about Sunday. What if she had gotten pregnant? What would her father do to her in order to kill her baby? Quickly she pushed the thought aside. *That won't happen. I am not pregnant and if we never see each other and are never close, we never will get pregnant.*

Moaning she fell across her bed. Tears flooded her eyes and she let them fall. "Please, God," she whispered. "Please let us get through this. And please keep Dustin and his family safe. Please don't let him tell. I can't bear daddy's wrath if Dustin should tell." Exhausted she fell asleep.

Chapter 23

As Dustin walked in the door at home he was startled by a loud "Surprise!"

He jumped back, "What in the world?"

Sara laughed. "It's your going away party. Boy your boss is good, you got here just on time."

Dustin stepped back. "Going away?"

"Yes," Mr. Davis stepped toward his son. "Going away to collage."

Dustin quickly backed away from his father, staying in the shadows so no on one would be able to see the blood on his face or back, nor the fact that his shirt was torn. He trembled at the thought of what Mr. Varson would do to Nicky if someone found out.

His father stepped closer to him then Sara laughed. "We ordered pizza and everything."

Dustin looked at Sara then at his dad and quickly backed away, and ran down the stairs.

His father frowned as he started to follow. Mrs. Davis stopped him with a hand on his arm. "Just give him a few minutes. He'll be back, he just needs some time."

Mr. Davis frowned at her. "He is going to see that he and that girl are not aloud to be married no matter what they want. It will not be legal till she is eighteen and he already told us that won't be till next summer. We both agreed that this is for his best and hers. They need to be apart and he is going to see that."

Mrs. Davis sighed. "He loves her." she whispered.

"Then they can be together when she is old enough. He will do this. I am not giving him a choice this time." Angrily he walked down the stairs.

Dustin jumped as his dad pushed open the door, and quickly pulled on his shirt. "I'll be up there in a little bit." he snapped as he quickly backed away, keeping his head down.

Mr. Davis frowned as he stepped in. "You may not see this, Dustin, but it is for your own good. After you and she are apart for a while things will get better, if you wait till she is eighteen, her father probably won't care. But you already told us that won't be till next summer and your mother and I have agreed that you need to move on with your life.

"I know. I just don't agree with you." Dustin bit his lip, it was hard not to look up and meet his fathers gaze. "I know you just want what is best for us, but I don't agree that it is to be apart. It seems that we have no choice though. I will go if I must, but come next summer we will be married." *If she is still alive by then,* he added to himself.

"Thank you for understanding." He turned to go then turned back to Dustin. "It bothers me that you are not meeting my gaze, Dustin. Are you trying to hide something?" He stepped closer to his son.

Dustin quickly looked up, but stayed back far enough he hopped his father couldn't see. "No, I'll be up in a little bit, I just needed to wash up before I felt like a party that's all."

Mr. Davis looked at him a moment. "If you say so." He turned and walked out. "Don't take to long. I know you are not thrilled about this, but please at least act like you don't hate me for making you leave her."

Dustin dropped his head again. "Yes, sir."

Mr. Davis turned to look at his son, "When your siblings can see, you meet my gaze. I will not allow them to see you sulking like a child."

Dustin stepped back before looking up. "Yes, sir." He heard the coldness in his voice and hoped his father wouldn't see it in his eyes.

Mr. Davis smiled. "Give your problems to God, son. He can handle them all so much better than you can."

Chapter 24

Friday morning Nicky's father loaded up her things in the car and he and her mother took her to the collage about three hours away. It was a public collage, but to Nicky's surprise they were across the road from a Christian collage. The collages she learned later did a lot of things together and many of the students, though they would be going to one collage, took classes at both. The collage was very conservative, it just didn't hold the name Christian in its name. Nicky later learned that the collages use to be divided as girls and boys collages, but now were simply more like a joined collage to make the campus bigger. They just didn't share the same name.

Nicky trembled as her father took her things to her room.

The dorm mom smiled as she opened the door. "I know you have requested a private room Mr. Varson, but the application was so late that all the private rooms have already been filled and we are so over run with students this year that I'm afraid your daughter will have to have a roommate."

Her father grunted as he looked down at Nicky.

Nicky trembled, sure her father was going to hit her as if it was her fault. She knew he wanted her to have a room of her own incase he thought he had to "come and take care of her." She trembled. Was she suppose to say something or let her father do all the talking?

The dorm mom looked embarrassed, "I can try to get one of the other girls switch if there is a problem. I just don't know what else to do."

Mr. Varson turned to her. "That is quite alright you won't need to do that. I'm sure my daughter will be fine. You are right her application was late."

Again Nicky trembled, *What is he going to do to me, beat me before he leaves long enough to last two months?*

The dorm mom smiled. "I hope you like it here, Nicky."

"Yes mama I am sure I will." Nicky trembled as her father frowned at her.

"Well I will leave you to your goodbyes and see you soon, Nichol." She waved as she hurried down the hall.

Nicky shuttered as her father put her things in her room and turned to her.

"You remember what I told you, girl." He gripped her arm hard. "You try to so much as look at a boy and I will brake every bone in your body. You'll wish you could die."

Nicky tried to stop trembling. "I remember, sir. I will not disobey you. If I do I will accept my punishment." She then dropped her gaze to hide the flash of anger and hate in her eyes. What did her father think she was? He knew she cared about Dustin. Did he think that she would just go running after the next boy she saw?

She looked up at him quickly as he slapped her. "You let anyone know what I do to you and you will wish you never lived."

"Yes sir." She tried not to whimper.

Angrily he pushed her to the floor and walked out. "I will see you soon, don't forget."

Nicky pushed herself up and nodded. "Yes sir." She spoke through gritted teeth. As the door closed she willed herself to relax. At least she would have a roommate.

"Thank you, Jesus." she whispered. Then moaned as she dropped to the floor. Her hand touched her stomach as tears flooded her eyes. "I know what we did, we shouldn't have, God, but please protect our child and bring me and Dustin together some day."

Slowly she looked at her new room and noticed that someone else's things were already there. She sighed. *I guess school is starting on Monday. There are probably a lot of students moving in this weekend.* She jumped as the door opened.

"You must be Nicky. They told me you would be in today." Nicky turned to see a tall girl with long jet black hair and deep green eyes step into the room.

Nicky smiled weakly. "Yep, that's me. And you are?" she reached out slowly to shake hands.

"My name is Holly." the girl answered as her eyes danced. "I'm glad you are finally here. I've been here since last night. My parents brought me, well actually they followed me. I brought my own car. I told my dad I needed my own car. I couldn't stand it if I had to depend on someone else to take me everywhere, besides you never know when you might need to go to town for something. It's a whole lot easier if you can just go and not have to hunt up someone with a car to take you. Did your parents bring you or did you drive?" She asked then rambled on before Nicky had a chance to answer. "My parents left early this morning, so I've been learning my way around the campus today. It's such an awesome place. I've never been anywhere like it before. The boys here are simply dreamy, at least all the ones I've seen. I shouldn't have any trouble finding a boyfriend here. And just think we have two whole collages of guys to choose from. What are you majoring in? I just started this semester also, incase you hadn't noticed that yet. I'm majoring in boys." she giggled. "No, I'm just kidding but I figure a Christian collage ought to be the best place to find a good one, a boy that is. And the collage across the road is a Christian collage. I can't wait till our schools get together. I hear they do that a lot. I'm just taking my basic classes. Figure if I'm not married by the time I'm done with that I'll decide what to major in." Holly smiled happily rolling off this whole speech without hardly taking a breath.

Nicky smiled. *This should be an interesting semester, I guess it shouldn't be a quiet one. I have a feeling I won't get board,* she thought to herself.

Chapter 25

Despite Nicky's fears she and her roommate got along great, though they were complete opposites - Holly was a loud outspoken girl who always seemed to be in trouble and most of the time she managed to drag two or three of the girls along with her, and Nicky was quiet and always careful to stay out of trouble.

Though quiet and shy Nicky was soon a favorite among the girls. Her quietness seemed to draw them. She was a good listener, and, as long as Holly wasn't around, what the girls talked about stayed quiet. She became a burden bearer for most of the girls in the dorm. This bothered Nicky slightly, when she thought about what would happen if the girls found out that she was pregnant, or if they found out about her father, she felt sick.

She soon became quit popular among the boys at the collage also. Nicky's shy quiet ways seemed to win the hearts of most if not all of the single guys on campus. They all desired to ask her out, though not many of them dared to try, as the first few who found the courage were bluntly refused. This became a great aggravation to Holly who was always trying to get the boy's attention, until she got a boyfriend, then she was constantly trying to hook Nicky up with someone.

Within the first month of school Holly and her boyfriend joined forces trying to get their roommates together.

Nicky refused to go anywhere with Holly. Her fear of her father and her ache over Dustin bothered her more and more. And as the next couple of months wore on her baby became even more visible.

Nicky trembled as she looked in the mirror one day and saw that her very tiny tummy was starting to bulge. She wasn't surprised by this, now that she was being aloud to eat. "Please, don't let anyone notice." she whimpered as she pulled a shirt on. "I don't want anyone to know. If daddy finds out he will without a doubt kill it whether I am willing or not."

Just then the door opened.

Nicky jumped as Holly stepped in. *What if she would have seen.* Nicky trembled as she stepped back. *I'll have to be more careful, if she sees my stomach she will know I'm preg, and if she sees my back -* Nicky stopped mid thought. *I don't even want to know.*

"Nicky," Holly started as she dropped onto her bed with a sigh, "why don't you ever go out with any of the guys here. You don't even give them a chance. They are all dieing to date you. Yet you don't seem one bit interested. Why not?"

Nicky sat on her own bed and looked out the window, though she had only been here a couple of months she couldn't even begin to count the number of boys who had asked her out. "I'm not interested in any of them. I've told you that before. I don't want to date. I'm here to study and that is all. I don't have time for boys."

She trembled in spite of herself. She would not let any man get near her again. She was not falling for anything. It wasn't worth the heart ache. Besides she only wanted to be with Dustin. What would he feel like if she was with someone else. Her stomach knotted painfully. What if he had forgotten all about her? Had he decided she was to much trouble? Maybe he had decided his father and hers were right. They should not be together.

Tears stung her eyes as she looked away from Holly. No matter what, Dustin was her man, even if she never saw him again. She would not fall for someone else. Whether her father liked it or not she was married and she would act like it even if she never was aloud to be with her husband. A tear ran down her cheek and she bit her lip hopping Holly wouldn't see.

"You're not even a little interested in any of them, none at all?" asked Holly with a teasing smile.

"No. I'm not." Nicky snapped.

"Even the ones you haven't met?"

"What are you talking about?"

"Oh, come on, Nicky. You know me and Derik have been trying to get you and his roommate to date ever since we have been going together. As far as I know you haven't even seen him. He never comes to the parties or anything, which wouldn't matter since you don't either, they go to the Christian collage and I don't think he takes any of the classes over here. In fact I don't think he has ever even been on this campus that I have seen. Come on, Nicky, just give him a chance, please. You won't be alone. We could make it a double date or more if you want, please. I can't stand to see you so lonely." Holly looked at Nicky with big puppy dog eyes, "Please, Nicky."

"No, Holly. I told you I'm not interested." Nicky snapped. Laying down softly she turned away. "I can't." she whispered.

Holly gave a sigh. "Well, you can't say I didn't try. Are you sure?" she tried once more.

Nicky laughed. "No, Holly, I'm not going with you on a date."

Holly looked at Nicky for a few minutes and decided the time had come to ask another question that had been bothering her. "Nicky," she hesitated, "are you, that is to say, did you, um, are you, I don't want to sound rude so please don't take it that way. I was just wondering if it's because-that is-" Holly stopped.

Nicky looked at Holly in surprise, it was not like her to be at a loss for words, nor was it like her to seem afraid to say something. She was usually quit blunt and didn't care if what she said hurt someone's feelings or not. She was "brutally honest" she had told Nicky once. "I'm listening." she assured her friend.

Holly looked at her for a moment, "Nicky, are you pregnant."

Nicky stiffened even as tears stung her eyes. Holly had noticed. "Why?"

Holly shrugged. "The other day when you were in the gym I thought it looked like it and, well, since you don't even want to talk to any of the guys here I was just wondering. Besides I heard you barfing your guts out yesterday morning in the bathroom."

Nicky turned away even more. "It is none of your business."

Holly bit her lip, she didn't want to make Nicky mad, but she was sure she had her answer. "It might help if you talk about it. It doesn't make you a bad person, Nicky. It's just one of those things that happen sometimes." Holly looked out the window then back at Nicky. "Who was it, or did it happen before you came?"

Nicky bit her lip. "I don't want to talk about it. Please, just don't say anything. I don't want anyone to know. I will tell you that it is not anyone you know, it happened before I came, but you have to keep it a secret, Holly. I know you are not good at keeping secrets, but this one you have to. Don't breathe a word to anyone, not even your boyfriend. You can't tell anyone!" Nicky was practically screaming in Holly's face. "Not one word!"

Holly stared at Nicky in surprise. She had never heard her so much as raise her voice, not even when she got hurt, and now she was practically screaming. "I won't say a single word." She gasped. "I promise."

Nicky stepped back from Holly and bit her lip. "I'm sorry I shouldn't have yelled. I just don't want anyone to know. I know I can't keep it secret much longer, but my parents will kill me if they find out from someone else. They are probably going to kill me anyway." She shuttered as her fathers words once again ran through her mind.

Holly sighed. "I'm sorry. I didn't mean to upset you."

Nicky shuttered. "I only have a week left till thanksgiving. I know they will find out then, but I don't want it to happen any sooner than that."

Holly trembled at the look of terror in Nicky's eyes. What was Nicky really afraid of? "Does he know?" she asked weakly. "Are you going to tell him?"

Nicky bit her lip and turned away.

Holly searched her mind for a way to change the subject then she smiled. "You want to go swimming?" she asked mischievously as a brilliant - or so she thought - idea began to form in her mind.

"What?" Nicky laughed looking at Holly and wondering if she heard right.

"Do you want to go swimming. We could go tonight after curfew."

"You are nuts." Nicky laughed.

But Holly was beginning to love her idea more and more. "No, I'm serious, we could sneak in after dark. The window in the poolroom doesn't close the whole way. And besides. I over heard talk that the pool will be drained over brake. Come on, it will help you feel better. No one will know. We could just go for a few minutes. Just you and me and a few other girls. It will be fun." Holly smiled as she thought it all out.

Nicky looked at her roommate and shook her head. "I know I will regret this, but I guess I owe you this one. Okay, I'll go."

"Yes!" Holly smiled. This will be the most fun we have had since school started.

Chapter 26

About half an hour after the curfew bell Nicky and Holly slipped quietly out of there room and down the hall, being joined as they went by most of the girls in the dorm. Nicky looked at Holly. "A few others?" she chuckled.

Holly just smiled. Most of the time Holly's ideas were only greeted happily by one or two girls, yet this one seemed to be all the girls idea of fun. Quickly and quietly they slipped out into the night, made a b-line for the gym and finding the window unlocked - as Holly had said- slipped inside. Not daring to turn on any lights, for fear of being discovered, the girls one by one jumped into the dark water.

Only a few minutes after getting into the water Nicky stopped. What was that noise she heard? Was someone walking around on top of the gym? "What was that?" she whispered motioning for the other girls to be quiet. The other girls hearing the fear in her voice stopped talking and listened.

The sound of someone walking over head could be heard loud and clear now. Then there was a creaking sound. Suddenly a rope came from nowhere and landed in the water. The girls froze to scared to even scream.

Then Holly who happened to be the girl nearest to the edge of the pool jumped out and flipped on the lights, screaming as she did not caring if they got caught. Her only idea was to scare whoever this was away. This, however, brought screams from all the girls as well as the boys who were just starting to slide down the ropes.

As the lights came on the alarm went off. This only frightened them more. Boys and girls scrambled for the ropes and the window in hopes of getting away before they got caught. Most of them managing to get out and halfway across the lawn before the staff showed up seemingly coming from all directions.

Everyone froze. They all knew it was to late to hide.

"Every one stay right where you are." the president of the collage called out. Then coming into the light shook his head. "I am disappointed in all of you." he sighed. "Separate into two groups. I want the girls under the trees over there and I want the boy over by the dinning hall." He looked at all of them as if they were a bunch of children. "And stay there until I get to you. Anyone caught braking this rule will be liable for being expelled."

Quickly and quietly the boys and girls moved to their designated spots. The girls stood dripping and shivering from fright and cold having left their towels, those who had brought some, in by the pool. The boys realizing this, and most of them still carrying their towels, spoke to the staff and got permission to give the girls some towels while the staff talked.

The boys quickly moved around passing the girls towels. Most of them who had girl friends sought them out and the others just sort of mingled. They all felt bad for frightening the girls and worse that they had been caught.

The girls felt awful for not being more quiet and making everyone get caught.

Nicky backed away from everyone trying to stay in the shadows. Fear gripped her, what would she do when her father found out what she had done. *Oh, well,* she thought at last. *At least I did something to deserve the beating I will get.*

Holly looked at Nicky and sighed. "I guess it wasn't such a good idea. Sorry."

Nicky shrugged. "You didn't know." she whispered. Looking up she took another step back seeing some boys approaching.

Holly turned to see what Nicky was looking at and smiled. "I think they are bringing us towels she whispered." Then she smiled even wider as she notices her boyfriend Derik and his roommate Dustin. She and Derik had been trying to match up their roommates for quit some time, maybe now it would happen. "Now you have to meet someone I have been trying to match you up with ever since Derik and I started going out. You can't go anywhere so you might as well be civil."

"Holly." Nicky groaned as she turned away. "This is the worst thing that could have happened."

"Derik," Dustin grumbled. "I do feel bad about scaring them but I don't think I should be going with you. It was your idea to come here. I agreed, I know, but if this is all a part of your scheme to get me a girl friend, I don't want any part of your matchmaking game. I told you I have me a girl at home and - "

"It wasn't matchmaking." Derik grumbled. "I had no idea they would be out here. Can't you just try to be social with a girl. Just five minutes won't hurt anything. If you think I am trying to trick you into meeting someone you want nothing to do with, which you have made quit clear, go back to the rest of the group. I'll go over here by myself." He stopped and turned to Dustin. "Just give me your towel and go back with the rest of the guys, but I promise this wasn't meant to be one of my tricks. I wouldn't have included the staff." he said sarcastically.

Dustin grunted. Slowly they approached Nicky and Holly.

Holly smiled as she looked into Deriks eyes. "Thank you so much." She turned to Nicky. "Derik, this is my roommate Nicky, I don't know if you have met her yet or not."

Derik smiled, "I have, but I don't think you have met my roommate, Dustin."

Nicky turned quickly at the same moment Dustin looked up at her. Their gaze met. Suddenly Nicky started shaking. She backed away quickly. "Oh, no." she whimpered before she could stop herself.

"Nicky," Dustin whispered as he stepped closer to her. It was hard to tell in the dim light, but he knew it was her. He reached out to her.

Quickly she backed away remembering the child she was carrying in the dark it was most likely not noticeable, but if he came to close he wouldn't have to see to know. She couldn't let him know. Her father was going to kill it as soon as he found out and then what would Dustin think of her.

"Nicky," he whispered again. "I can't believe it's you."

"What are you doing here?" she whispered.

"I go to the Christian collage across the road. Just came over to get a dip in the pool." He stepped closer to her again as though wanting to touch her and make sure she was real. "What about you?"

Nicky turned away so he couldn't see her.

"I think you boys better get back with your group." Mr. Par spoke from behind them. "Now!"

As Dustin and Derik turned Mr. Par frowned. Mr. Davis I didn't expect to see you here.

Dustin looked down. "I'm not perfect." He muttered.

"What we are to do with everyone I don't know. We can't expel the lot of you. We wouldn't have a collage left."

Dustin turned to look at Nicky again as Mr. Par escorted him and Derik back to their group. At that moment the light shone on her and his stomach knotted. She was pregnant. There was not doubt in his mind about it.

Chapter 27

The next day all of the students met with the staff in the dinning hall. It was two days before brake and the staff was at a loss as to what to do with the one hundred students from both collages, who had snuck out to swim.

All the students nervously awaited there fait. The president stood slowly. "Students," He began in a trembling voice as though he was unsure he was doing the right thing. "because there were so many of you who disobeyed the rules, we have decided not to expel you, but rather you will all have extra jobs assigned to you and you will all be getting your grades cut by ten points.

The jobs are to be done before thanksgiving brake and the Christmas party our collages usually have is canceled. You will be divided into groups and assigned your jobs. These groups will contain both boys and girls and you will all have to get together and decide on a time that works for all of you to get your jobs done before you leave.

You will each find a note in your mailbox telling you what your group is to do and who you are working with. This concludes our meeting. All of you return to your classes and there had better not be any more shenanigans the rest of the year." He sadly stepped down as the students rose to leave.

Dustin looked around hoping to find Nicky, but only saw her as she and Holly hurried out the door.

Later that day Nicky trembled as she opened the paper in her mailbox telling her what she would be doing. Her heart stopped. The paper read. Derik Morton, Dustin Davis, Holly Parth, Nichol Varson : Mop the South Port entire gym and wash down all it's walls inside.

Nicky groaned in spite of herself. She wanted to be with Dustin, but her fear of what he would think of her and what her father would do to her made her feel even sicker than she already did.

Holly ran up behind her. "Can you believe it. We actually get to work together. I'm so excited. And now you have to spend time with a guy whether you like it or not. Judging by the way you acted last night you won't mind, hu. I'm sure he won't. He was head over heals for you."

Nicky turned away quickly so Holly couldn't see her hurt. "Nothing gets past you." she muttered.

Holly smiled. "Derik and Dustin want to have supper together and discus a good time to meet. I told them that was fine, they are coming here."

Nicky looked at Holly, "I can't." she whispered.

Holly laughed. "Yes you can. You'll be fine. I don't think he'll bite."

Nicky tried to blink back her tears, "You don't understand, Holly."

Holly laughed again as she ran up the stairs to get ready. "Don't understand what?"

Nicky bit her lip then looked right into Holly's eyes. "He is the father of my child."

Holly stumbled back as if Nicky had hit her. "W- w - w - What!" she gasped. "He's what."

Nicky dropped to her bed. "What do I do? What do I say to him."

Holly dropped down beside her. "Maybe you won't have to say much, but don't worry. He is a great guy. He'll take care of you."

Nicky pulled away. "Holly, you don't understand. Dustin Davis is my husband!"

Holly stared at Nicky. "This is something I don't want to figure out. Why you here if you are married? Why aren't you two together? And if that is the case then you don't need to worry. He'll be thrilled that you are having a baby.

Nicky turned away from her roommate. "There is to much to explain." she whispered. "I guess we might as well get this over with, but don't you dare say a word. Not to Derik or to Dustin about this."

Fifteen minutes later the girls stood outside the dinning hall and waited for the boy. Nicky kept her head down. She didn't want to face all the questions she was sure were coming.

Will he believe me when I tell him the baby is his or will he think I have been sleeping around? I don't know what to say to him. Tears blurred her vision.

"Here they come!" Holly squealed.

Nicky groaned in spite of herself and slowly walked toward them with Holly. *I don't want to do this.* She felt tears sting her eyes as she slowly lifted her eyes and looked at Dustin.

He smiled at her. His heart felt as though it was going to explode. It really was her. "Nicky." he whispered. He wanted to put his arms around her and pull her close, but he forced himself to hold back. "What are you doing here?"

Nicky felt her face flush. She wanted to run to him, she wanted him to hold her and love her, but she was afraid he wouldn't want her to. "My father sent me here to get away from you." she whispered. She didn't want Holly or Derik to hear.

Finally he stepped closer to her. "I wish I would have known you were here sooner. I can't believe we have been this close and not known it."

Nicky looked into his eyes, but stepped away from him. "We can't - it's against school rules to hug or even touch. You know that." she stepped back even more. "Besides, we're already in enough trouble."

Dustin smiled. "You are right. I'm sorry. I just - I have missed you Nicky. I've been so worried about you, not knowing what -" he stopped as he looked into her eyes. He stepped closer to her and pulled her in front of him. "Nicky?" he whispered again.

"Hay, come on brake it up you two." Derik called. "You don't need to get in even more trouble. Let's go get some supper and figure out when we are going to do this clean up, I want to get it over with as soon as possible."

Nicky trembled. "I didn't think we were aloud to leave campus."

Derik shrugged. "They told us to meet and figure out when so they shouldn't object to us going out to dinner to decide."

Nicky bit her lip but didn't dare say any more, for fear Dustin would figure out something was still up with her father.

Dustin looked up at Derik. "No, I think Nicky is right. We should at least ask. We don't need to get into any more trouble."

Derik sighed as he looked around. "There is Mr. Par. I'll go ask him. Will that suit you?"

Dustin grinned, "Only if he says it's fine."

Derik laughed in spite of himself. "Well I guess we'll just have to see."

Nicky trembled. If her father found out, she would be in serious trouble, but what was she suppose to do. She couldn't say anything, some one would figure something out.

Derik ran back. "He said it's fine as long as we are back by curfew and don't brake any rules while we are away."

Holly smiled. "Yes! I am so glad. Let's go get pizza."

Derik smiled at Holly. "Sounds good to me. How about you guys." he turned to Dustin and Nicky.

Nicky bit her lip, but slowly nodded.

Dustin shrugged. "Fine with me." he didn't care where they were going as long as it would give him and Nicky some time to talk.

As they all climbed in the car Nicky trembled even more. She didn't want to get into any more trouble. She didn't want her father to show up and who knows what he would do.

"Nicky," Holly called. "Are you going or not. Come on."

Nicky bit her lip, but slowly slid in the back seat with Dustin.

As they drove off campus he smiled and slid closer to her. "I've missed you." he whispered as he slid his hand in hers.

Nicky bit her lip as tears sprang into her eyes. She didn't want to talk where Derik and Holly could hear. She pulled her hand away and dropped her head. "I can't." she whispered.

Dustin bit his lip. What was wrong? Was she still afraid of her father? What had he threatened to do to her that would make her act this way, even when he was hours away?

Later that night as they pulled back on campus Dustin once again slipped his hand in hers. He leaned closer to her and whispered. "I still love you, Nicky. I mean it. Please, don't shut me out."

This time she didn't pull away, but quick tears sprang to her eyes. "Dustin," she whispered. *How do I tell him?* she wondered. Slowly she turned away. "I'll see you tomorrow."

Dustin and Derik climbed out at there campus. "Sorry we got you guys messed up in this." Derik smiled at them. "I guess it was a pretty dumb idea, but this way we get to spend more time together before we all have to leave for brake."

Nicky smiled. "You and your girlfriend just think alike. But you are right it was a very dumb idea."

Holly flushed. "It would have been fine. We just weren't careful enough."

Dustin smiled into Nicky's eyes. "I'll see you tomorrow at three."

Later that night, after Holly was asleep, Nicky lay awake wondering what she should do. How should she tell Dustin about the baby? She hopped he hadn't noticed tonight. She was just drifting off to sleep when she heard a soft tap on her window.

She walked over and carefully opened it trembling when she saw a man below. Was it her father?

"Get out here." he hissed.

She bit her lip as she pulled her head back in. It was her father and she had a pretty good idea she knew what was coming. Slowly she pulled on a jacket and, glancing at Holly to be sure she was still asleep, she climbed out the window and followed her father into the trees close by the dorm.

Chapter 28

Nicky trembled as she and Holly walked into the gym. The boys were already there and had the mops and buckets out.

Dustin grinned as he looked at Derik. "Well, where have you two been. Wanting to leave us here to do all the work."

Derik held his back. "I think we already did the toughest part." He teased.

Holly shrugged. "I was just waiting on Nicky, but I wouldn't have minded if you guys would have at least started with out us. At this rate we are going to take all night. And classes got out a little late, I wasn't really waiting that long on Nicky."

Derik smiled. "We did. We got the water ready, so if Nicky and Dustin want to work on the floors, you and I can wash down the walls. Does that sound good?"

Dustin glanced at Nicky.

She nodded, but kept her head down. *Why did he have to do this today?* She had struggled through the day to keep Holly from seeing the marks on her neck, now she would have to try even harder to keep them from Dustin. Her stomach turned and she struggled not to throw up.

As Holly and Derik went to the other side of the room Dustin turned to her. Now they would have a chance to talk without anyone hearing in.

Slowly he held out a mop to her. "I was hoping we would get a chance to talk."

She looked away as she reached for the mop, jerking when there hands touched. Her heart lurched. "I've missed you." Her voice trembled.

Dustin reached out and touched her cheek. "Nicky," his voice was soft yet full of questions and pain. "I'm sorry I didn't know you were here. If I would of I would have tried everything I could to be with you more."

Nicky shuttered as she slowly looked up at him. "I'm sorry." her heart broke as she saw the surprised look on his face. She didn't wonder why. The cuts on her cheek and the welts on her neck would be very plain to him. Suddenly her stomach turned again. "I'm sorry." she gasped as she turned and ran out the door and down the hall to the bathrooms.

When she came back in Dustin looked up at her then looked away. "When were you going to tell me?" he asked when she was close enough to hear. He didn't want Derik to hear or Holly, though he was pretty sure Holly already knew she lived in the same room as Nicky.

Nicky flushed and stepped back. "Tell you what?" she tried to look away, but he gripped her arm and stepped closer to her. Slowly he touched her stomach. "Nicky?" he whispered.

Nicky burst into tears. "I didn't want you to find out."

Dustin stepped back. "Why?" His heart dropped to the floor. "Is it not mine? Who else have you been with?"

Nicky pulled away. "It's not like that." she whispered looking quickly around to be sure no one heard. "I didn't want you to have any more reason to hate me. It's yours, but -" She looked around again, to be sure that no one was listening or could see them and pulled up her shirt just enough he could see her stomach.

"Nicky!" he forgot to keep his voice quiet.

She dropped her shirt and turned away. She sat down on the floor and put her head on her knees. Why did her father do this to her? All she wanted was to be free from him. Tears ran down her cheeks and she turned farther away so no one would see.

Dustin dropped down beside her. "What did he do to you and when? More to the point, why? Did he come here yesterday. You weren't like this last night were you?" He gripped both her shoulders. "Does he know?"

Slowly she looked up at him, "He found out about the pool, then when he got here last night and I wasn't here, that made him even more upset. I don't know if he knows I was out with you, but he knew it was with some guys and he was not happy. He got bad drunk while he was waiting for curfew, I guess I should have known it was coming when I snuck out to go to the pool. He warned me before he left me here that he would find out about everything I did."

Dustin looked away. "Does he know about the baby?"

"No." she whispered. "Any time he has come here it has been at night, and I have been trying not to let it show otherwise."

Dustin pulled up her shirt to look at her stomach again. He felt sick. Her whole belly was black and blue. Welts lined it and wrapped around to her back. "Then why did he do this to you."

"He wanted to be sure that if I was 'getting around' as he called it, that I wasn't going to get pregnant." Seeing the pain in Dustin's eyes she burst in to sobs. "I didn't want to tell you, because I knew he would find out at brake. When he knows he will kill it. I didn't want you to know so you wouldn't have to feel the loss."

Dustin pulled her into his arms. "I'm so sorry, Nicky. I shouldn't ever have let this-"

"Don't!" she broke him off. "It won't change any thing. I'm sorry for what I will not be able to keep." she looked away. "Even if it is still alive now it won't be when brake is over."

"Hay come on you two." Derik called. "We want to get done today not next week." Then his voice changed. "Guys hurry up there is someone coming, it looks like Mr. Par."

Dustin helped Nicky up and quickly started mopping. "Is he still here?" he asked without looking at her.

"He said he would be back tomorrow afternoon to get me for brake, and I wasn't coming back unless I could behave myself. He told me not to set foot off campus till he came with mom tomorrow. I don't think she knew he was here." she dropped her head.

Dustin bit his lip as Mr. Par walked in. "Well I am glad to see that you four are making a good team and actually working. We have had some trouble with some of the others." He smiled at them. "Dustin, I came with a message for you. Your father wants you to go home in the morning, so you are excused from your classes tomorrow."

Dustin looked up quickly. "Did he say why?"

Mr. Par shook his head. "Just said he wanted you to head home in the morning. I think they might be expecting bad whether and your mother would worry or something like that. And some family is coming in or something."

Dustin smiled. "Thanks. I'll probably leave around eight then."

Mr. Par smiled. "He would probably like you to call him tonight and let him know your plans."

Dustin grinned. "I guess I could do that."

As Mr. Par left Dustin turned to Nicky. He watched her for a few minutes. Fear gripped his stomach as he thought about what would happen to her if her father saw her again. He knew he had to stop that from happening. The child she was carrying was as much his responsibility as hers. "We'll work something out, Nicky. I mean it. You don't ever have to see him again. And we'll get out of here before he comes for you."

Nicky looked up at him quickly. "How?"

Dustin shrugged. "We'll figure it out. But some how, this time I mean it. This is our child and our life and he is not going to kill it. I'm taking you home with me and we are going to start our life together like we should have three and a half months ago."

A scared feeling welled up inside Nicky, but she didn't want Dustin to know. "And if he find me, then what?"

Dustin bit his lip. "You have to trust me. Don't give up. The only way for hope to be lost is to give up. We'll get a restraining order on him. Tell the police the truth Nicky, and everything will be fine."

Nicky bit her lip as she thought about the possibilities. "I will if I have to, but I would rather not."

Dustin put his arms around her. "We are leaving in the morning at eight. I'll come and pick you up. Everything is going to work out this time Nicky. Dad will help if we need him to. I will not let him hurt you or our baby anymore. And don't worry, God will take care of the rest."

Nicky shuttered but slowly pulled away. "Then we better get this done."

Chapter 29

Wednesday morning Dustin stopped outside the girls dorm and waited.

Slowly Nicky walked out. Tears filled her eyes as she and Holly embraced. Fear gnawed at her stomach. Would she ever see Holly again? Would her baby be alive after brake, was it alive now?

Dustin felt tears sting his own eyes as Nicky waved good bye and Holly blew her a kiss. "I'll see you guys soon even if you decide not to come back to school you better come back to visit."

Nicky smiled. "We will." she slid into the car and glanced at Dustin. *My husband.* she told herself. *We are going to start our family, as long as I don't lose hope.*

The three hour drive was very quiet and Dustin could feel the fear in Nicky and himself. It was thick enough you could cut it with a knife. "God, please help us." he prayed. "You know what is going to happen. Please keep us and our child safe."

Nicky bit her lip and looked out the window. "Dustin, what if your family is not fine with this either. What if-"

"Don't worry, Nicky. We will be fine." he glanced over at her.

Nicky whimpered then turned away.

"Nicky," Dustin whispered as he reached out to her. Suddenly he pulled his hand back. Was that blood on her neck?

Nicky turned quickly so Dustin couldn't see. "It's nothing." she whispered.

Dustin pulled off the road and stopped. "Nothing, is it?"

Nicky dropped her gaze not wanting him to see her agony.

"Nicky, look at me." His voice was soft, but stern.

Slowly she looked up at him.

"What happened? That was not there yesterday. Did he come back last night?"

"I - just -" she looked down as tears filled her eyes.

"Nicky." Dustin said again. This time he reached over to her pulled her jacket off her, then slowly raised the back of her shirt.

Gasping she tried to pull away. "Please, Dustin, you don't want to see. Don't!"

Dustin let go of her and turned away slamming his fist on the stirring wheel. "Why?" his voice came out a growl. "You said he wasn't coming back till today."

She dropped her gaze ashamed to tell him the truth. "He hired someone to do it. It's not the first time."

Dustin dropped his head down to the wheel. "Did he do anything else to you?"

Nicky trembled. "Not like - he didn't rape me if that is what you want to know."

Dustin looked into her eyes. "But he did hurt you that way, didn't he?"

Nicky looked away. "Yes." she burst into tears as she admitted the truth to him. "I'm sorry."

Dustin pulled her into his arms and let her cry. "It's not your fault, Nicky. Don't blame yourself. We might just go to the doctor first and make sure everything is okay. I want to be sure he didn't hurt you more than you think."

Nicky looked away. "We can't. He'll kill me."

Dustin reached over and squeezed her hand. "I will never stop loving you, Nicky. I will always love you. Remember that. Don't give up on me and he won't be able to get to you. Don't let your hope get lost. As long as you hold on we'll make it."

Nicky smiled, "I will." She reached to pull on her jacket and flinched.

Dustin saw, "What?" he whispered, concern in his voice.

Nicky shrugged as though it was nothing, but winced again as she moved her left arm. "I just hurt it that's all." She looked up at him with fear in her eyes.

Dustin smiled weakly. "Are you telling me the truth?"

Nicky bit her lip as she looked away. "I - it did get hurt and it is my fault."

Dustin reached for his phone. "I think we need to get it checked out to be sure. We should be home in an hour, I'll see if we can get you in to see a doctor today."

Nicky shuttered but finally nodded. "I'll trust you." she whispered. It took all her strength, and she thought her fear would make her barf, but she didn't. "I just hope dad doesn't find out. I don't want him to even know where I am."

Dustin shrugged. "I don't think it's up to him anymore." He looked at her then looked away. "I'm turning him in."

"NO! You can't you promised."

Dustin turned to face her and took both of her hands in his. "You are carrying our child and you have already made it clear he wants to kill it. I am turning him in and if there is anyone else on his payroll you need to tell me know. I am not going to let him hurt you or our child any more."

Nicky bit her lip and turned away. "I don't have a clue who all he has hired."

Dustin flipped open his phone. "I'm calling mom to get the number for the doctor. We'll start there then see what to do next."

Chapter 30

Dustin pulled to a stop in front of his parents home. He got out and came around to her side, opening the door he helped her out. He felt her body tremble as she stood beside him. Looking down at her his heart fluttered. If her father found her again now, what would they do? She was to weak to withstand his beating.

She looked down slowly. "What will we do when he finds out I am here? What will your parents say?"

Dustin shrugged as if it didn't matter. "The important thing is that the doctor said our baby is fine and I am going to do my best to make sure that you are fine."

Nicky trembled. "If he sees this sling on my arm, there is no telling what he will do. He'll think I told for sure."

Dustin stiffened as he put his arm around her. "At least it isn't broken." he whispered.

Nicky bit her lip and dropped her gaze. What will your dad do when he sees us together.

Dustin shrugged again. "We'll know soon. I don't supose it will take him long to figure out where you are. Especially if he had people down there hired to watch you. They probably called him as soon as we left."

Nicky trembled as she walked with him to the house. When they got to the door he turned to her. "Nicky, I want to pray with you before we do this." he whispered. "We need God's help."

Nicky trembled as she walked unto his embrace. Together they prayed for protection and help. Then, for the first time that day, they looked into each others eyes and smiled.

Mrs. Davis looked up and smiled as Dustin and Nicky walked in. "I was beginning to think you weren't coming home today." she said to Dustin. Then looking at Nicky she smiled, "I'm glad to see you here?"

Nicky smiled then trembled. "He brought me home from school. We ended up next door to each other down there." She trembled again then with out warning she threw up.

She groaned as she pulled away from Dustin. "I'm sorry." she whimpered.

Mrs. Davis smiled. "It's okay honey. Why don't you go on into the living room and lie down. Dustin, I think your father is out back. Why don't you go get him. I think we all need to talk, now."

Dustin looked down at Nicky.

"I'll be alright." she whispered.

"Are you sure?" he whispered. "I don't think this is going to be easy."

Nicky looked up at him and smiled. "I don't think your dad will react the same as mine will."

Dustin smiled and turned to go out.

Mrs. Davis soon came into the living room. "How are you feeling?" she asked.

Nicky smiled weakly sure that Mrs. Davis knew she was pregnant. "Fine. A little stiff but fine. I'll be glad when this arm is better. It's a pain not being able to use it."

Mrs. Davis smiled to, "You right with your left hand?"

"Yep." Nicky smiled. "But it is only a sprain it should be better before brake is over." Her mind raced. She had to think of something else to say before his mom asked if she was pregnant. Or did she already know?

Mrs. Davis smiled. Then turned as Dustin came in.

"I couldn't find him mom. Are you sure he was out there."

"Maybe he had to go somewhere. I thought that was where he was. Oh, well, I'm sure he will be back soon."

Dustin smiled at Nicky. Just then Sarah walked into the room. "Nicky!" she cried in surprise. "What are you doing here!"

Dustin's eyes glittered as he teased his sister. "Oh, I see how it is you'll talk to her, but you don't even notice I'm home."

Sara wrinkled her nose at him. "Hi, Dustin. I'm so glad to see you." she returned his teasing. "Well, who wants to play a game." she cried. "If you are waiting on Dad you are going to be waiting a while. Mrs. Jenkens came by a little bit ago and said that someone needed his help. He said I was suppose to let you know, mom."

Mrs. Davis smiled at her daughter. "Thank you for the message, delayed though it may be."

Sara smiled.

About dark a knock sounded. Nicky looked fearfully at Dustin knowing it was her father.

Mrs. Davis stood and walked slowly toward the door. The kids were playing in the basement and she was glad. This was no time for them to come up and be under foot. If it was Nicky's father they needed to have a serious conversation without the kids around. She bit her lip. She had hopped that her husband would be here, before Mr. Varson showed up. "Dear Lord, please help us." she whispered as she slowly opened the door.

Mr. Varson stood there anger on his face. He looked down at Mrs. Davis. "My girl here?" he asked in a voice as cold as ice.

At that moment Dustin came up behind his mother. "Yes she is and she is staying here."

Mr. Varson stepped up to Dustin as though he would hit him. Then seaming to change his mind he said, "I just want to see her and ask why I wasn't told she was coming home with you till the school called me."

Dustin stiffened. "I'm surprised you waited this long to come. Did the school really call you or some one you hired to hit her? And she doesn't want to see you. Maybe you should just go sleep it off. Then maybe you could actually talk to someone."

"Watch yourself young man." his mother warned.

Slowly Dustin stepped aside allowing him to enter. Dustin could smell the whisky on her father's breath and he trembled. What was he going to do to them?

As they entered the living room Nicky jumped up. Her whole body shook. "Daddy." she said managing to keep her voice steady.

Her father took a step towards her. "Why did you leave?" his voice was gruff.

Nicky was shaking so hard she felt if she spoke her teeth would chatter. Dustin stepped around her father and put his arm around her. "Sara." he said softly.

Sara looked at Dustin then left the room quickly. She had caught her brothers look. She didn't understand it yet he seemed scared. She hurried outside in search of her father. She didn't know why, all she knew was she had to find him.

Dustin darted a look at his mother and she stepped quickly out of the room, "I need to go check on the kids." she said calmly. "So, I'll just leave you all to talk." She hurried down stairs and picked up the phone, praying the police would get there in time.

As soon as they were gone Mr. Varson stepped up close to Nicky. "You going to answer?" he asked coldly. "Or do you need a little bit of encouragement?" he reached out and grabbed her.

"No!" she screamed, trying to duck away from her father. As she did he noticed her arm was in a sling.

Anger blazed from his eyes as he released her arm, striking her face as he did. "You worthless fool. You told didn't you!" he stepped closer to her causing her to back up, as she did she fell into the couch.

Nicky looked up at her father. "No." she said softly. "I didn't tell. I promise I didn't. Dustin just took me to the Doctor because I was sick. He was worried about me. They found out that my arm had a bad sprain, they think I feel down a flight of stairs. That's all."

"Don't lie to me." he grabbed her arm and pulled her to her feet. "You'll pay for this."

Nicky trembled as her father raised his hand to strike her. "Daddy, please." she whimpered before she could stop herself.

Dustin suddenly stepped up to Mr. Varson. "If you want to hurt someone, hurt me."

Mr. Varson looked at him strangely, "What are you talking about?" he asked.

Dustin looked him straight in the eye as he reached out and pulled Nicky from her fathers grasp. "Just what I said. If you want to hurt someone hurt me. Nicky hasn't done any thing to you. Leave her alone."

Mr. Varson laughed scornfully. "Hasn't done anything wrong?" he almost bellowed. "Will you tell me what she is doing here then. I seem to remember telling her not to see you again and I seem to remember telling you the same thing. Doesn't your Bible say for children to obey their parents." his voice sounded mocking, yet dangerous. "She hasn't obeyed me, yet you are telling me she hasn't done any thing wrong." he grasped Nicky's arm. "Get out to the car or face your punishment here-" he stopped as looked down at her. "No!" He screamed. "You worthless -" he slugged her stomach, before she could see it coming.

Nicky trembled but held her ground. "I'm not leaving." she said firmly. She blinked back tears as she put her hand over her stomach and barfed.

Her father smiled at her wickedly as if he expected this. "Then," he sounded as if he enjoyed tormenting her, "get your clothes off."

"What!" Nicky stumbled back shocked.

"You heard me. If you think I'm going to let you stay here so you two can have your fun, then you are going to have it right now." his eyes gleamed with anger. Then he looked up at Dustin, "What are you waiting for?" he looked at him closely. "I meant what I said."

Dustin stepped away from him pulling Nicky with him. "You are drunk." he said boldly. "That is not the reason she is staying here. She is to sick to be close to anyone right now and she has you to thank for that. She is staying here because she is my wife, whether you will accept that or not. She is not going home with you, ever."

Mr. Varson let out and angry roar and lunged at them. Nicky screamed in fear as her father grabbed her and pushed her to the floor. Dustin jumped at the man but Mr. Varson swung around and cracked him across the jaw. "That's what you get for talking to me like that you little twerp." he screamed then grabbing Nicky's arm he pulled her up. With out hesitating he pulled out a whip witch he had hidden in his shirt. Raising it he struck her several times. As he released her arm Nicky fell to the floor beneath the heavy blows.

"Daddy, stop." she cried in fear. "Please stop."

Instead of stopping her father laughed wickedly and slapped her harder. "I will kill that child, make no mistake in that." Nicky still facing her father backed away in fear. As her father raised the whip she pulled her arm up over her face and tried to turn so the whip would hit her back. It caught her side mid turn. She screamed in pain.

Her father reached down and pulled her to her feet. "Are you going to get to the car and go home?" he asked dryly.

Nicky looked into his eyes. "No." she snapped.

Her father let out and angry cry and raised the whip. Holding on to Nicky's arm she caught the full blow of the whip. Screaming in pain she tried to pull free. Her father pushed her to the door. "Get out and I won't hit you any more." he said wickedly.

"No." she moaned weakly. Her father raised the whip again.

This time Dustin leaped on the man causing him to drop the whip. Nicky's father twisted and turned in anger. Dustin lost his hold. Her father flung him to the floor beside her. "You!" he screamed. "You did this to her and you'll pay for it. She was warned."

Now it was Dustin's turn to tremble. He backed away from the angry man. Her father raised the whip and snaked it in Dustin's direction. Dustin raised his arm to block the strike and the whip wrapped around his wrist. Her father gave it a jerk pulling Dustin forward.

Dustin cried out as her father grabbed him and pulled him up. "You want to take her punishment young man?" he said dryly. "You've got it."

He struck Dustin across the face, with the whip, letting go of him at the same time.

Dustin fell to the floor.

"Daddy, no." cried Nicky. "leave him alone." as her father raised the whip to strike Dustin again. Nicky flung her body against him knocking him off balance.

Leaping up he grabbed her. "You're a dead girl." he growled in her face.

Nicky felt his anger and smelled the beer on his breath. In fear she tried to back away. Her father picked the whip up, in anger he slashed her back. Nicky cried out in pain. After only a few blows she fell to the floor to weak to move. Her father towered over her, anger blazing out of his eyes.

"You and your child are going to die." he growled as he raised the whip again.

"Don't hit her again." Dustin groaned as he tried to get up.

Her father turned on him in sudden shock, he thought he had knocked the boy out. Grabbing his arm he hauled him to his feet striking his face several times then he raised the whip to Dustin and flung him to the floor. Suddenly a gun shot sounded. The whip flew from Mr. Varson's hand.

"Don't hit my boy again." Mr. Davis sounded angry.

Dustin looked up in surprise. "Dad." he cried.

Mr. Davis looked down at Dustin with a frown. "Quiet son." he said coldly. "What's going on here?" he asked looking straight at Mr. Varson.

Nicky's father raised his head. "I came for my girl." he stated dryly. "If you think I should do nothing about the fact that he got her pregnant, when they weren't suppose to even be seeing each other, then I suggest you discipline him. And also that you quit letting him see my girl." his voice sounded threatening. "I'm calling the police with a charge of kidnapping if she thinks she is staying here. She isn't old enough to be on her own and she does not have permission to stay." he looked Mr. Davis in the eye. "It's up to you. I will not hesitate to call you in on this."

Mr. Davis cleared his throat. "I recon that is up to her." He turned to Nicky. She had backed away into the corner and there she sat with her head down. "Nicky." he said coldly, "Do you want to go home?" He took a step toward her. "If you don't you are more than welcome to stay here. I'm sure your father will be understanding if you don't wish to go with him right now. "

Nicky didn't dare look up as tears burned her eyes. She knew she couldn't endanger the lives of Dustin or his family and she wasn't about to. How she wanted to scream out the truth to Mr. Davis, but she was to scared. Without looking up she slowly nodded and as she did she felt her heart braking. The only thing that scared her was how she was going to protect her child. But what else could she do? If she said no her father had the ability to kill Dustin and his whole family.

"Nicky!" cried Dustin feeling his heart brake right along with hers. What had her father done to make her suddenly give up.

She didn't look up, instead she laid her head down on her knees, not wanting Dustin to see her hurt. Nicky fought hard to keep back her tears, yet some of them escaped.

Mr. Varson reached over and pulled the girl to her feet. As he did she once again barfed.

She bit her lip as she tried to pull away, all the while keeping her head down, but her fathers grasp was strong. Pulling her with him he headed to the door. "Get out to the car." he growled. "I'll deal with you when I get out there."

"Hold on a minute." Mr. Davis said. "I want to know what was going on here." looking straight at Mr. Varson he added, "You might as well tell me cause you aren't going anywhere till you do. I think we all need to sit down and have a talk. We are all adults and we need to act like adults. Let's all sit down and talk this out rationally."

Mr. Varson turned to him. "He attacked me." he said dryly. "I have to defend myself and protect my girl." he grip tightened on Nicky's arm.

Mr. Davis nodded. "So you didn't hit her at all?" His question sounded innocent yet Nicky cringed. She knew her father would think she told now.

Her father shrugged. "Why should I have hit her?" he asked dryly. "I told her I came to take her home and your boy told me she wasn't going with me. I asked him what he meant and he attacked me. Did you think I would just let her stay when I told you to keep your son away from her?"

Mr. Davis looked at Nicky, "Do you want to go home with him Nicky?" he asked softly.

Nicky trembled. Her father gripped her arm tighter and gave it a twist. She whimpered. Then bit her lip.

Dustin stepped up to Nicky's other side, "Why don't you let her go so she can answer for herself, instead of trying to get her to answer what you want her to." he said crossly as he grabbed her other arm, and taking her father by surprise, managed to pull her away from him.

Nicky glanced up. Then just as quickly dropped her head again, but it was to late. Dustin reached out and lifted her chin. "Nicky." he gasped. Her jaw was covered in blood. Glancing at her father he knew why. He was wearing brass knuckles. Nicky had had no way of knowing. When she had tried to stop her father from hitting Dustin he had slugged her instead.

Mr. Davis stepped forward. Looking at Nicky he asked crossly, "Your father do this to you?"

Nicky trembled. "It was an accident." she whispered.

Mr. Davis looked at her closely. "If you don't want to go home you can stay right here. It's up to you."

Nicky trembled as she looked at her father.

"Do you want to go with him Nicky?" Mr. Davis asked softly.

Nicky looked down and slowly nodded.

Dustin stared at her in surprise and grasped her arm.

She looked up at him with tears in her eyes.

"Nicky," he whispered. "You can't just give up. You are carrying our child inside of you. You already said he was going to kill it. Is that what you want?"

Nicky looked away, "I can't let him hurt your family." she whispered.

Dustin gripped her arm tighter. "You are my family, Nicky. You and the baby you are carrying." He looked into her eyes. "Don't give up, Nicky, please." he whispered.

"I have to go." she whispered back. "If I don't -"

"Think about what will happen to you if you do, Nicky." Dustin pulled her into his arms. "Not just you, but also our baby."

Mr. Davis stood watching a moment then put a hand on Dustin and Nicky's shoulder and turned them to the living room. "I think we all need to have a long talk."

Nicky bit her lip, but Dustin pulled away. "Dad, could you and I talk in private just a minute first.

Mr. Davis looked at him hard. He motioned toward the bedroom and turned back to Nicky and her father, "We will be back soon."

Nicky trembled as they left the room. She felt her father turn toward her. Tears stung her eyes knowing what was coming.

He pulled a bottle out of his shirt and drank it. Then he stepped closer to her. "You will pay for this." he growled. Grabbing her arm he slammed his fist into her stomach. Then pulling back he kneed her.

Nicky moaned as she dropped to the floor.

Her father laughed wickedly. "You will never escape me. And you will never have a child!"

Nicky whimpered as her father grabbed her again. "You need God." she burst out. "Then you wouldn't have to drink."

Her father grabbed her arms and spit in her face. "Let me tell you one thing right now girl, I don't need nor do I want your God. There is no hell, and if there is I would rather go there then be with a bunch of hypocrite Christians in heaven."

Nicky shuttered. "What? There won't be any-"

"Shut up!" her father slugged her jaw. "I'm to young to die anyway. I'll have plenty of time on my death bed. Until then I want to enjoy my life. I don't want t be bothered with a bunch of rules. I don't need your God and I will never accept him!" Suddenly he grabbed his chest and gasped.

In the bedroom Dustin turned to his dad quickly. "You saw everything, why don't you turn him in? Aren't you required to as a foster parent?"

"Dustin," His fathers voice was calm, "I already have. Your mom called the police they should be here any minute."

Suddenly Nicky screamed. "Dustin, come quick!"

Dustin and his father ran out of the bedroom. Mr. Varson lay on the floor gasping for breath. Nicky grabbed her fathers arm. "Daddy!"

As Mr. Davis grabbed the phone to call 911 Dustin ran to Mr. Varson and rolled him over. His lips were turning gray. Gasping Dustin tried CPR. In five minutes the house was crawling with emergency responders.

Nicky trembled as she stepped away from her father. "Please God, he isn't ready to meet you. Please give him one more chance." Tears ran down her cheeks as she watched them all rush about. Finally one of them shook his head.

Nicky bit her lip. "No!" she cried. "NO!"

Dustin pulled her close to him. "I'm sorry." he whispered. "Do you want to call your mom or do you want me to?"

Nicky bit her lip. "I don't want to talk to her." she burst into sobs. "The last thing he said was he was to young to die and he would have plenty of time to repent on his death be. He didn't have any time. He didn't even have five seconds."

Dustin bit his lip as he held her with one arm and slowly dialed the phone. This was one call he never wanted to make.

"Mrs. Varson?" His voice shook slightly. "This is Dustin Davis. I'm afraid I have some bad news." He stopped as heard the phone drop. "Mrs.

Varson!" His heart dropped to his toes as he heard a gun shot. "Mrs. Varson!" He pulled the phone back.

Nicky grabbed the phone in time to hear the last gun shot. "Mom!" she screamed.

Dustin pulled her into his arms. She felt the warmth of his love and whimpered. She knew she shouldn't feel relieved and she felt awful that she did, but she couldn't help it. She felt so relieved that her father would never pull her out of Dustin's arms again that she started to cry.

Dustin pulled her back gently. "Nicky, we need to go check on your mom." he whispered.

Nicky looked into his eyes, "No, we don't. She is dead. Didn't you hear the shots?"

Dustin sighed and stepped over to an officer.

As they pulled up in front of the house Dustin held her back. "Maybe I should go in first or maybe we should let the police go in first."

"We'll go together. This is my problem, I need to be the one to go in." Slowly she walked up the steps not prepared for what she would see inside. As she opened the door she bit her lip and turned away.

Chapter 31

Nicky quietly made her way to her parents bedroom. Tears stung her eyes as she opened the door.

Dustin pulled her close. "You don't have to do this now." he whispered. "It can wait. Till later."

Nicky looked away sadly. "I have to find out if there is any way to get in contact with their family. Their funerals are in two days. I've never met any of my grandparents, I don't have a clue where to start, but I have a feeling they need to know." she looked away as tears ran down her cheeks. "You would wouldn't you, if it was your child."

Dustin pulled her close.

Nicky turned away and pulled open her mothers cedar chest. "I just need some answers." she whispered. "There is so much of my life I don't understand. I have to find out what happened. I need to know why they never let me meet them. Did they have a bad home life? Did their parents abuse them, and if they did, do I even want to meet them?"

She stopped and looked up at him. "I have to know."

Dustin smiled as he sat down beside her.

"Then lets see what we can find."

Nicky reached in and smiled as she pulled out some old baby shoes and a small bag with a few soft curls in it. The bag was marked "Nicky's fist curl." Slowly they removed one thing after another.

"What exactly are you looking for, Nicky." His voice was quiet, but she could tell he was concerned for her.

She looked down, "I'll know when I find it." she whispered. "I know you probably think -" she stopped as her hand touched a small book. Slowly and carefully she pulled it out. Under the book were papers, and more books.

Fear ran through her as she looked up at Dustin then back down at the papers. Carefully she opened the book. The writing was clear and steady and it took Nicky a moment to realize it was her moms. The date was March 15, 1987. She gasped, that was just two days before she was born. "I found it." she whispered. "Listen." Her voice trembled as she read.

"Dear Journal, Today was the most awful day I have known. I am sick of my parents trying to run my life, I guess that is what finally drove me and Rich to where we are. I know that I shouldn't have got pregnant, but they shouldn't try to make my decisions for me either.

All I want is to have a good home with the man I love. I'll tell you all that has happened, but I think I shall write it down as a story just incase it should fall into the wrong hands someday. That way you, my precious journal will know the whole story not just part of it."

Nicky gasped as she looked up at Dustin.

Dustin looked over her shoulder then looked into her eyes. "Are you going to go on?"

Nicky took a deep breath.

"This story is so long I don't hardly know where to begin. I guess I'll start with the night Richard asked me to marry him. I couldn't believe it. I was so scared and surprised. Well here goes my attempt journal, I hope your can read this someday.

Rachel stood for a few minutes at the door before entering the dining room. Her stomach knotted painfully. For weeks she had kept this secret from everyone, but there was no way to keep it secret anymore. Her family and her boyfriend must know. Biting her lip she thought of the best way to brake the news. Would it be best to tell her family or him? Perhaps she should tell them all at once and get it over with.

Yes, that's what she would do. It would be easier since he was here for supper tonight anyway. Taking a deep breath and squaring her shoulders she pushed open the door. The smell of food and the anxiety she felt almost made her throw up. Her parents smiled at her and Rich flushed to the roots of his dark hair when he saw her in the doorway.

Rachel stood as if rooted to the spot, everything she wanted to say wouldn't come out. No one had told her that he was already here.

'Hello Rachel,' Rich said. His voice cracked a little as he looked into her eyes. Then to her complete astonishment he slipped out of his chair, came up to her and took both her hands in his. As he knelt down in front of her, her heart stopped. Was this for real or was she just dreaming. Then his voice broke through her thoughts, 'Rachel Hayland,' at that his voice almost broke, 'will you marry me?'

Her heart stopped then thundered on. She stood trance fixed for what seemed like hours to Rich, who still knelt grasping her hands and waiting for her answer, though it was only a few minutes. Taking a deep breath and blinking back tears she whispered, 'Yes, I will.'

Rich smiled, slipped a ring on her finger and stood. Looking into her eyes they sealed their vow with a kiss. Her parents smiled. *So this is why no one told me he was here?* she thought to herself.

As they ate supper her stomach cramped. She needed to tell him about the baby. He had every right to know. Now however, she felt she should tell him before she broke the news to her parents. Once again she felt her stomach cramp. What if he decided he didn't want to marry her after she told him?

Later that night they sat together on the front porch while her parents were inside.

'I didn't have any idea you were going to ask me marry you.' Rachel commented. 'It was a shock, but a nice one.'

Rich just looked at her. His eyes seemed to say something to her but he wasn't about to say it to her face. Then he smiled and she was sure she must have just imagined the look.

'Rich,' she whispered, 'I need to tell you something.'

'I'm listening.' he answered as he leaned on the railing.

She looked into his eyes, 'If you don't want to marry me after I tell you I'll understand and I won't blame you.'

He looked back at her. 'Why don't you just tell me? I won't change my mind. I will still love you.'

Taking a deep breath she turned her head as though to hide her shame. She whispered almost to quiet for him to hear, 'I'm pregnant.'

A tear rolled down her cheek and she kept her head turned so he would not know. Then he did something that surprised her.

Taking her face in his hands and turning her to look at him he said 'I know. I've known for a while.'

'You knew. Why didn't you ever say anything.' she looked at him in shock.

'I was waiting, hopping you would tell me. How long have you known?' he looked at her with hurt in his eyes.

'A couple of months and you?'

'About a month. I saw the test in your purse the night we went bowling with the group.'

'You rummaged through my bag?' she cried. 'You should never have done that!'

'I didn't exactly rummage though it, you had gone to the bathroom and Steve bumped into it and knocked it off the seat. Some stuff fell out and when I went to pick it up I saw the test laying in there. I couldn't help but look. Why did you take so long to tell me. Were you afraid of what I would do?'

'Not exactly. I just wanted things to be the way they always have been. I guess I was afraid you would hate me.'

'I would never hate you, Rachel. I love you. It isn't your fault you are pregnant, at least not completely. You didn't do it on your own. I am just as much to blame. Stop trying to put it all on yourself. Don't feel guilty. You should be excited.'

'But it's wrong.' she whispered. 'Mom and dad will know. We'll be found out. God knows our sin.'

Rich looked at her. 'I thought you gave up on that God stuff. Or have you changed your mind?'

'No, I just-I guess I'm just afraid of what my parents will say. I wanted to tell you first. I was just so scared I wanted to-'

'We are not doing that. It's not even an option. This is our baby and we are going to have it. Rachel, we are going to be parents. You should be thrilled.' Rich looked into her eyes. 'I don't want you to have any thoughts of aborting.'

Rachel smiled. 'Well I guess I am a little excited, now that I told you. I'll be more excited after I tell my parents.' A worried look crossed her face.

'Well you've told me, now shall we tell your parents? Might as well break the news tonight while their still happy about our engagement don't you think.'

'I suppose.'

Hand in hand they walked into the house."

Nicky looked shocked. "I can't believe it. He was so against me being close to a boy and they were pregnant before they got married. I already knew that but I still can't believe it." She bit her lip as she looked down.

Dustin looked at Nicky. "Don't worry, Nicky, they aren't going to hurt you any more."

Nicky looked into his eyes. "But what about my grandparents. What if they-"

"Don't, Nicky." Dustin pulled her to him. "You are borrowing trouble. Everything is going to be fine."

Nicky took a deep breath and again began reading. "Well, as you might have imagined, journal, my parents weren't at all happy, as a matter of fact they where heartbroken…

'I hope you are planning to have the baby and not abort it or some silly thing like that.' Rachel's father said. He looked straight at Rich, 'You better live up to your mistakes.'

Rich stiffened. 'What we do is our business. It's our child not yours.' (He never did take well to criticism.) 'We are going to get married and we are going to raise our child. We don't need your help if all your going to do is give negative remarks just because we didn't go about things the way you wanted us to.'

Rachel's father looked at him for a few moments. 'Sorry. I shouldn't have said what I did. I know you are both responsible adults. I was just concerned, that's all.'

The next few weeks went by with a lot of strain between Rachel, her parents and Rich. Rich seemed to think her parents were to protective. Her parents seemed to think Rich didn't care about Rachel and was demanding to much out of her. Pour Rachel was caught in the middle, with hormones raging out of control, she felt as though she couldn't do anything without hurting someone.

Finally about a month before the baby was born Rich and Rachel talked things over.

'Your parents are trying to run to much Rachel. I thought we wanted to be married before the baby came. I thought we would have been married already. Yet every date we picked they had some problem with. What is going on?' Rich was clearly upset.

'I don't know. I wanted to be married long before this too. I think they want to keep us apart physically. They think if we are not married that we won't be together. It's all wrapped up in their beliefs. You were a Christian once you know -' Rachel kept her head down to hide her tears. This was not all her fault. Why was he acting like it was? This was not how she wanted it either. She wanted to be with him, not her parents, when the baby came.

'That's ridicules.' he almost screamed, 'How did they figure we got pregnant in the first place. They couldn't stop that.' Rich looked down at

Rachel, 'Let's elope. We can leave and never come back. We could get away from your parents and mine with all their religious stuff. We can go some place and not let them know. We could be on our own. What do you say, Rachel? Let's get away from them breathing down our necks about God. Let's do things on our own.'

Rachel hesitated. 'What about the baby? Moving would mean having to find another doctor. Do you think it will be safe?'

Rich put his arms around her. 'We'll find another doctor. We'll be safe.' he pulled Rachel back and looked down into her eyes. 'I want to be there when the baby is born. You know if we stay here I won't be. Your mom hasn't let me do anything with the baby. She has been the one to go to all the appointments with you and everything. If something were to happen here, she wouldn't even let you call me until it's over. You know that, Rachel. We've talked about this before. This is our baby, not your mothers. I want to be a part of our baby's life and birth."

Rachel smiled at him. 'When do we leave?'

She knew what he said was true and talking about it to her parents hadn't helped. When she had tried they just cut her off and made things more miserable. And besides she did want to get away from her parents and all their religion. She'd had a relationship with God once, but ever since she had backslidden with Rich, well, life just seemed more fun this way. Though she was aware of an empty feeling inside she pushed it away. Her and Rich would fill that void with the life they made for themselves. She was sure of it. She would come back to God when she was ready.

Rich looked down into her face. 'Now! Let's go now. We can stop by the bank on our way out. I'll close my account. We can live for a good while on the money I have saved up.'

Rachel smiled, though she was still afraid. 'Lead the way.'"

Again Nicky stopped. "They couldn't stand stuff about God. I wonder why?"

Dustin shrugged. "Well, your mom wrote that life was more fun. I guess that is what I lot of people think. They try to fill that empty void in their life with drugs or alcohol or parties. They don't want the true happiness that only God can give. They want to do things their way and not be under any rules, not seeing that they are imprisoning themselves, to their lifestyle."

Nicky shuttered, but started to read again.

"We wanted an adventure and that is what we got. There we were, journal, about to have a baby and we moved seven hours away from home.

We didn't take hardly anything with us except the clothes we had on. We made a few stops before we left town. One to the Justice of the peace, so we would be leaving married, and one at the bank. Then we were on our way.

When we came into town we just drove around the neighborhood, it was quiet and peaceful. 'This place looks nice.' Rich smiled. 'Shall we make this our new home.'

I said I liked the neighborhood so we started looking for houses. When we passed a service station Rich saw a sign that said help wanted so he stopped right there and went in commenting that it was worthless to try to live somewhere if you didn't have a job.

When he came back out I could tell thing had gone well. He climbed in the car, flashed me his big grin and asked. "Ready to find a home, Rachel?"

I smiled, 'You bet.' was all I said, but I could tell he was thrilled to get a job that easy.

'He was impressed by my willingness to work as well as my experience. I changed the oil in a car for him and he said I was hired. What do you think about that. I start tomorrow.'

'I'm glad. Then we can find a house and have our baby here? We don't need to go on any further?'

'You bet. Everything is going to be fine.'

Well, journal, that is how we came here. It was the first house we saw and we liked it. It was up for rent and we could move in right away. So right now he is at work and I am in labor I think. I'll close for now, but hopefully I will find the time to write again soon."

Nicky looked up in shock. "I can't believe it."

Dustin smiled. "You seem to be saying that a lot today."

"Well I can't. I just can't believe that is how this all started. I wish I would have known a time when they were happy."

Dustin smiled sympathetically. "Maybe you should stop."

"I can't." she looked up at him. "Did they ever talk to their parents again? Did they know about me? What happen to make things the way they were? I have to many questions to stop now. Did they ever go to church again? Mom said in here that her and dad were Christians once. I wonder what happened."

Dustin smiled. "Well, I guess you better read on."

Nicky smiled as she turned the page then she frowned. "The next entry is dated February 15, 1990. Why didn't she write all that time?"

Dustin shrugged. "There is only one way to find out."

Nicky bit her lip as she looked at the page. The writing was shaky and this time Nicky had no trouble knowing it was her moms. She cleared her throat as she read.

"Dear Journal, I know I haven't written in almost three years, but I just haven't had the time. Nicky is growing so fast, and now with this little one on the way we are looking for a new place. I hope we find one soon.

Rich is so worried lately and I don't blame him. This baby doesn't seem to be moving much and I know it is not growing as it should. The doctor say that if things don't get better we may need to run some test - I have to go now journal. I think I'm having labor pains. Oh no!"

Nicky turned the page. "That is all there is. There is no more written down. What happened to the other baby?"

Dustin watched her silently as she rummaged through the papers on her lap.

Nicky pulled out an envelope and smiled. "Dustin, this is addressed to Mr. and Mrs. Hayland. I wonder why she never sent it?" Quickly Nicky tore open the letter. Scan it quickly she started to shake.

"Dustin, listen.

Dear mom and dad,

 I know I have hurt you by leaving the way I did and not contacting you in so long, but I am not sorry one bit. I still hate you for the religion you tried to push on me. I don't want your God. If he is so loving then tell me why he took my child before he even had a chance to live. No child is a blessing.

 Nicky is an impossible child always asking questions. She is six now and I am glad she is out of the house at school. It gives me more time to work on things I want to do.

 I have started designing again and will soon be going to New York with my new fashions. I know you think I am awful for designing the clothes I do, but I don't care.

 We don't want to see you and we will never let our daughter see you. We are both in agreement to keep her as far away from the church world as possible and also agree that we will make sure she never has a boyfriend so she is not burdened as we were, with a child.

 Rich and I hate you and if you ever see his family you can let them know we hate them too. If God can't hold his church or family together, why should we trust him."

Nicky dropped the letter on the pile of papers. "I don't believe it. All that anger, just thrown at her parents. Like it was there fault. And at God. It's probably a good thing he took their other child or daddy would have killed him like he tried to kill me." Nicky jumped up. "I don't want to do this anymore. I don't want to know anymore about my past."

Dustin jumped up and grabbed her arm. "You started this, Nicky, and I think you were right. You do need to let your grandparents know. You need to meet them. Maybe there is more to the story. Every story has two sides. Don't blame yourself for this. It is not your fault. What your mom said in that letter was just blowing off steam. She didn't mean for anyone to ever read it."

Nicky trembled as she picked up the envelope. "Well, I guess this is the best thing I am going to get for a start, I just hope they haven't moved or anything."

As she walked to the phone Dustin saw her trembled and he sighed. Was this the best thing for her? What if she was right and her grandparents were abusive also?

When Nicky walked back to him she was shaking so bad he thought she was going to be sick. "They are coming." she whimpered. "Both of my grandparents, the Haylands and the Varsons." she looked down to hide the fear in her eyes. "I gave them directions to your house."

Dustin smiled. "It's going to be fine, Nicky."

She smiled but stepped away from him. "Let's get out of here. I don't want to ever see this place again."

"I'm sorry Nicky. Just trust the Lord. He will take care of us."

Nicky whimpered. "I want to, Dustin, I'm just so scared."

Dustin pulled her into his arms and let her cry. "I know." he whispered. "I know."

Chapter 32

At seven that night a car pulled into the Davis driveway. Nicky looked at Dustin and trembled.

Dustin put his arm around her and she felt him stiffen. *So he is worried to,* she thought.

When Mrs. Davis led them into the living room Nicky looked up and gasped. Her grandfather Varson was the exact image of her father. She trembled. Would he be like him in more way than just looks?

Dustin stood and shook hands with them all. "Mr. and Mrs. Varson, Mr. and Mrs. Hayland, we are glad you could come. I'm Dustin Davis and this is my wife, Nicky." He motioned to her and slowly she stood.

"I'm glad to meet you." she tried to keep her voice steady. "I am sorry it is under these circumstances though."

Mr. Varson smiled. "Well, you look just like your mother, young lady. The same beautiful eyes and blond hair, but you have your fathers chin. He laughed, set stubbornly his always was."

Nicky trembled as she stepped away from him.

"Now, don't tease. You'll frighten the poor girl." her grandmother Varson chided. To Nicky she added. "We are so glad to finally meet you."

Her other grandparents said the same, but seemed more reserved.

Dustin motioned to the couch and chairs around the room. "Please all of you sit down. We can all get better acquainted."

Nicky trembled as she sat on the couch next to Dustin. She still was not sure she wanted to get to know these people. What if they hurt her too? She bit her lip then forced her mind not to judge, just because of her father.

Her Grandmother Hayland smiled. "Now Nicky, tell us about yourself. How old are you? How long have you and Dustin been married? What church do you go to? Where do you live?"

Mr. Varson laughed. "You might as well ask her to start at her first memory and go from there."

Nicky stiffened. "I really don't want to talk about me yet." she turned to her grandfather Varson. "But I do have a question for you, well actually it is for all of you." she looked around the room including the rest of her grandparents. Slowly she pulled out her mothers journal and the letter she had found.

"I found these in momma's things. The journal tells about when her and dad got pregnant and when they ran away. The letter is later. I don't know if she was ever going to send it or not."

Dustin took the journal and read the last few entries. They all sat there in shock.

Nicky looked at Mr. Varson. "Why did dad hate God, and church so much?"

Mr. Varson looked at his wife and shook his head. "It all started a long time ago. Your father was not always against God. There was a time when your father was so on fire for God you wouldn't have believed it."

Your right about that, Nicky thought to herself. "What happened?"

Mr. Varson cleared his throat. "We had some problems in Church. I was teaching the youth at the time. We were going through a devotional on the ten commandments. When we came to the one on Sabbath day desecration it raised a lot of questions.

I tried to let the young people know why it was wrong and give them scripture, like the verse that says he who is guilty of braking one command is guilty of braking them all. And I tried to reason with them to get them to see it was a serious problem in our day.

I asked them if they would like to be in heaven with a murderer or a child molester. Then I tried to get them to realize it didn't matter if we thought we were good, because we didn't lie or cheat. God's word gives us exact directions for getting to heaven, the church just wanted to convenience themselves.

Well, what I taught was looked down on by most of the church, the pastor included and I was asked to leave. I handled the situation wrong. I was young and head strong.

I guess the best way to tell you is some people respond to tough situations differently than others. Some people draw closer to God, some push away. Your father was determined to push as far away as he could get."

He sighed deeply. "The problem is that people don't even see what is keeping them out of heaven, or how close they can come and still miss it. They don't realize it only takes one sin to keep them out of heaven. Just one. Instead they try to see how much they can get by with and end up lost."

Nicky bit her lip. "What do you mean lost."

Mr. Varson shook his head sadly. "Lost in a devils hell for an eternity. Lost with no hope of ever being saved again. When they turn God away for the last time they will forever be lost."

Mrs. Varson turned to Nicky. "Did they ever come back to God? Did they ever turn back to him?"

Nicky looked down. "I'm sorry I have to tell you this, but no."

Mr. Hayland cleared his throat. "What about you, Nicky? What was life like for you? They must have changed there minds some to let you marry a preachers kid."

Nicky bit her lip. "It - No. I wish I could tell you otherwise, but daddy's last words to me were that he didn't need my God, and he was to young to die. And mom shot herself. I'm sorry this is how it turned out, but this is how it is." She looked away quickly.

Dustin put his arm around her. "It was like you said, Mr. Varson, he turned God away for the last time. He like his alcohol and beating his daughter to much to turn to God."

"Dustin!" Nicky hissed.

Her grandparents looked at each other. Mr. Varson cleared his throat. "Will you talk about it, Nicky?"

Nicky shuttered as she looked at her grandparents faces. Not for anything did she want to think about or relive any moments in her life right now. She knew she would need to sometime, but not now. Slowly she shook her head. "No, I don't want to talk about it. Maybe someday, but not today."

Chapter 33

"You can't be serious!" Mr. Varson stared in shock at his granddaughter.

Nicky stepped back as Dustin walked up behind her. "Nicky, the funeral starts in like thirty minutes. Why aren't you ready?"

Nicky bit her lip as she turned to face him. "I'm not going. I have no desire to go."

Dustin took her hand and led her into the kitchen. "Nicky, you need to do this. I know you don't want to ever see him again, but you need to."

Nicky pulled away. "Dustin, how can you say that? I hate him, even if he is dead. I know I shouldn't and that I should be grieved, because he went to hell, but I don't feel sorry he is gone. I'm grieved that he went to hell but I am not grieved that I will never see him again. And I don't want to go and hear someone preach him into heaven, when I know he didn't go."

Dustin pulled her close. "I wish I knew what to say."

Nicky bit her lip. "Don't make me go." she whispered. "Grandpa doesn't understand. He doesn't know what daddy has done to me, but you do. Please don't make me go and see all of his drunk friends and all the people he has hired to hurt me."

Dustin looked away. "I'm not going to force you. I can't force you, but I don't want to leave her here alone either."

He looked at her closely.

She bit her lip thinking of what could happen if she was alone. "I'll go, but I don't want to sit up front and I don't want to see anyone."

Dustin pulled her into his arms again. "You don't have to."

The funeral service was unlike any Nicky had ever been in.

Mr. Davis preached, and he didn't preach her parents into heaven. Instead he told the true story of their souls. When he came to the end there was dead silence in the sanctuary. "Men and women I admonish you, don't wait to come to church being carried by six men. Don't wait till you have time. Don't wait till you are done with all your partying. Mr. Varson thought he would have plenty of time on his deathbed to get right with God. He also thought he was to young to die, but death came in a moment. He had no time and though he thought he was to young, you are never to young to die. Don't wait friends or you will be forever, entirely and completely lost. There is no going back. You will be lost. In a devils hell forever. Lost."